The View from Penthouse B

BOOKS BY ELINOR LIPMAN

Into Love and Out Again

Then She Found Me

The Way Men Act

Isabel's Bed

The Inn at Lake Devine

The Ladies' Man

The Dearly Departed

The Pursuit of Alice Thrift

My Latest Grievance

The Family Man

Tweet Land of Liberty: Irreverent
Rhymes from the Political Circus

The View from Penthouse B

I Can't Complain

The View from Penthouse B

ELINOR LIPMAN

Houghton Mifflin Harcourt
Boston · New York
2013

Copyright © 2013 by Elinor Lipman

For information about permission to reproduce selections from this book, write to Permissions, Houghton Mifflin Harcourt Publishing Company, 215 Park Avenue South, New York, New York 10003.

www.hmhbooks.com

Library of Congress Cataloging-in-Publication Data
Lipman, Elinor.
The view from penthouse b / Elinor Lipman.
p. cm.
ISBN 978-0-547-57621-3
I. Title.
PS3562.I577V54 2013
813'.54 — dc23
2012018088

Book design by Melissa Lotfy

Printed in the United States of America
DOC 10 9 8 7 6 5 4 3 2 1

Who better to dedicate this particular book to
than my wonderful sister,
Deborah Slobodnik

ACKNOWLEDGMENTS

As ever, I thank my remarkable and steadfast friends, Mameve Medwed and Stacy Schiff, for improving every chapter and for their unflagging attention to matters great and small in real life, too.

I am grateful for the kind brilliance of my editor, Andrea Schulz, and my entire Houghton Mifflin Harcourt team, especially Megan Wilson and Lori Glazer.

I am immensely grateful to the Bogliasco Foundation and its Liguria Study Center for the kind of month abroad where this author and her chapters felt as if they didn't have a care in the world.

And like a certain fictional sister with both a giant heart and a head for business, my agent extraordinaire, Suzanne Gluck, wins daily, ongoing gratitude.

And for everything a son could be, I thank Benjamin Austin.

The View from Penthouse B

1

Fort Necessity

SINCE EDWIN DIED, I have lived with my sister Margot in the Batavia, an Art Deco apartment building on beautiful West Tenth Street in Greenwich Village. This arrangement has made a great deal of sense for us both: I lost my husband without warning, and Margot lost her entire life's savings to the Ponzi schemer whose name we dare not speak.

Though we call ourselves roommates, we are definitely more than that, something on the order of wartime trenchmates. She refers to me fondly as her boarder — ironic, of course, because no one confuses a boarding house with an apartment reached via an elevator button marked PH. In a sense, we live in both luxury and poverty, looking out over the Hudson while stretching the contents of tureens of stews and soups that Margot cooks expertly and cheerfully.

She takes cookbooks out of the library and finds recipes that add a little glamour to our lives without expensive ingredients, so a pea soup that employs a ham bone might start with sautéed cumin seeds or a grilled cheese sandwich is elevated to an entrée with the addition of an exotic slaw on the plate. We mostly get along fine, and our division of labor is fair: cook and dishwasher, optimist and pessimist.

Margot has turned herself into a professional blogger — or so she likes to announce. Her main topic is the incarcerated lifer who stole all her money, and her readers were primarily her fellow victims. I use "were" instead of "are" because visitors to www.thepoorhouse.com dwindled to zero at one point. The blog produces no money and has no advertisers, but she says it is just as good for confession and self-reflection as the expensive sounding board who once was her psychoanalyst.

When asked by strangers what I do, I tell them I have something on the drawing board, hoping my mysterious tone implies *Can't say more than that*. So far, it's only a concept, one that grew out of my own social perspective. It occurred to me that there might be a niche for arranging evenings between a man and a woman who desired nothing more than companionship. The working title for my organization is "Chaste Dates." So far, no one finds it either catchy or appealing.

Best-case scenario: I'd network with licensed matchmakers and establish reciprocity. They'd send me their timid, and I'd send them my marriage-minded. Might there be singletons with a healthy fear of intimacy versus the sin-seekers of Match.com? I hope to find them.

Everyone I've confided in — my younger sister, Betsy, for example, who has a job in banking in the sticky, bundling side of mortgages — hates the idea and/or tells me I'm thinking small. She's the sister who is always alert to rank and ambition. Her husband is a lawyer who didn't make partner, left the law, and teaches algebra in a public high school in an outer borough of New York. You'd think she'd brag about that, but she doesn't. Occasionally I catch her telling someone that Andrew went to law school with this president or that first lady and neglecting to mention his subsequent career. I usually tell her later, "You should be proud of what he does."

"Algebra?" she snarls, despite the fact that, unlike the progeny of a lot of New Yorkers who spend a fortune on tutors, both of her children excel in math. Edwin was a public school teacher, so I expect a little more sensitivity. These conversations push Chaste Dates further into oblivion. Still in mourning, I am easily overwhelmed.

· · ·

Margot is divorced from Charles, a too-handsome, board-certified physician with an ugly story, who calls our apartment collect from his country club of a prison. He was/is a gynecologist, now under suspension, with a reckless subspecialty that drew the lonely and libidinous. Patients came with an infertility story and left a little ruddier and more relaxed than when they arrived. Who were these women, Margot and I always marvel, who knew how to signal, feet in stirrups, that a doctor's advances would be deemed not only consensual but medical? Yes, Charles partnered with a sperm bank, whose donors were advertised as brilliant, healthy, handsome men with high IQs, graduate degrees, and above-average height. And, yes, the vast majority of his practice *was* artificial rather than personal insemination. But for a few, the main draw was Charles himself, a silver-haired, blue-eyed, occasionally sensitive man, the kind of physician women put their faith in and develop a crush on. Overall, it was lucky that Charles suffered from borderline oligospermia — in layman's terms, a low-to-useless sperm count. Did he know? Of course. We're not sure how he framed these trespasses, but some patients must have told themselves that a doctor's fleshly ministrations, midcycle, were donorlike and ethical in some footnoted way, imagining the top-notch child and possible romantic entanglement that his DNA could yield. His bedside talents were such, apparently, that satisfied customers came back for subsequent treatments. Luckily, only one procedure took, only one child was conceived, one son eventually revealed through due diligence. Charles might still be practicing amorous medicine, except that his unknowing bookkeeper charged the paramours a fee commensurate with an outside donor — five thousand dollars, the going rate at the time — and thus committed fraud of a punishable, actionable kind. "Fraud" on the books; "malpractice," "adultery," "grounds for divorce," and "sin" everywhere else. Margot left the day he was rather publicly arrested. Her settlement was enormous. She bought her penthouse, invested the rest catastrophically, and resumed the use of her maiden name.

Edwin died one month before turning fifty, without getting sick first, due to a malformation of his heart valves that proved fatal. One morning I woke up and found that he hadn't, a sight and a shock that I wonder if I've yet recovered from.

Even twenty-three months after his death, his absence is always present. People assume I am grateful for the memories, but where they're wrong is that the memories cause more wistfulness than comfort. It's hard to find a subject that doesn't summon Edwin, no matter how mundane. All topics — music, food, movies, wall colors, a stranger's questions about my marital status or the location of the rings on my fingers — bring him back. I haven't seen much progress in two years. Keeping someone's memory alive has its voluntary and involuntary properties. You want to and you don't. You're not going to hide the photos, but neither will you relocate the images of his formerly happy, healthy, smiling face to your bedside night table.

Amateur shrinks are everywhere. "Ed wouldn't want you to be staying home, would he?" — to me, who never called him Ed. And, "If it was you who had died, wouldn't you want *him* to find someone else?" They mean well, I'm told. I think Edwin actually *would* be glad I haven't remarried, dated, or looked. He wasn't a jealous husband, but he was a sentimental one.

It's good to be around Margot, an amusingly bitter ex-wife. She loathes Charles, so I join in. We enjoy discussing his felonious acts, a subject we never tire of. Hating Charles is good for her and oddly good for me. We often start the day over coffee with a new insight into his egregiousness. Margot might begin a rant by saying, "Maybe he chose to be an ob-gyn just for this very purpose. Naked women, legs open, one every twenty minutes."

The summing up of his character flaws often leads one of us to say, usually with a sigh, that it's just as well Charles didn't father a child inside their marriage. Imagine trying to explain his behavior to a son or daughter of any age? Imagine having a jailbird for a father. That, of course, reminds me that Edwin and I tried, but without success and without great commitment. For years, Margot urged me to consult Charles, but who would want to be seen by a brother-in-law in such an intimate arena? Knowing now about his modus operandi, that I might have given birth to my own niece or nephew, I am forever thankful that I resisted. Lately Margot is juicing up her blog by admitting that her ex is the once-esteemed physician-felon who was a tabloid headline for a whole season. As the subject tilts from the recession to his unique brand of adultery, she's won new readers. Though she's not much of a stylist, her writing is lively and her pen poisonous in a most engaging way.

Living here is interesting and soothing. It's a beautiful apartment with what Margot calls "dimensions." Hallways veer this way and that, so you can't see from one end of the apartment what's going on in the other. The building has doormen, porters, and a menagerie of fancy purebred dogs. Edwin and I lived more modestly in a ground-floor, rent-controlled one-bedroom on West End Avenue. The Batavia shares its name with a Dutch ship that struck a reef off the coast of Australia in 1629. Amazingly enough, most of its shipwrecked passengers survived.

2

I Next Considered

MY ONCE-RELIABLE FREELANCE job was writing copy for bill inserts issued by utility companies, the slips of paper that offered tips on insulating and reducing customers' carbon footprints. Occasionally I'd get to write 250 to 300 words about a heroic, lifesaving deed, usually CPR or a Heimlich maneuver performed in the field by a hard-hatted employee. When customers switched to e-bills, my assignments dwindled to nothing. Every day I read front-page stories about professionals combing every inch of second-fiddle job listings, and there I am.

I don't like to blame what pop psychologists call "birth order" for my situation and motivation. If I did, I'd have to accept that being the middle child has a major influence on how I approach the world and those gray areas that fall loosely under the heading "relations." Still, I wonder if some of my professional dead ends had to do with my growing up between perfect Margot and formidable Betsy.

I majored in education in college, a safe and appealing concentration — until I got into the classroom. Even as a student teacher, I dreaded every minute, every smart-aleck eighth grader, the smoke-filled teachers' room and its burned coffee, the married gym teacher who liked me and his guidance-counselor wife who did not.

I lived at home, in Hartford, which might have contributed to my less-than-amorous twenties. Like today, I helped around the house and read the classifieds. After my retirement from education at twenty-two, I took the summer off, sleeping late in my childhood bedroom, the empty parakeet cage and *The Partridge Family* poster reminding me that time had passed. I lunched with unemployed high school girlfriends who hadn't moved away, either. My father, one of dozens of vice presidents at one of the city's insurance company's world headquarters, gave my anemic résumé to what in those days was called Personnel, despite my objection that I didn't want a job because of nepotism or mercy.

Soon enough, when asked in a social setting what I did, I could answer "administrative assistant." My boss wrote the magazine-size glossy annual report and I typed it all up, correcting his grammar and punctuation. Within six months, he told someone in Personnel, whether out of admiration or annoyance, about my eye for typos, and soon I had my own cubicle, dictionary, thesaurus, and pencil sharpener, proofreading insurance jargon all day long in what felt like solitary confinement.

I lunched with my father almost daily until there wasn't a single cafeteria worker who hadn't heard him say a half-dozen times, "This is my daughter, Gwen-Laura. She works here now." I'd nudge him and add "His *favorite* daughter" in such a way that always elicited a chuckle and at the same time signaled to our audience that Jim Considine loved all his daughters equally. It was at one of our lunches that he asked if I had any desire to get my own place. Margot, for example, struggling to make ends meet, had nonetheless found that garret in the Bowery. And Betsy, too, was happy living with people her own age.

I reminded him that Betsy was still in college, living in a dorm, so I didn't think she should be held up as a paragon of residential courage. I said that I *did* want to be on my own, a white lie I hoped would soon be the truth. Again, looking back, I wonder: birth order. Middle child. Brown-haired daughter between two hazel-eyed blonds. Maybe I needed extra parental attention to make up for . . . well, for nothing.

Every one of the three Considine girls, we would discover after first my father's death, then my mother's, thought herself to be the favorite child.

As Margot contemplates various angles for a possible memoir, I'm thinking of writing something, too. My premise is good: A woman widowed relatively young moves from her small apartment into a choice piece of Manhattan real estate. It would be a retelling of *Little Orphan Annie,* updated and without the orphans. She would find companionship and eventually love, and along the way, travel the world through the good graces of her husband's generous life insurance policies. I know I'd enjoy casting myself in a Cinderella story, fully recovered from my sorrows — which I guess makes it fiction. Margot and I often discuss our books; sometimes we pause midconversation and wonder aloud if the conjuring is half the fun, at which point we vow to start our respective works that very week.

We have updated résumés at the ready. Margot's is livelier than mine. She even makes her first job (second-tier secretary in Obstetrics at Saint Vincent's) sound consequential. What was actually socializing and flirting has become "mentored and liaised with interns and residents." It was where Charles first spotted her, and possibly what reinforced his career choice. To test the relationship, to make her overscheduled and exhausted boyfriend miss her, she jumped ship to an AM radio station, putting up with the on-air banter of the two male drive-time deejays who soon worked her into their act. Her receptionist's role on *The Mitch and Mike Show* expanded the morning they buzzed her on the intercom while on air and asked, "Margot? We were wondering what you had for supper last night?"

She answered casually, even lazily, "Spaghetti and tap water." Hilarity ensued. After that, "Let's Ask Margot" became an hourly sure bet. "Margot's wearing a fetching — what is that called, doll? — a nearly see-through blouse today." She would yell back, "It's voile. And the bodice is lined so you cannot see through it one iota." The guys would deliver a mock apology. *So sorry to offend her highness! Her bodice is lined! She's rolling her eyes at us now. Wish you could see her! Two words, guys: Bomb. Shell.*

Off air, Mike and Mitch were kind and harmless, she maintained. They explained that it was called "shtick," that their wives understood; and it came with a raise. She received fan letters and the occasional marriage proposal. Mike and Mitch read the cleanest ones on air, prompting even more letters — listeners trying to outdo, to empurple, to rhyme.

Even now her name occasionally rings a bell with a middle-aged commuter who asks, "You're *that* Margot? From *The Mitch and Mike Show*?" I think it marked her — in a good way. Not that her self-esteem was ever low, but more than anything else, it was Mike and Mitch who gave her a feel for a pedestal beneath her feet. I am sure that one of the reasons she is relatively cheerful today is that this new Depression reminds her of her happy twenties, sleeping alone on a Murphy bed in what is now NoLiTa (but previously had neither nickname nor appeal) and making soup out of chicken backs and necks on a hot plate. "I used to walk my skinny little paycheck to my bank, deposit all of it, and keep forty dollars for spending money! For everything! For lunches and subway fare and maybe one movie a week. I never felt deprived because all my friends lived that way, too. Those were the days!"

Those were also the days when daughters married right out of college, especially when young doctors were doing the asking. Margot explained her ambivalence at Thanksgiving, with just the immediate family present, planned that way so she could explain why she'd turned down Charles's proposal.

He didn't understand who she was, Margot insisted. Or who she'd become. Margot Considine was something of a household name; well, at least she felt that way when Mitch or Mike teased and complimented her, and the station's phone lines lit up. Our father paused in his carving mathematically precise slices of breast away from the bone and turned to our mother. "Did a daughter of ours just say that she didn't want to marry a perfectly nice man from a good family, a physician no less, because he didn't listen to her being teased by two buffoons?"

"I'm afraid so," said our mother, still in her apron, a gift from me that was festooned with horns of plenty in honor of her November birthday. And then, borrowing his wry tone: "Let's use psychology. Let's agree that she is too important and famous to marry anyone, let alone a mere doctor in training. We'll pretend we don't want her to give Charles the time of day. That should help."

Margot said, "What about the fact that he's going to be a gynecologist?"

Dad said, "I owe most of what is great in my life to that honorable profession."

"But would you want your favorite eldest daughter to be married to one?" Margot asked. "Aren't you wondering if a man whose patient population will be 100 percent female is the best candidate for marriage? Or monogamy?"

We waited. Our mom said, "Jim?"

Margot continued. "Because it seems to me that one of two things would follow: either temptation or burnout."

"Ask him," our dad said. "He must already know if temptation goes along with the job."

Charles insisted that the answer was no. He'd learned in his first week of residency, performing dozens of pelvic exams a day, to disassociate. How could she confuse the emotional with the clinical? He had eyes only for her.

Margot said she needed a week to think things over, then said yes. As befitting the beautiful eldest daughter, the wedding was large and formal, black tie and prime rib. I'd been fitted for contact lenses and wore an orchid behind one ear. Charles's eight groomsmen danced with Betsy and me so obligingly that I now suspect it was a condition set down by the bride or her parents. But that night, it felt like popularity.

• • •

Although Margot appears strong and cynical, and is quick to joke about her divorce, I think she needs me here. I have assumed the task of accepting Charles's collect calls, two a month, a frequency we negotiated despite her reluctance to accept even one. I argued for that small act of charity. "At least he didn't die," I remind her.

At first, his calls were heartbreaking. He told me how much he missed Edwin, his favorite brother-in-law, which I really shouldn't have believed, but I'd so rather have heard that than the frequent questions about poor me, my state of mind, health, welfare, and rotten luck.

Whether it's the group therapy in prison or just the hours and hours of boredom that have made him reflect on his life and marriage, he speaks in a new pop psychology idiom and in a new revelatory fashion. "I wasn't emotionally available to Margot," he announced, his greeting. "Which is so typical of a surgeon."

I said, "But you're not a surgeon," which he corrects. What did I call hysterectomies and Caesarians if not surgery? He'd spent thousands of hours in the OR during his training. And his point was not his board certification but his surgical personality. He may have been a little robotic and selfish . . .

This sounded new. Apparently, at his particular prison, where alpha-male white-collar criminals of the CEO variety served time, many group therapy sessions turned to wives, girlfriends, mistresses, conjugal visits — what went wrong and how did felons woo when reintegrated into society?

"So you're saying that your being robotic and surgical was the cause of your patient hanky-panky?" I asked him.

"You two are close," he continued. "So I'm assuming you know that during the time that the unfortunate conception took place, Margot and I were separated."

I said, "I would've known if you two were separated!"

"No one knew. I was sleeping on my office couch. It wasn't that we were unhappy. I think it was just that Margot had bouts of romantic ambition, with those two deejays forwarding her fan letters for years; *love* letters from her commuter-suitors, real or imagined. I think any little argument we had, any little dry spell, made her wonder what if . . . ?"

I said, "We discuss you a lot. I'd have known about a separation, especially if it exiled you to a couch in your office —"

"You discuss me a lot?" he repeated, sounding pleased.

"That can't surprise you! You get married and you feel secure and you think it's forever, then suddenly your husband's in prison! Gone. You're alone. Of *course* we talk about you."

Someone, presumably a guard, was telling Charles that his time was up. "Thirty seconds," he negotiated. "This is important." And then to me: "I don't have time to be anything but blunt, so here goes: Aren't you talking about yourself? About you and Edwin? Because if you substitute 'in the ground' for 'in prison,' you're describing your own situation. He's gone and you're alone —"

I hung up without answering. I didn't want bluntness or insight or analysis. And the news of a long-ago separation was confusing. Charles was one of our top two villains. If there had been mitigating emotional circumstances, I'd have to realign everything.

I had moved into the Batavia three months after Edwin died, as I was pondering whether to renew my lease. The teaming up was our sister Betsy's idea, who asked calmly while she was treating us to our semi-monthly dinner in her Upper East Side neighborhood, "Have either of you discussed the possibility of joining forces?"

I asked what she meant.

"Gwen moving into the Batavia."

Margot asked, "Do you mean *buy?*"

I knew, embedded in that question, was her hope that Betsy the banker knew something she did not — that Edwin had left me previously undetected funds.

I said, "Oh, sure. I'd be just the one to spend a million or two on a one-bedroom."

"I meant," Betsy said, "*obviously,* beyond obviously, that Gwen could move into your outsized apartment."

I said, "I think Margot would have asked me by now if that idea appealed."

Margot was writing on the edge of her paper place mat featuring the Chinese Zodiac. "What are you scribbling over there?" Betsy asked.

"Math," said Margot.

I said, "I know the second bedroom is your study . . ."

Betsy said, "What does she need a whole study for? One blog entry a week? She can move her laptop to the dining-room table."

Margot looked up finally. She asked, "Can you afford . . . ?" and named a figure that was thirty dollars below my current rent.

I said yes, I could.

Betsy asked what percentage of the common charges and utilities did that figure represent. Half?

Margot said firmly, "It represents what I'm comfortable asking my widowed sister to put into the coffer." She asked again if I could manage the figure she'd named.

"I can."

"And do you want to?"

My first, unspoken answer was no. How could I abandon the apartment that still had Edwin's voice on the answering machine and his DNA on the piano keys? But then I pictured the inlaid marble floors of the Batavia's lobby, its frescoed walls, its bank of filigreed brass mailboxes, and its companionship. "Yes," I said. "I want to."

Margot said, "Then I can, too."

Though I could talk about Edwin and even his death without getting choked up, I still lose my voice and composure in the face of unexpected acts of kindness.

Margot saw this. She added, "We'll be good for each other. I've always secretly envied you and Betsy sharing a room."

Betsy laughed. Even when Margot went to college, she fought to keep her bedroom sanctified and empty for her visits home.

I said, "It'll be temporary. A few months?"

"Why go and set some arbitrary deadline?" asked Betsy. "This could work out beautifully for all sides and all pocketbooks."

Margot said, "Maybe she'll get sick of me. Maybe after your last child goes off to college, Gwen will be ready to move in with you and Andrew."

"That sounds about right: I'll go from sister to sister till I die, young and unexpectedly."

Margot explained to Betsy: "What happened to Edwin — it makes her feel doomed herself."

Betsy reached across the table and took my hand. I knew what was coming: the speech about life's possibilities. She began, "I know you don't like to hear this, and I know you think it's too soon to imagine that one day . . . someone —"

Eyes closed, I shook my head to stop her. I had no appetite for what I knew she was about to say, that my life wasn't over. And by "life" she would mean one lived in the company of a man or men.

"Later, Betsy," said Margot. "She needs time. I'll remind her occasionally that she's still alive."

I slept at the beautiful Batavia that night, not in the second bedroom but on the other half of the king-size bed that Margot had brought from the marital home in New Jersey, hoping that one day she'd need something expansive. Because of her large wardrobe of nightwear and spare toothbrushes, I didn't stop at home first. We stayed up talking past midnight, Margot confessing what she thought were the bad habits and rituals that I might find annoying in a roommate. Not one was unfamiliar or discouraging. I offered a few feeble warnings of my own, that I'd leave dishes in the sink and lights on; that I had insomnia, a dry cough; still wore my retainer at night and was apt to leave it —

"Not one a deal breaker," she said, and reached across the broad expanse of mattress to pat my pink satin–clothed forearm. It was kind of her not to make me admit my most obvious shortcoming: I would be a sad roommate who couldn't be counted on for any fun at all.

3

Feedback

W E DO GO OUT — Margot to dinner parties hosted by friends who understand she can't afford to reciprocate, and I to free museum nights and occasionally, still, to my widows' support group at the Y. Otherwise, Manhattan is beyond our budgets, with its double-digit appetizers and skimpy wines by the glass that cost three times as much as whole bottles from Trader Joe's. For a woman who can be counted among the bereaved (marriage over, brother-in-law deceased, money gone), Margot excels at keeping both our chins up. She announces almost gleefully every novel down-market activity she engages in. Last January, for example, her New Year's resolution was to read supermarket circulars, scissors in hand. It opened up a world she hadn't ever entered — double and triple coupons. I told her about the bruised-fruit-and-vegetable shelf that some stores offered, where a barely shriveled Holland red pepper or wilting head of radicchio, ordinarily beyond us, could be had for ninety-nine cents. She was amazed to learn that if you get on a bus after you've paid for a subway ride, it's considered a transfer and deducts nothing from a MetroCard.

We have a terrace and roof garden at the Batavia, open to all, frequented more often under dark of night by me, who doesn't want to chat with strangers about why I'm here. There are miniature victory gardens up there, necessitating an honor system among residents when the tomatoes are ripe and the basil luxurious. There are picnic tables, lounge chairs, fire extinguishers, hoses for watering the plants, and signs everywhere posting admonitions per the FDNY about a ten-foot clearance between building and briquettes.

Margot feels proprietary toward the space because it is practically outside the penthouse windows. Just for a change of venue, even when it's chilly, we cook there. If there's an unseasonably warm evening, we take our hot dogs or ground chuck to the roof at an hour when most have already eaten and left. Hovering in the lighter-fluid-scented air is always the question: How long before someone notices and complains about my unofficial occupancy? I worry about Margot's across-the-hall French-speaking neighbors in penthouse A with whom we share an umbrella stand, and the strange man below us in 12D who has mentioned on more than one occasion that he hears an extra set of footsteps in the night. "Someone not sleeping well?" he likes to ask just as he steps off the elevator.

Margot thinks I'm worrying too much. After one particularly un-friendly *bonjour* from Madame LaPlante across the hall, I asked, "What if someone writes a letter to the board saying that money is changing hands in penthouse B, against co-op rules?"

Margot was at her laptop. She paused, took a deep, long-suffering breath, and said, "We've been through this. I was on that board. I've participated in discussions about illegal boarders and lingering guests. And you know what always makes it okay? Our collective social conscience. Someone always grouses, 'What is this, Park Avenue? We're the *Village*. Emma Lazarus lived on this street!'"

"In that case," I said, "why not just come clean and make me official?"

She rose and headed for the kitchen with her empty mug. "Too late," she called over her shoulder. I followed her and asked why.

"If I said you were paying me rent, I'd have to renege on what I already told them."

"Which was what?"

From the open fridge, her back to me, she murmured, "You won't

16

like it." She opened the spout of the milk carton, sniffed it, and handed it to me for a second opinion.

"'What did you tell them?" I asked again.

"I told them that money does *not* change hands. That you don't have any; that I was taking you in, not charging rent, doing all of this out of the goodness of my heart because otherwise you'd be homeless. Of course they knew I didn't mean *homeless* homeless . . ."

I said, "That is a very depressing label to stick on someone, especially when it's not true. Wasn't it enough to just say, 'She's my sister'?"

"I'm sorry," said Margot. "But all they have to do is take one look at you to know you're not penniless or pathetic." She paused. I sensed a turnabout coming. "Like your big sister, the divorcée and pauper," she added.

Then it was my turn to say something soothing. We often ended a conversation this way. One of us would sound a morose note, and the other would try to staunch the leak of self-esteem. A joke, a compliment, a summary of attractive traits. As kids, we never got along this well.

Here was the beginning and end of my entrepreneurship. I finally took a little leap with my alleged agency, announcing Chaste Dates on Craigslist. My first and — as it turned out — last client made what he called "an appointment" the same day the ad appeared. His caller ID said "private," and his voice was clipped. In person, at a well-regarded Midtown steak house of his choosing, he seemed in a hurry and wasn't answering my questions about where he lived and worked. Noting that his hands were tanned except for the white skin circling the fourth finger of his left hand, I asked if he was married. His answer was "No . . . Well, I was. I'm recently divorced but had" — he looked down at the telltale pale flesh — "a hard time with the, um, final, um, separation. I wore my ring on a fishing trip recently. It was sunny the whole time."

I looked down at my own wedding ring, switched just this one night to my right hand.

"Is dinner really necessary?" he asked.

"Aren't you feeling well?"

"I just was hoping to get onto the main course."

I pointed to the list of entrées under "secondi" on his open menu.

"What about *your* menu?" he asked. "What are we talking about, pricewise?" Then he added, in the least flirtatious voice that ever employed the phrase, "I find you very attractive."

Having been warned a dozen times by my sisters that I'd better be ready for exactly this kind of misunderstanding, I lowered my voice to the level of the hoarsely insulted. "Are you talking about prices for things done in a bedroom? Because if you are, there's been a misunderstanding."

He said, unperturbed, "Your ad's under escort services, isn't it?"

I said — Margot and I had role-played this exact situation — "First of all, the ad was only meant to be a soft opening. I wanted to test the waters, to see if there was any market out there for an evening of innocent company that is in no way sexual. I would've put *that* in the ad, except even that's in bad taste. Furthermore, what did I ask you about your potential date?"

He said he didn't remember.

"Then let me remind you: I asked your age, occupation, and hobbies, and whether it matters to you whether a dinner companion shares your interests or roots for your teams. I also asked whether you were a vegetarian or an omnivore. If we were that other kind of business, I think I'd be asking you — I don't know this from experience — about your physical preferences in a partner, wouldn't I? Hair color, breast size, skin pigmentation?"

My dinner companion looked at his watch, then gave the knot of his tie a twist, loosening it an inch, which I took to mean *This is merely dinner. I'm off duty now.*

"Are you really a golf instructor at Chelsea Piers?" I asked.

"Off the record?"

"Of course."

"I am *not* a golf instructor at Chelsea Piers."

"Are you in a line of work where you wear handcuffs?"

"Wear? I'd say no."

"I meant are they on your person?"

He said, after staring for a good long time, "Yes."

"Are you a policeman?"

That made him laugh. I reminded him that we were off the record. What was the harm in telling the truth?

After another longish stare, he said, "Vice."

I said, "Wouldn't the world be a better place if you put your energy into saving children from abuse and making sure they got breakfast and a hot lunch?"

"No question."

As stipulated, he picked up the tab. I try to avoid red meat, but this night I felt obliged to order the porterhouse and two glasses of a pinot noir that were seventeen dollars apiece. Sergeant Mulvaney said, raising his glass of Coke, revealing a shamrock tattoo on the inside of his right wrist, "I have a thought. My father is a widower, and a sweet guy, but he can't afford these prices. Do you ever — just for fun — match up a single gent with someone nice, say Catholic, a good housekeeper — someone whose kids aren't messed up?"

"He's how old?"

"Late sixties. Good shape. Great guy."

I said, "No, I'm retiring."

He said, grinning — and I'm quite sure joking — "But it's always good to do a favor for a cop."

"Most people would say, 'Sure. This is how one succeeds in legitimate matchmaking. Maybe you'll send me a rich uncle.'"

"And what do *you* say?"

"In over my head," I told him.

Margot was fascinated. I had to repeat the evening's conversation practically word for word. "You should have told him our outlaw story," she said. "They love when the bad guy gets caught and is paying his debt to society."

19

She meant Charles. I didn't correct her, didn't say "that would be *your* outlaw story" because by this time we held joint custody of each other's tribulations. I said, "Not in this situation, not with someone on the alert for crime. The law enforcement part of it would have been okay, but the rest? It would've brought us back to the topic of sex."

Margot said, "I've never known anyone who thinks so much before she speaks. I'm the opposite. I say, 'Hello, nice to meet you, my ex-husband is in prison and I lost all my money in a Ponzi scheme!' I can't help it. It just comes tripping off my tongue. And no offense, but what comes tripping off your tongue is 'Edwin this and Edwin that. He was born missing a part of his heart.' Men don't find a late husband such an interesting topic."

We then role-played. Margot said, "Pretend there's a lapse in the conversation. You say, 'I have an interesting situation in my own family: My sister's husband was an obstetrician specializing in getting women pregnant, but it was more like a one-man sex ring.' Say that. And say 'gynecologist.' Guys love that. You can't lose. It's riveting, and while it appears that you're talking about Charles, the guys will pick up on the subtext."

"Which is what?"

"Fucking," said Margot. "No matter how you spin the inseminating, they'll find it a little stirring." She was staring at me now in an appraising fashion. She asked if I realized that I visibly shuddered when she uttered the word "sex" in the context of conversation with a potential date.

"Do not," I said.

"Do, too. And I'm going to work on the other words that also render you silent."

"Such as?"

"Death. Dying. The month in which it happened. The *year* in which it happened. And one more time: sex."

"Why bother?" I asked.

She said that she and Betsy had talked after our last dinner. Not that they were worried . . . not that I was a drag to be around. But they

20

had talked about something that she, the live-in sister, could work on to desensitize me to several words and concepts.

"To what end?" I asked.

"Normalcy," she said. "Progress. Moving forward."

"It was situational," I told her. "Having dinner with an undercover cop set me back a few months. What was I thinking? That I could be a G-rated madam?"

Margot shook her head. "We have to move forward, both of us. What if I was stuck in the past, crying every day about my stolen money? I'd be figuring out a way to break into prison and commit murder."

Crying every day? All she did was exaggerate. She wasn't going to murder Bernard L. Madoff. There, I'd said it. I'd pronounced the name aloud. How's that for a start on desensitizing? Let's stop the psychoanalysis and the drama. I didn't need it. I didn't cry that often anymore.

4

Edwin

THOUGH I USED TO leave my retail employment off my résumé, I look back on it now with pride and nostalgia. To escape the long solitary confinement of my proofreading cubicle, I became a buyer-in-training, despite being not terribly well suited or well dressed enough to catch the eye of managers who might promote me. The job was the result of more parental networking, a propitious conversation between my mother and a stranger at a bridge tournament. And though a wrong turn professionally, it turned out to be the high point of my romantic history because Edwin and I met on the mezzanine level of Nordstrom in Farmington, Connecticut, in what now seems another life.

It was luck or kismet or just being on the right shift at the right time. The store's famously unreliable piano player, Viktor, had come to work drunk.

"No, sorry, I do not take requests," we sales-associates-in-training heard him say. He ranted about the stupid clichéd songs Americans always requested, which then led to a sarcastic rendition of "Chim Chim Cher-ee." He punctuated his tirade with swigs from a Styrofoam cup, its contents clearly alcohol. When he stopped playing altogether and started muttering, presumably obscenities in Russian — acoustics were wonderful in his area — two security guards rushed over.

"Sir," said the lead guard, reaching for his walkie-talkie, a hand on Viktor's shoulder.

"Don't touch me!" Viktor yelled.

"I think it's time for your break," said the guard.

Have I mentioned that we all knew Viktor, and all knew he was an émigré from Irkutsk who liked to assert his new American right to swear in two languages at anyone who policed the state, even if the state consisted of Nordstrom, Lord & Taylor, and Emporium Armani?

Those of us in adjacent departments were edging as close as we dared, tucking our IDs into our pockets so we could mingle with the curious shoppers.

"Don't let him drive!" someone called to the guards.

"Name a musician who owns car," Viktor yelled back. "And where in hell would I park in U S of A even if I owned little Japanese shit-box?"

A guard sniffed the contents of the Styrofoam cup and pronounced with too much glee and stereotyping, "Vodka!"

"Beeg detective," Viktor sneered.

Now the head of HR was at the top of the escalator and racewalking toward the piano. We displaced salespeople moved several yards into the crowd, back toward our departments.

The reason a random Russian's separation from the store is relevant to my social history is that while all of this was unfolding, a customer named Edwin Schmidt was buying athletic socks in the shoe department. He first heard the music stop, midpassage, then a discordant bass clunk of keys as if a big, angry fist had attacked the keyboard. Then he heard raised voices. He abandoned the package of socks under consideration, hopped on the up escalator, and came toward the noise. Arriving as both guards were raising Viktor from the piano bench, he stayed after the crowd had dispersed and gestured toward the piano's keyboard and to the HR woman *May I?*

"Play?"

"A few pieces I know by heart."

He admitted later that he was showing off, starting with a gorgeous

Liszt impromptu that drew sighs from the assembled shoppers and rubberneckers. The HR woman smiled the smile of someone who thinks it's her lucky day and her own bit of genius recruiting. "Do you play other stuff?" she asked. With barely a pause between pieces, Edwin switched into a beautifully mournful rendition of "All You Need Is Love."

"Are you a professional?"

"Yes and no. I'm a music teacher."

The HR woman asked where, what time school got out, and whether his weekends were free. He said West Hartford, three p.m., and yes. Did she need references?

"My office is downstairs, a right turn after the restrooms. Come by on your break?"

"So I should keep playing?"

"Let's get you into a jacket and tie first — follow me — and then we'll call the next hour an audition."

Before he left, with a gift certificate toward the purchase price of his new sports jacket and a voucher for our café, he'd played Rodgers and Hart, Rodgers and Hammerstein, Stephen Sondheim, more Beatles, and more impromptus. He returned that night with sheet music, and without being told, played songs that conjured snow, snowmen, winter. It was our huge February coat sale.

No wedding ring on those talented fingers, my coworkers and I all noticed. "Gay," a few ignoramuses concluded because of his artistic gifts. I wondered aloud to Meredith and Taisha in Hosiery if our maestro was available. Both young and adventurous, they claimed the next move was up to me. When I did nothing, Taisha — safely married and on my behalf — strode to the piano and asked if he was married or seeing anyone. He looked up. She must have mentioned my name because there was a direct gaze into Hosiery, then a switch to a song I didn't recognize.

I might have turned away, but Meredith was there, backup to Taisha's bold overtures, prompting me to answer. I smiled and shrugged — *Sorry, can't name that tune.*

His right hand crossed over his left to punctuate his answer with one last chord. He called across the mezzanine, "It's 'Always,' by Irving Berlin. He wrote it for his wife."

I'm sure our three faces fell. Taisha must have said something like "So you *are* married?" Even from a distance, I could see him trying to take back the impression the lyrics had falsely suggested. He said something to Taisha, who then yelled to me, "Get over here, missy! Time for your break."

"Lipstick," Meredith commanded.

Was there ever a less subtle exercise in matchmaking? I made a slow walk over to the piano, trying to look unruffled and innocent, as if I didn't know what their conversation had been about. With a sly smile Edwin announced to the passersby, "I'm now going to play 'A Pretty Girl Is Like a Melody,' also by the late, great Irving Berlin."

I was thirty. No one had ever played a song for me without my first having requested it. Over coffee, I asked him to dinner at my new, barely unpacked studio apartment, and he accepted. Sometimes you see gestures that tell you everything about a person's character and temperament, and that night I saw many such signs. First among them was his good humor after my scallops turned out to be ammoniated and nearly inedible. Edwin turned down my offer of substitute tuna sandwiches and celery sticks for a spontaneous outing to an Italian bistro in my neighborhood. We discovered that we shared two movies in common (*Casablanca* and *Dirty Dancing*) on our list of top five. From that first night, I could so easily see myself across the table from him, who'd be relaxed and lenient about whatever I served. I could also see us taking trips together, nothing strenuous or exotic, Edwin sliding onto unoccupied piano benches aboard ships and in restaurants, his staying calm when flights were canceled and luggage lost. I'd get a piano. He didn't make an overture in the direction of a kiss, so I did that myself, knowing that Meredith and Taisha would scold me for a lost opportunity. He took it well.

He proposed on the one-year anniversary of Viktor's termination with a ring that needed to be sized, so we waited until it was back from the jeweler's to announce our plans. It had been his grandmother's, willed to Edwin upon her death. It was white gold and not exactly my taste, but I grew to love it. The diamond was flawless, and noticed by every single customer of the chatty sort whose purchase I wrapped in tissue or whose credit card I ran.

He always claimed he spotted me first, across a crowded mezzanine, but I think everyone knew that was Edwin evoking Ezio Pinza in *South Pacific*. He stopped his freelance playing, and I returned to fixing other people's sentences when we moved to Manhattan and its Washington Irving High School; with our combined incomes and rent-controlled one-bedroom, we didn't need second jobs. His students loved him.

It was only nineteen years later when the school's award-winning a cappella group brought the mourners to tears with "Amazing Grace." It surprised me and broke my heart all over again when they closed with a slow, sweet "Always." Everyone grasped its meaning: The way we'd met, at a Steinway grand, had been Edwin's favorite illustration of how music could change a life.

5

We Add Anthony

I SHOULD HAVE KNOWN we were leading up to a large lifestyle change at the Batavia when Margot sold her diamond engagement ring, as well as an enameled bullfrog with topaz eyes that she had never liked. Immediately she regretted another transaction — selling a string of pearls that she'd worn at her wedding, an engagement gift from her in-laws. A few times she arrived at breakfast looking a little glummer than usual, and when I asked what was wrong she said, "I dreamed about my engagement pearls again." I told her that the pearls were a metaphor for her old life. Their replacement would be a metaphor for her new one.

"How's that?" she asked.

I looked up from my cereal and newspaper. "I think it's obvious: When your ship comes back in, or your book gets published, you'll replace them and you'll feel a kind of victory over hardship every time you look down at your bosom."

What I happened to be looking down at was an advertisement on page two of the *Times*. To distract her, I jabbed at the paper and asked, "Do you believe this: 'Mary-Jane with Cut Out Detail' — four hundred and ninety-five dollars! Who buys shoes for five hundred dollars these days?" I held up the page. The shoes were pictured and very beautiful, and looked to be of the softest silvery leather.

Margot put on her reading glasses, leaned over, and read from the fine print at the bottom of the ad. "Bal Harbour, Beverly Hills, South Coast Plaza, Las Vegas, Honolulu, Dallas. Ha! As if there's any money left there."

Margot thinks that no one in the United States, regardless of employment or liquidity or reserves of gold bullion, has anything left. She puzzles over the society snapshots in the Sunday Styles section, its smiling couples still raising money for the arts, still raising debutantes, still in black tie and designer gowns, still in possession of the jewels from the days before the black Fridays and Mondays.

This particular exchange sticks in my mind because of the phone call that interrupted it. As soon as she noted the caller ID, Margot left the table and headed into the den.

I heard only murmuring, followed by laughter. Then she was back, still on the phone but now speaking to me. "Are you home tonight?" she asked. And then back to the caller: "My sister is a matchmaking consultant. She's often on duty at night."

I said, "I'm home."

"Do you know where we are . . . ? That's right. North side of the street. Just give the doorman your name. He'll point you to the right elevator."

"Who's coming over?" I asked, as soon as she clicked her phone shut.

"A man. An acquaintance." And then — too gently, too psychiatrically: "His name is Anthony. You'll meet him and you'll form an opinion."

"About what?"

"His suitability."

"For what?"

She picked up her coffee cup, pantomiming *refill*. The swinging door between us closed, and I waited for her return.

After a conspicuously long absence — *she's bringing water back to a boil for her French press*, I thought; *not dodging my question, not stalling*. Finally she returned, an English muffin split and toasted on a plate. She walked by me, clearly heading for her desk. "Bills to pay," she said.

I called after her, "Now I'm really nervous. Now I'm thinking you need your apartment back. And this Anthony is a therapist who makes house calls, who's going to be present when you break the news to me."

She backtracked and scolded, "Where do you get these ideas? I don't want my house back! I want more people around, not fewer."

"Including me?"

"Gwen! You're the reason I want more people around! I like the company. I think we can accommodate another."

Thus I learned that Anthony was interviewing for residency. And as much as I was looking unhappy and worried, and as often as she'd promoted democracy and equality — this, she was telling me, had to be her decision and her pocketbook's.

"Did you think about consulting me before you advertised for a roommate?"

"I didn't advertise. It just happened. Literally on the street."

"Not a panhandler, I trust."

"Of course he isn't a panhandler! He was picketing outside what used to be his office. I can't remember — which one went under? Merrill Lynch? Goldman Sachs?"

"Lehman Brothers."

"There was a whole bunch of them picketing. He had a baby in one of those slings that hang around your neck."

"A baby? How are we going to have a baby here?"

"It was a borrowed black baby for extra effect! One of his coworkers, a fellow picketer, was there with her twins, so he took one. His signage didn't hurt, either, in terms of catching my attention." She demonstrated — exaggerated scrutiny, eyes bugging out.

"What did it say?"

"To most people, his slogan would have meant nothing. But it's what stopped me cold. And when I tell you, you'll understand what drew my eye."

29

"'Will work for food?'" I asked.

"No," said Margot. "Much more . . . coincidental. And relevant. Believe it or not, the sign said NEXT STOP: THE POOR HOUSE! You can imagine how that hit me! I had to ask him if he knew about my website, didn't I?"

"Did he?" I asked.

"Absolutely not. Which made it all the more kismetish. I gave him my card so he could check out my blog," she continued. "He did. Right on the spot! On his phone! By this time, I'd kind of joined the picket line, so I was filling in the personal and domestic blanks. These financial types are always good with their gadgets, so he's reading and marching and talking and patting the baby's back. Eventually I left, and there was an e-mail waiting for me when I got back here. 'By any chance, do you have a room to let?' I said no. He didn't give up. He wrote back, 'Even for a month or two? Even a sofa? Pretty please.'"

"So you said yes?"

"I said, 'Come over for a drink and meet my sister.'"

"How old?"

"Young."

"*How* young?"

"Late twenties."

Decision obviously made, I asked, "Whose bathroom will he use?"

"The powder room. He says he'll shower at his gym."

"If he can afford gym membership —"

"That's all he *can* afford!"

"But you haven't made a firm commitment, correct?"

"Gwen. Let's be practical. Remember the stuff Daddy took care of? Wouldn't it be nice to have someone who knew his way around a fuse box? And who could unscrew jar lids? How about transferring a turkey from oven to cutting board? Remember that fiasco?"

When I didn't respond, she added, "Besides finding a job, and selling my jewelry, what's easier than bringing in an extra boarder for fifty dollars a night?"

I did the math: at least $1,800 a month.

30

"Negotiable," she added.

I asked if he could afford it and how long we could depend on that.

"He pays more than that now for half of a barely two-bedroom. As for how long, we'll see how we like him."

"Does he know about me?"

"He knows I live with my sister."

"I meant does he know I was recently widowed?"

Margot stared at me, a long, unhappy, corrective gaze. "'Recently'? Is that accurate? Because when a person says, for example, 'I was *recently* elected to Congress,' and someone asks when, and the answer is 'two years ago,' it means he's already running for reelection."

I recited what the literature liked me to believe, that everyone is different; everyone heals at a different rate, so to me, "recently" was accurate.

"Let's be open to this, and let's look at it this way: Even though we don't have much to spare, we're being charitable in our own way."

"Charitable implies that you're giving him a couch at no charge."

"Not true. He's not broke. He just doesn't want to pay for a hotel when he's between jobs and apartments."

Bereft of arguments, I asked, "You really think we have room?"

Margot gestured toward the far end of the long mahogany dining-room table, and I was obliged to follow her gaze to the six empty chairs and faraway bowl of wizened apples. "I'm expecting him at six tonight," she said. "I'll be roasting a chicken and I was hoping you'd make your corn bread and a green salad."

A whole roasted chicken and corn bread from scratch that would exhaust a half stick of butter. Anyone could read the welcome sign implied in that.

Anthony did not have the hedge-fund personality I was expecting. To begin with, he arrived with a rock star's tousled brown hair, a dimple in each not well-shaven cheek, and homemade cupcakes. "For you. For later. I don't want to overshadow whatever dessert you planned." He also exhibited something of which we were in short supply lately:

a sense of humor. As soon as he retold the picket-line-meeting story, with some new flourishes, I recognized that we might be getting some entertainment with our meals. He did a spot-on impression of Margot, how she'd led with her business card, cutting in and joining the picketers. I sneaked looks over at her to gauge any degree of offense she might be taking; she was not only enjoying herself. She was also laughing.

I wondered if he was too cheerful for a man who'd lost his domicile and his job. But how to ask? He must have sensed that I was trying to be a responsible interrogator because he volunteered, "I haven't told you everything. I'm divorced, and it's embarrassing because what I did was a felony."

"Oh shit," said Margot. "Not another."

"No, no, nothing homicidal. Not even what most people would consider criminal. I was doing a friend a favor. Actually, it was my Spanish tutor. I wanted to improve my Spanish and be the guy in the office they could send to South America. She was here on a student visa." He shrugged. "I married her so she could stay."

"And now she's divorcing you?" Margot asked.

"Immigration and Naturalization took care of that. We didn't convince anybody that it was a real marriage. They're much better detectives than I gave them credit for. And I'm a terrible liar."

"And it wasn't like a movie where you marry each other so she wouldn't be deported, and then you fall in love?" I asked.

"Ha! More like fell in hate. I had to get a lawyer and make a deal: tell the truth and save my own skin."

I said, "That was very generous of you to marry her as a favor."

"Actually, it was more stupid than generous. My mother is clamoring for an annulment. My friends thought the whole thing was moronic. The alleged bachelor party the night before the wedding was more or less an intervention. They threatened to rat on us, and I'm not so sure one of them didn't."

"She must have been a great Spanish teacher," I said.

Anthony laughed.

"She wasn't?"

"Sorry. I was laughing because I've never had such a compassionate question thrown into my fake-marriage confession."

Margot said, "What is it about men? Do they think about the people they'll hurt? Are they such slaves to their sexual impulses?"

"Actually," Anthony began. "If there had been some of that, we probably wouldn't have gotten caught."

I said, "I think my sister was talking about her ex . . ."

Anthony's face registered *Do I ask?*

Margot said, "Gwen? Do you want to do the honors?"

"Which honors?"

"The abridged version. About Charles?"

I said, pretty much in a drone, "Her ex is a physician whose patients came to him for artificial insemination, and a couple of times . . . it wasn't so artificial."

"Unsafe, adulterous, brazen, fake inseminations!" Margot cried. "And do you want to know the worst part?"

Anthony nodded.

"Once a week, on his receptionist's day off, I sat in that outer office while he did his dirty work!"

I said, "You never told me that."

"I never tell anyone. The whole thing is humiliating enough without it having happened on my watch."

"You don't know that!" I said.

"*Did* you know?" Anthony asked Margot.

"I certainly did not! I'd have killed him! I couldn't even go to his trial. I threw him out the minute the DNA results came back on the baby who came out of it. Who, by the way, is already a teenager. And guess what his name is? Charles! Named for the gifted physician who cured his mother's barren womb."

I said, in the silence that greeted Margot's outburst, "Her ex is in a minimum-security prison. He calls every other week."

"Collect," said Margot.

Poor Anthony. "Wow," he said. "I'm sorry. Are you sure this is a good time for you to be taking in a stranger?"

Margot said, "I know that it seems as if every topic has a touch of the tragic, but now you've heard the worst."

"Dessert?" I asked.

"Not yet," said Margot. "Are your parents alive?" she asked him.

"They are. Both."

"Still together?"

"Still together."

"Are you estranged from them?" I asked.

"Not estranged, just far away. They moved to Arizona when they retired. For the climate. My dad has asthma."

"Otherwise you might have moved home when you lost your job?" I asked.

"Maybe," said Anthony. "But unlikely." He hesitated. "They lived way out on the island. Hauppauge."

"How far is that via the Long Island Railroad?" I asked.

Margot said, "This is getting very boring. Shall we open another bottle? Gwen, tell Anthony about your business idea while I get dessert."

Alone with Anthony, I said, "It's nothing. A fleeting idea I had for an escort service of the platonic kind."

From the other side of the swinging door, Margot yelled, "Strictly G-rated. Believe me. She'd find men who take presentable members of her widows' support group out to dinner and maybe get a peck on the cheek when they part at the coatroom." She returned with her own dessert concoction: baked fruit cocktail, a 1950s recipe that cost no more than the dented can its principal ingredient came in — and one white cupcake cut into thirds. "I took you at your word, that the cupcakes were a hostess gift. They're adorable."

Out of politeness — surely a cake mix, not worth the calories — I helped myself to my one-third of the cupcake. I tasted it, finished it, closed my eyes, and smiled.

34

"Like it?" he asked.

"It's unbelievable."

"I'm glad. Not everyone likes coconut."

Margot claimed her portion and moaned as soon as her mouth closed over the first bite. She pronounced something with her mouth full that I didn't get until she repeated it: "Butter."

"Correct," said Anthony.

"Whose recipe?" I asked.

"Mine. I've had a little too much time on my hands."

"You could make a killing with these," Margot said.

Anthony said, "Everyone who bakes a good cake thinks that. The cupcake market is saturated."

I asked what the other flavors were. He said, "I think I brought red velvet, mocha, rum-raisin . . . chocolate-chocolate, of course. Um . . . I think I included one I call carrot and burnt sugar."

Margot murmured in my direction. "I think this is going very well, don't you?"

Anthony was gathering dishes and stacking them with the expertise of a young man whose parents had raised him doing chores. Backing through the swinging door, he said, "I'll let you two conference."

Margot said, "We only need a minute." As soon as he was gone, she said, "Do you love him? What if we put a bed in the storeroom? He can put his stuff in a pantry drawer."

"Did you say 'Put a bed in the storeroom'?"

"With all our junk out of there, it's got bedroom potential. I happen to know that my sellers used it as a maid's room."

"Were they slave owners?" I asked.

Minutes later Anthony agreed to take the closetless one hundred square feet that was currently housing all the boxes I'd never unpacked. Whatever downsizing had brought him to our door made him agree without whining to quarters big enough for only a narrow bed and stubborn built-in pantry drawers originally meant for table linens.

"I'm very grateful," Anthony told us. "And I'm sending out résumés by the dozen every day. And don't worry about the size of the back room, because it looks to me like home sweet home."

"How long do you think—" I started to ask, but Margot interrupted with "We're glad we can help a fellow victim of the recession and personal setbacks."

Grinning, Anthony asked if we felt as if we were taking in a foster child.

I looked at my sister. Did I mention she was wearing a soft, cream-colored blouse that showed off her lovely neckline? Her skirt was straight and not that easy to sit down in; her shoes were oxblood patent leather and open at the toe. I couldn't help but wonder if she was thinking *foster child* at all.

6

Anthony's Interests

H E MOVED IN thirty-six hours later with his laptop, backpack, duffel, weights, compact discs, and muffin tins. From our basement storage unit, now housing leftovers from my former life, he selected a futon, a rug, a quilt, a floor lamp, and a framed French movie poster of *The Producers*. He said his parents were relieved; they liked the sound of two mature ladies watching over him. Should they send a gift basket of fruit or products indigenous to Arizona? "I took the liberty of suggesting wine," he said.

Neither Margot nor I have ever thought of ourselves as fascinating, but suddenly we were. Anthony approached our meals and conversations as if he'd scored an orchestra seat to a sold-out show. He is more communicative than almost all the men I've known. We think it's his age — that he spent four years in coed dorms and after that shared cubicles and conference tables with women. His questions aren't rude or overly personal; they all have a getting-to-know-you quality, and we are flattered at his unflagging attention. Not to be discounted: He is also a newcomer to our signature topics of fraud, extortion, and sudden death.

"Tell me when I'm prying," he says. We haven't yet. As polite women, we try to turn the tables conversationally. He'll say, "You already know about my marriage and divorce. Nothing more to report there. Classic green-card arrangement. Happy childhood. Played T-ball, flag football, a little tennis, a lot of soccer. Never progressed beyond jayvee. College, Wall Street."

"Siblings?"

"One sister, younger. For now an au pair."

"Where?" we ask.

"Upper East Side. Fifth Avenue, in the nineties. Park view."

"Here! New York City! When do we meet her?" Margot asked.

"I never see her. She's a slave."

"Nice children at least?" I ask.

"Two lawyers with one baby."

"Boy or girl?" I ask.

Anthony says, "Umm. Girl? I forget. She has one of those androgynous names like Tyler or Taylor."

We move in that direction every so often — our interviewing Anthony — but mostly we experience him as moderator. It's part gregariousness and part something else, sociology or anthropology, as if he's never had the chance to discuss the stages of life beyond his own. He is happy here. And he is easy to have around, both thoughtful and helpful. He's freed us from stereotyping and hating men who have anything to do with Wall Street or wealth management. As far as being handy, he has exceeded our expectations. In the first twenty-four hours of his residency, he put batteries in our remote control, set our clocks ahead to daylight savings time, and gave new life to what we thought was an inoperative ice maker. He always has the right cable needed for various transfers of information that we didn't even know we wanted. He can see and talk to his far-flung friends while sitting at his computer, and he is the king of uploading and downloading, of searches and hunts.

He likes his room, or at least its location on the other side of the kitchen, somewhat segregated. When he's home, we often find him at the kitchen island, on a stool with his laptop and vitamin water. "Praying at the altar," he says with a smile. He bakes a double batch of cupcakes every week, some for us, and the rest as offerings to his dates.

I'm not sure where he meets these young ladies, but he must, wherever he goes. His phone vibrates and barks fairly constantly. He is exceedingly polite in our presence. Whatever calls, e-mails, and texts pour in, Anthony doesn't return them until dinner and conversation conclude.

He asked both of us, after weeks under our roof, if we dated. He hadn't noticed too much traffic of that variety, coming or going. "None of my business, of course," he added.

I don't mind answering his questions, which would be awkward if he was a man my age instead of the kid in running shorts and flip-flops, eating leftover Chinese food straight from the refrigerator. His youth provides the comfort level. He is like a teaching assistant in a psych course called Spinsterhood. So I admit, "I might be a candidate for Chaste Dates myself. But less so now than a year ago."

Margot yells to him from the dining room, "Now tell us who you were out with last night."

"The lucky lady who got the pink cupcakes," I add.

Anthony does a very sweet thing at this moment. He takes me by the hand and leads me into the dining room, where he says, "Please be seated."

I do, but he continues to stand, Chinese food abandoned in the kitchen. He says solemnly, "I just realized, when Margot asked me who I went out with last night, that I've put you on the wrong track."

"Which is what?" I ask.

"Let me put it this way: Young ladies don't appreciate cupcakes. They're all on diets. They dump them or regift them." He pauses, smiles. "On the other hand, dudes scarf them down."

Margot and I are still smiling expectantly, not realizing that his announcement is whole and complete, if not eloquent.

"Hmmm," he says with a theatrically perplexed hand to his chin. "I see that I haven't made my point."

"You're not going to be baking cupcakes anymore?" I ask.

Anthony says, "Let me put it this way: Dear ladies, I'm gay. I thought you might have guessed that already, but apparently not."

Margot says, "Well! I am a little stunned." She puts her coffee cup down, hitches one nightgown strap back in place. "But not in a bad way."

"Did the INS guess faster than we did?" I ask.

"Quite. Like immediately."

I said, "I hope you know we are very, very pro-gay. I think I can speak for both of us."

"She certainly can," says Margot. "In fact, I can't believe how lucky we are. We get a man under our roof, a man's opinions and his mechanical ability, but without any sexual tension whatsoever. It's almost too good to be true."

"And vice versa," he says.

Margot and I did not realize how fascinated a homosexual man would be with the details of a life lived under the banner of gynecology. Another thing we failed to anticipate was that anyone with even a modicum of intellectual curiosity would Google the family scandal that brought Margot — and consequently we her boarders — to this beautiful home.

Most of the Charles-centric conversations took place between Anthony and me when Margot was out or asleep. I was feeling a little guilty and disloyal discussing her traumas behind her back, but Anthony pointed out that the holes in my knowledge were rather astonishing. I had not attended the trial of my brother-in-law? *Really?*

I said that he and Margot were separated by then and she was virtually in hiding so I spent those days with her. Besides —

"I know," he said — was it a little wearily? — "your own personal tragic loss."

I said, managing to smile, "My footnote to everything, right?"

"Understandably."

"And the basic facts were bad enough — the cheating and the fornicating. Did I really need all the details?"

As ever, he was at his laptop. He asked if I drank beer and I said yes, sure. Did he mean now? We had *beer*?

"We do, Miss Gwen. My treat."

With refreshments served, he pulled the second kitchen stool closer to his laptop and said, "Sit. Shall we?"

The headlines he produced referenced Charles — not by name but by variations on "Jersey Sperm Doc" and "Fertility Chuck."

Anthony said, "Based on what I'm seeing, it was huge. Hard *not* to know the details."

I thought I had paid some attention at the time, but apparently I was deaf to many nuances. I had missed one of the biggest bomb-shells, which was the appearance, live on the witness stand, of women who'd paid five thousand dollars for unsterile fertility procedures conducted on a leather couch in the doctor's private office. Yes, they admitted in cross-examination, it was consensual. Yes, they had been draped. No, there had been no kissing or fondling. And yes, they had been desperate to have a child and yes, maybe they had sobbed when told that the donor didn't show up on the appointed day. And yes, both parties had agreed that they shouldn't let the window of opportunity pass.

"What a jerk," Anthony grumbled. "And where was his nurse?"

I angled his laptop toward me and began clicking the NEXT arrow at the bottom of the breathless stories. I sipped my beer straight from the bottle and said, "Maybe I *should* know more. I'm the one who accepts Charles's calls from the pokey. Maybe I've been a little too nice."

"There's more." Anthony took back possession of his keyboard and typed something into a search box.

A timeline and birth certificate were before me, and a photo of the son, probably in third or fourth grade — assuredly a school photo, its background a web of blue and pink laser beams.

This is the world now. This is how Anthony, within minutes, found a son spawned by Charles: He went on Facebook and "friended" him.

7

Notice

A YOUNG WOMAN WITH short, cowlicked blond hair and dark roots was asleep on our living-room couch, lavender spaghetti straps visible above an heirloom granny afghan we considered too dowdy to display. I might have yelped, but there was something about the way her shoes — red ballerina flats — were neatly, almost mathematically, lined up at the approximate spot where her feet would land upon rising that seemed trustworthy. Should I wake her? Or wake Margot or Anthony to fill in the blanks? It was not yet seven a.m., so I decided to grind some coffee beans and let that racket serve as the alarm clock. First, though, I tiptoed closer to the sleeping intruder for clues, at which point I solved the mystery myself. Next to her, having floated to the floor, was a Post-it note in a familiar hand. It said, "Meet Olivia, my sister. Will explain. xo A."

I felt that the calm and mature thing to do was not to wake anyone but to carry on. I retreated to the kitchen and poured myself juice. Yesterday's *Daily News* was on the island, open to a photograph meant for critical analysis: a shot of Mrs. Bernie Madoff furiously exiting a Burger Heaven on Lexington, take-out bag in hand. The headline, circled, read GOTTA BEEF, RUTHIE? Margot, who'd added devil's horns to Ruthie's baseball cap, would be blogging about that culinary comedown later, I was sure.

And then, in the doorway, taller than she'd looked horizontally, taller than her brother, was our unexpected guest, red plaid boxer shorts below a lavender camisole, pink-encased smartphone in one hand. She introduced herself: Olivia Sarno, sister of Anthony. I said, "I know. Your brother left a note on you. I'm Gwen."

She asked what time it was. I pointed to the digital clock on the microwave — 7:05 — which caused Olivia to mumble, "Oh, shit."

"Too early?" I asked. "Or too late?"

"Late. But, you know — so what? I gave my notice yesterday." Then, with a grin and a slide onto the nearest kitchen stool, she said, "Fuck 'em, don't you think? How about a little comp time for once?" She pulled the newspaper closer, pointed, and said, "Oh, right. Anthony told me that one of you lost all of your money to this Madoff guy."

"Margot. Still asleep. And you're the au pair sister?"

"Not for long," she said. "Two more weeks."

I asked if she'd like coffee, which made her jump off the stool and say, "I'll get it! Here? Filters are where?"

I said, "Sit down. You're a guest." I pointed to the cell phone in her hand. "Do you want to call your employer and tell her you'll be late?"

"Tell *him*. She's out the door already. Her hours are insane."

She volunteered that the baby's mother took a mere two weeks off for maternity leave. "Noel was the one who took family leave, six weeks. Until I got hired," she said.

"Noel is the husband?"

"Noel . . . would be the husband."

From what he liked to call his "wing," from the chin-up bar he'd installed over the pantry door, Anthony called, "That's right. The husband. And paramour."

Ten athletic grunts later, he was in the kitchen, barefoot and wearing only sweatpants. He crossed to the refrigerator, opened it, and took out butter and a carton of eggs. Olivia and I watched him crack too many eggs into a bowl and beat them rather mercilessly. "Hers," he finally stated, pointing. "My sister's paramour."

43

The eggs met the melted butter with a sizzle. "Want me to tell Gwen what's going on, or would you prefer your own spin?" he asked.

Olivia said, "Go ahead, Anthony. Knock yourself out." She asked me which bathroom she should use and could she borrow a towel. I led her toward mine, and when I returned to the kitchen, I said, "She seems pretty much . . . together."

"You are correct," said Anthony. "Oh, is she ever together. I see it, too. Miss In Charge. Miss What Goes Around Comes Around. She doesn't understand the damage she can do."

"*She* can do? Even though her employer made sexual advances? I'm missing something here."

"I didn't say sexual predator. I said paramour. My stupid sister is in love with him! They were *welcome* sexual advances! Very! And she's enjoying it because she hates the wife!" With a dishtowel around the skillet handle, he bumped the pan to an unlit burner and muttered, "Why did I start this now? They'll be cold by the time she's dressed."

"I'll have some," I said.

He opened the dishwasher and began emptying it with too much clanging.

"Leave it. Tell me the rest. What is Olivia's version?"

"She took the job because of him — hot, according to her — and because she felt sorry for the baby, having a mother who held her like she was holding out her arms for a stack of clean towels. Classic!"

I asked how old Olivia was and how long she'd been working for this couple.

"Twenty-four. And on the job for six months, seven? Something like that. She knew right away. She told me — confessed after a half pitcher of sangria one night — that she had a crush on the dad. And you know what I said? I said, 'Well, that makes the job a little more interesting, doesn't it?' Like I'd say to a kid in high school who had a crush on her math teacher. Who knew it was mutual? Who knew that the guy who married a ballbuster attorney in Armani was going to fall for a scruffy little college dropout?"

"You've met these people?"

"No, he has *not*," said Olivia. She was back, now in jeans, a parka patched with duct tape, and a fluffy pink scarf framing a face that was — though scrubbed and unadorned — beautiful. *Employment agencies might take cautionary notice*, I thought. *Bad idea to have early-morning, unaffected beauty so evident in a live-in nanny.*

She turned to me. "Did he tell you that I'm in a very sticky situation? That my boss confessed he was in love with me?"

Anthony said, "Which I'm not buying."

Olivia said, "Noel told me that he couldn't deny it any longer, that he knew I felt the same way, that he and his wife hardly ever had sex since Skyler was born. And not because Davida was working 24-7, or because she had no sex drive after the baby was born — all true, by the way. And now, because of me" — a squeak of a sob escaped — "and he was in agony."

Anthony snickered.

"Not that kind of agony. He meant emotional agony. Psychic agony."

Anthony turned to me. "Would you believe it? A lawyer? Of the do-good variety? In this day and age? What an asshole!"

"What would you have done if you were in love with him?" Olivia demanded. "Push him away? Say, 'Take a hike'?"

"Yes! For legal reasons! For — I don't know — for Nanny Cam reasons! You should've said, for the record, 'If you ever do that again; if you ever suggest what I think you're suggesting, I quit.'"

Olivia said, "Yes, Anthony. I know how pissed off you get when a hot guy comes on to you. Puh-lease."

Anthony said, "I gave your eggs to Gwen. That's your juice on the island. And you can take a cupcake — over there, in the Tupperware. Then get going, though I forget why I'm sending you back there, especially if what's-her-name —"

"Davida."

"If Davida's left for the office and her poor, misunderstood, horny, middle-aged husband is waiting for you under their designer duvet."

"He's middle-aged?" I asked.

45

"He's thirty-four!" said Olivia. "They were only married like a week when Davida got pregnant. Big mistake! She was all nice until they marched down the aisle. She spent the entire honeymoon on the phone with her associates and paralegals — some big federal case that was going to trial."

"So now what?" Anthony demanded. "He's going to admit to the world, 'I'm a walking cliché. I'm divorcing my mean wife and I'm in lust with my nanny.'"

Olivia turned to me. "Did my brother tell you about his own personal, ridiculous wedding? How he married someone he didn't love and never could? So you'll excuse me if I don't take your advice, Tony Baloney. Sometimes this happens: Two people fall in love, for real, even if one of them is the help. Some people, some sympathetic people, might even view it as fate, that of all the applicants the agency could've sent, of all the potential au pairs, why me? What force in the universe put my résumé at the top of the pile?"

I admit: I liked that. I didn't want to say it aloud, but I was starting to see the miserably married, love-starved, paternity-leave-taking, and pro-bono-inclined Noel as sincere. I also didn't want to admit how I was factoring in Edwin. What if he had already had a wife when I first saw him at the Steinway grand? What if he'd played an Irving Berlin love song that was a metaphor for a future together and later, over our first innocent coffee, had confessed his marital misery? Would I have rebuffed him? I put an unfrosted carrot cupcake in a Baggie for her. Some biologically based need to pair things up made me pack a second one. Olivia thanked me. "Anthony's been telling me how great you and your sister have been."

I detected a signal between brother and sister, a prompt involving some point of etiquette. I saw her squint in a failure to understand, and then clarity dawned.

"Um . . ." she began. "I didn't have a chance yet to say I'm sorry for your loss. Anthony told me last night about your husband."

I said, "Thank you. It's never too late to hear that."

"Call me, Liv," said Anthony. "And don't do anything more lunatic than you already have."

"It'll be fine. Noel texted me. The baby's still asleep. He'll go to the office when I get to the apartment."

And just when I thought he'd regained his composure, Anthony said, "Give him my congratulations. At long last, he gets a vagina that doesn't leave for the office at dawn."

"Isn't that nice?" Olivia threw back. "Just what a dickhead says to his sister."

"Someone's gotta speak the truth," he said. "Someone's gotta say, 'This can't have a happy ending, no matter what your pheromones are telling you.'"

Olivia, already at the front door, returned. "Oh, really? Well, how about this, Mister Marriage Counselor: Noel's father took him aside and said, man to man, 'Does Davida make you happy?' And when Noel just stared back all red-eyed, his father said, 'Do what you have to do. Do it while the baby is too young to understand what a divorce is. And don't tell your mother I said this.'"

Anthony said, "Even with my bullshit, doomed, bogus, illegal marriage, Dad said something like 'Son, even if your heart's not in it — and I'm not saying I want you to be a heterosexual — but I'm thinking of your vows. For better and for worse, under God, and all that . . .'"

I didn't have a brother, and even with all our sisterly fights growing up and our recent turns for the tragic, we weren't a dramatic family. At 7:25 a.m. I was transfixed.

"Dad said that? Dad wanted you to stay married to that crazy Ecuadorian?"

"In effect . . ."

"Such a liar you are," said Olivia, and with a kiss to each of her brother's cheeks, she rushed away.

8

Professional Standards

ANTHONY WAS EXPLAINING to me why a service called Chaste Dates, screaming "abstinence," was doomed out of the starting gate. What normal man, gay or straight, is going to agree to an evening at which any form of sexual activity is precluded from the get-go, he asked.

Did he not think there were normal men who — because of various personal setbacks or performance anxieties or extra pounds — could've reordered their social priorities?

Margot walked into the room at that exact moment and asked, "Like the chief executive herself?"

I said, "We've been over this, Margot. I'm not you and I'm not in the market."

She made a grand sweeping gesture, a half curtsy, in my direction as she asked Anthony, "Have you met my sister, Queen Victoria?"

Her attention shifted abruptly with a ping from the sideboard, her laptop signaling that someone had entered the PoorHouse's chat room.

"I'll be right back," she said, laptop under one arm, as she circled back for her wine glass on the way out.

Anthony next did what he often did during a lapse in the conversation — dropped to the floor to do push-ups. He was tireless about his athletic activities. His props were everywhere: a jump rope, hand weights, ankle weights, dumbbells. From the floor, he exhaled one word as if it were a whole depressed sentence: "Women."

"What about women?"

Between breaths he asked, "May I be honest?"

I waited.

"Your sister has a website that gets one hit a week. And you have an imaginary dating service."

"So?"

"I'm only speaking for myself, for what I might do."

"Which is . . . ?"

"Shake something up! Get a loan! Advertise! Margot could get a publicist. Or blog on a site that would pay her and that had readers. Or get a book deal. Or — hate to say it — work outside the home."

Did we not feel professionally inadequate enough without his holding a mirror up to our limited entrepreneurial skills? Was Mr. Advice himself employed? I managed to say "Tea?" to escape further discussion of anything. After a hundred push-ups, he was panting and sweating. I knew he'd say no to a hot drink.

I joined Margot in her bedroom to read over her shoulder. The latest entry, by someone with the screen name HardUp, was *Let him eat shit!!!!*

"What's that about?" I asked.

"Someone heard the lifer is getting special meals in prison. So, of course, we're all guessing — kosher? Low fat? Atkins? Or just fancier than what's on the menu. Also, Ruth is commuting between Manhattan and Boca, where she's delivering meals to the housebound." Margot consulted an open page of the *New York Post* next to her laptop and read aloud, "With frequent pit stops in North Carolina to visit her jailbird hubby."

"How many chatting tonight?" I asked.

"So far, three of us."

I asked if she wanted me to log on and join the discussion. And should I recruit Anthony?

"You're enough. Are you registered?"

I said of course I was. Give me two minutes and I'd jump in.

By the time I logged on from my room, the chat had gone silent. Margot yelled from down the hall, "Write something!"

I typed *Maybe he's bribing the guards for better food!*

HardUp wrote *w $$ he stol & hid!*

I could see that no one proofread what he wrote and there was a shorthand I should learn. A visitor named SadDad added a string of symbols that I took to be epithets, then exited, signaled by a cute little sound effect of a door hinge squeaking.

Margot yelled, "You can leave now!"

I typed, in the spirit and letter of the culture, *have 2 go.* But I didn't leave. I kept reading.

Alone @ last wrote HardUp.

Anyone w/ u? Margot wrote back.

Jess asleep was his answer.

What about Thur? Margot wrote.

Can't wait HardUp wrote back.

Who was HardUp, who was Jess, and who was Thur? I couldn't ask Margot because she'd know I was spying and eavesdropping. But this much I could deduce on my own: HardUp and Margot met alone in cyberspace more often than I or any other chatter knew.

Inevitable, I suppose, given the way romance germinates in this century, that Margot would attract admirers among her following. Luckily, she introduced the subject by asking the next evening, over turkey meatloaf, mashed potatoes, and carrot coins, if we thought it was a bad precedent to have coffee with a person she'd met in a chat room.

"Depends on which chat room," said Anthony.

"Mine. Where else would I be?"

"Man or woman?" he asked.

"Man. At least I think so."

"Which screen name?" I asked.

"HardUp."

"No clue there," said Anthony, with a wink for me.

"Does he have a real name?" I asked.

"Roy."

"He asked you out for coffee in front of everyone else?"

"He did ask, but in a private box. That thing that Anthony helped me set up."

"IM," Anthony explained.

"He could be a serial killer," I said.

"Thank you, Grandma," Margot said.

Anthony said, "You and I could go with her and sit at the next table like undercover agents." He smiled. "Or we can sit in the squad car, and Margot can wear a wire."

Before I could think of a comeback that demonstrated I was less of a wet blanket and perpetual Victorian widow than I was being portrayed as, Anthony added, "It's not too different from Match.com or Nerve or OkCupid, sending perfect strangers out into the world."

I said there were professional standards to consider. If the others found out Margot was dating one of their own, they'd think she was playing favorites. There might be some hurt feelings.

"What dating and what others?" she asked.

I reached back and came up with "SadDad."

"Hmmm. Let me see. HardUp versus SadDad?" said Anthony. "No contest."

Margot said, "I can see that no matter how many times I say 'Roy,' you two are going to enjoy calling him by his screen name."

"Which says a lot about a person," I argued.

"Have you ever laid eyes on this guy?" Anthony asked.

"He e-mailed me a photo so I'd recognize him at Starbucks," she said.

"*And?*" asked Anthony.

"And what?"

"Good-looking?"

"I didn't form an opinion."

Anthony said, "Translation: butt ugly."

"I'm sorry I brought this up," said Margot.

"Did you ever talk to him?" I asked. "I mean live. On the phone?"

"Once."

"Who called whom?"

"He called me. But it wasn't a personal call. He asked — sort of joking — if anyone in the five boroughs wanted to buy Girl Scout cookies, and if so, send an e-mail to thus and such address. I wrote him to say that I fully supported Girl Scouts and sold their cookies myself throughout my childhood, but it would be best not to use the website for commercial gain. He felt bad about violating the rule, so he called. I mean, I'm listed. You don't need a gumshoe to find me."

"Why is he selling Girl Scout cookies?" Anthony asked.

"His daughter is, so he's helping. Nowadays, parents get involved. You know this phenomenon, right? Helicopter parents? Hovering over every little activity and every piece of homework?"

"Is he married?" I asked.

"That I don't know."

"Still, you're having coffee with him," I said.

"Did you ever know such a babe in the woods?" Margot asked Anthony. She tapped me on the wrist. "It's *coffee*. Even if it was more than coffee, even if we were going out for a drink, for martinis, for mojitos, for — God forgive me — dinner, there are people around! I'm not going down any dark alleys. We are cohorts, fellow soldiers, victims. I think I can be friends with a man who's married. Who knows? He might bring his wife along. Or his boyfriend! What do I know?"

Anthony said, "My money's on him being divorced or separated, with joint custody of the kid, and the website makes him feel as if you're friends and he's ready for the next step." I noticed a charitable tilt of his head in my direction, which Margot wasn't interpreting.

"What?" she asked. "Just say it."

He said, "Have you ever heard of those parties where single women

52

invite their nonstarter ex-boyfriends so they can meet all the single friends? Like a rejects party?"

"No," I said.

"I have," said Margot.

"So what I was thinking was if you don't feel any chemistry and this Roy is, in fact, available . . ." He now points at me, all subtlety abandoned.

I said — and how many times was I required to announce this? — that I was not looking for a boyfriend.

Anthony said, "Not a boyfriend." He smiled. "Just a good time."

"He's actually right," said Margot. "Your circle of friends seems to have shrunk to nobody."

I asked, "Why would I be looking to make friends with an angry, penniless blogger?"

"A good time has nothing to do with friendship," said Margot. "Jesus! A good time means — you tell her."

Anthony said, "Recreational sex."

I declared, in an effort to improve my image, "I can find my own recreational sex partners, thank you."

"Some day we'll tell Roy about this conversation," said Anthony. "How we hemmed and hawed and practically took a vote on whether Margot should meet him in broad daylight for a cup of coffee."

"This is New York City," I said. "This isn't Grover's Corners. People leave their homes and are never seen again."

"That's a *no* vote," said Anthony.

"What choice do I have," Margot asked, "if I want my two boxes of Thin Mints and two of Do-si-dos?"

"My money says he's already got a crush on you from your *très charmant* blog entries and that very nice headshot on your home page," said Anthony.

Margot yelped, "Really? That was taken when I was, like, forty!"

I said, "I don't think you've changed."

"Me, neither," said Anthony. "In fact, I think you look younger in person."

Margot laughed, giving me permission to follow suit.

Anthony said, "Some great guy is going to come along and sweep you off your feet. You'll see. You, too, Gwen. Both sets of feet. And neither one is going to be an adulterer or a penniless blogger or a serial killer."

That was so Anthony, our optimist. Margot and I said we wished the same for him.

9

We'll Never See Those Pearls Again

I T ISN'T JUST CHARLES who hovers and haunts from prison, but his mother, Lenore, who does so from Brandywine Senior Living in New Jersey. She declares in frequent phone calls that the money Margot lost was her son's and therefore rightfully, morally, and every which way hers.

"Then what's your point?" we hear Margot ask. "What part of zero would you like to collect?"

That is when her ex-mother-in-law changes the subject from bill collection to marriage vows. What, she demands, did Margot mean when she stood before God and said the words "for better or for worse" if not that she would swim alongside Charles when he found himself in hot water?

Margot was weary. She used to deliver a litany of her ex's broken commandments, but now says only "C'mon, Lenore. You have to accept that your boy did some pretty unforgivable things."

As Anthony and I eavesdrop, we can guess Lenore's question because we hear Margot answering "*Why* is it against the law? Do you mean did he go to prison for personally inseminating patients? Not officially. But he was convicted of fraud and lying to a grand jury and" — she makes this up since Mrs. P's legal knowledge is pitiful — "they got him on statutory medical rape." She winks at me when she says this and I give her a thumb's up. With a large dose of the entertainer in her, she is braver when her roommates are present.

We think Lenore is establishing a paper trail or perhaps is just bored because she writes weekly to Margot. Her letters maintain that Charles's activities were not shenanigans but science. He was only trying to help desperate women get pregnant! If Margot had gone to the trial as she was supposed to, she'd understand that he had acted out of mercy. And surely Margot knows the pain of childlessness.

That is the cruelest cut of all. Anthony and I literally wrestle the phone from Margot's hand to keep her from calling Lenore and escalating the battle. We pour her a drink and we agree: mean. So mean. An old woman distilled to her essence: cruel and stupid and immune to fact and reason.

And the latest! Lenore wants her pearls back, the long-ago engagement present she now says were family heirlooms merely on loan! The nerve! We know this is a lie. Margot went with her then-future mother-in-law to lunch, which was followed by a surprise errand in the diamond district. First Margot tries reason: "Lenore, do you remember our lunch? In the café at B. Altman? And then we walked over to your family jeweler and we picked them out? Brand-new ones?"

Lenore disagrees. Those were family pearls being restrung by that jeweler, a Jewish man on West 47th Street. If he was still alive, he'd back her up. They were merely picking them up or perhaps they were choosing a clasp. Margot says the worst and most frustrating part is that if Lenore was hooked up to a lie detector, she'd pass — so wholeheartedly does she believe that the pearls were in her family for generations and therefore subject to recall.

Margot might have stalled or dissembled with "They're in a vault and I never can get to the bank when it's open." Or "Charles took them back when we got divorced. Didn't he tell you?" But she was so stunned and so furious that she yelled the truth. "Well, guess what, Lenore? I sold them." And for good, vitriolic measure she added,

"And I had to sell my engagement ring, too. Was that your property as well?"

It has become, as we say around here, World War Three.

We don't have to be psychologists to see what's ailing Lenore. Her son the doctor is now her son the felon. Displacement has made Margot — rather than the judge, jury, prosecution, or DNA results — the enemy. She is not interested in the fine points of the divorce settlement. All she knows is this: Her boy went to medical school, worked around the clock, and was so run down during his internship, residency, and fellowship that he caught every cold and needed emergency surgery on what was perilously close to a burst appendix.

Have I mentioned that Lenore divorced Charles's father for adultery on a grand scale? What we know is Charles's version, which was alleged by his mother on his sixteenth birthday during intermission at *Man of La Mancha,* that Mr. Pierrepont supposedly forced himself on every secretary he ever hired and had a genius for recruiting the young and the willing. Eventually, he fell in love with the least wifely of the set, a woman named Juliet, of all things. He eloped to Florida, had two little girls — now in their twenties, if we haven't lost count — and kept in touch with Charles and his sister only in the form of birthday cards, child support, and attendance at college graduations.

Due to the budgetary necessity of eliminating sessions with her therapist, Margot is encouraged by me to obsess aloud about Mrs. Pierrepont. I contribute because I know and resent Lenore myself. She came to my wedding, and we had Thanksgiving dinners together at Margot's table for twenty-plus years, but she neither attended Edwin's funeral nor sent condolences in any form.

We are quite sure that Lenore's companion, Teddy, who is estranged from his own children due to *their* alleged financial wrong turns, eggs her on. Margot says Lenore was always obsessed with money, perhaps the fault of her living through the Great Depression, and our own recession is bringing it back into focus. Some of what I've learned in my widows' group applies to Margot and her ex-mother-in-law—that daughters-in-law are not to be trusted. Daughters-in-law are suspect. Money earned inside a marriage belongs to the son alone, no matter his crimes or who did the breadwinning.

Discussing Margot's mother-in-law problems leads me to posthumous appreciation of my own in-laws, Edwin's lovely parents, who died before I could meet them. They married late, had Edwin in their forties to their great delight. He was adored but not spoiled; they gave him not just piano lessons but also pipe organ lessons and daily chores to promote responsibility and neatness. They let him have a succession of canaries, a dog, and two cats despite their own allergies. Their wedding portrait had a place of honor on our bureau throughout our marriage, and only recently did I replace it with our own.

Betsy is a great ally on the topic of Lenore at our semimonthly dinners—tonight around the corner at Elephant & Castle, where the three of us share two entrées (sliced steak and salmon *en papillote)* and each of us orders a wedge of iceberg with blue cheese and bacon, which Margot and I pledge to make at home.

Our banker baby sister is unsentimental and unsympathetic to exactly the right degree in dispensing advice re Lenore. "Hang up on her," Betsy instructs Margot. "Or, better yet, don't answer."

"Then she writes letters," I say.

"Threaten to sue her for harassment, or whatever would get her to stop."

"I could," Margot muses. "I throw made-up legal terms at her all the time. I don't think she'd run any threat by a lawyer, because she'd have to pay him."

"Do we think she's fronting for Charles?" Betsy asks. "I mean is he the one who wants the pearls and the money?"

Margot says, "He has plenty of money. You'll remember I only got half. And he can't spend a cent of it at Otisville."

"Maybe it's not the money," I say. "Maybe it's the pearls themselves. Maybe he has a girlfriend he wants to propose to. Men in prison, especially the famous ones, always attract girlfriends. I think there are even websites for women who want to meet the incarcerated."

"All a moot point," says Margot. "I'll never see those pearls again."

Betsy asks how much Margot got for them.

"I don't even know. It was a lump sum for what he called the lot — three pins, some bracelets, an old locket, and my engagement ring."

"I hope you got a second opinion," said Betsy.

When Margot only sips her martini, Betsy asks again, "Did you shop the stuff around?"

"I didn't. The guy seemed honest and his ad said 'No higher prices paid.'"

I could read Betsy's expression. It was saying *I wish you'd come to us. I'd have bought them. You'd know where they were and you could even buy them back as if I were your own private pawnbroker.*

I change the subject because I know that the pearls are a symbol for all that has gone wrong financially and romantically for Margot. I wish I too had stepped in to save them, had figured out in some nineteenth-century way — Marry a robber baron? Sell my hair? — to have been the safety net beneath Margot's jewelry box.

I bring up one of our favorite topics, our own parents, and we three smile wistfully. In contrast to every Pierrepont, our own father was of the faithful, even romantic breed of husband. It took our own entries into adulthood to interpret the gestures and glances passing between our parents, which had meant nothing to three little girls. Not that there were flamboyant public displays, but now we smile at the excuses that took them early to bed, and the noise we were told in the morning was Daddy tickling Mommy. We love reminding one another that while our mother was always polite, always careful around Margot on the subject of Lenore, there were never two greater polar opposites on the scale of maternal reasonableness.

After we reminisce, we grow solemn. One of us always says, "Why couldn't Mom and Dad have lived to a ripe old age instead of Lenore?" We wish we'd had them longer, that they'd have lived to see Betsy's boys grow up. "It's probably better that they didn't live to see me become a widow or what Charles did to Margot," I'll usually say.

"Not to mention what *Madoff* did to Margot," Betsy adds.

In truth, we know our parents would have survived our catastrophes exceptionally well. They would have been stalwarts and rocks in these times. We stir our coffee and perpetuate the lie, nodding sadly. *Yes, it's a good thing for them and their huge hearts that they didn't live to see our troubles.*

10

Delicado

H OW HAD MARGOT neglected to share the startling news that Dr. Charles W. Pierrepont, released absurdly early for good behavior, was living at the Batavia? Not in our apartment, naturally, but in one of the dark ground-floor studios off a back hallway, which was once the domain of nannies, cooks, and maids. This staggering intelligence came to light when bills addressed to Charles showed up in our mailbox. Margot's reaction was not "Forward them to Otisville," but a brusque "Give them to the doorman."

Handing the waylaid bills to Rafael, Anthony asked if he had the doctor's, um, current address.

"One D," said Rafael, pointing toward the archway between the elevators. "I'll make sure he gets them."

Two hours later, at dinner, Anthony said — in a tone that implied *inculpatory evidence withheld* — "Maybe I missed this in previous conversations, but I just learned that your ex-husband is out of the Big House and living in the Batavia."

"Do you mean Charles?" Margot asked.

"Indeed Charles. He seems to be living downstairs."

"What do you mean — 'living in the Batavia?'" I asked.

"One D. The servants' quarters," said Anthony.

We both looked at Margot, who only said, "No one's eating the applesauce. I used up those McIntoshes that were going bad."

I asked, "Of all the apartment houses in all the world, is it possible that he moved into ours?"

"It's not a coincidence," she said. "His room — you could hardly call it a studio — used to be his sister and brother-in-law's, the one who works at the UN — their pied-à-terre. It's like four hundred square feet! We stayed there a number of times instead of driving home after a show. It's the reason I bought here — that little space gave me a taste for more of the Batavia."

I said, "I'm stunned. I can't believe you didn't tell us."

"Is this suddenly an amicable divorce?" Anthony asked.

"It's nothing," said Margot. "I couldn't very well tell him not to move into his brother-in-law's apartment, could I? I avoid him and he has to avoid me because he has an ankle bracelet. I didn't bring it up before because I was too embarrassed to tell you."

"Does it have a kitchen?" Anthony asked.

"We are *not*, N-O-T, inviting him to dinner," Margot said.

"It's not that. I was just wondering, real-estate-wise. How come I didn't know there were studios on the first floor?" he asked.

I said, "I thought he had another six months on his sentence."

"People like him get released early," Margot said. "All of a sudden two guards appeared out of nowhere and said, 'Get your things, Doc, you're going home.'"

"I thought you haven't talked to him since he got out," I said.

"He called me from his mother's house his first night home to ask if I'd freak out if he moved onto West Tenth. Collect! I refused to take the call. He called back on his mother's dime."

"I hope you said, yes, you certainly *would* freak out," I said.

"I surprised myself. I found myself thinking it was a good sign."

"Of what?"

"Alimony payments! Some song and dance about how his accountant couldn't write the checks after his office was closed because of mold contamination. Anyway, he's at least three months behind. He threw in that he'd be catching up as soon as he moved out of his mother's house. And if he lived here, he wouldn't even need a stamp."

"Who's paying maintenance on the studio?" Anthony asked.

"He is! Charles isn't broke. He's got the other half of what I let go up in smoke."

"If he has plenty of money, why is he living in four hundred square feet?" I asked. "Why doesn't he get a real apartment?"

"Ahem," said Anthony. "Perhaps the answer is sitting across the table from us."

"You don't think I accused him of that? 'You're not moving here because you're holding out some kind of ridiculous hope that I'll take you back?' Of course, he said no. It was all convenience, the brother-in-law's pied-à-terre, instantly available."

"Can he work now?" Anthony asked.

"Not as a doctor. Not till he gets his license back," I told him.

"Gwen knows more than I do," said Margot.

"Except for the news that he moved in downstairs!" I yelped.

"Is this so bad?" Anthony asked. "I mean you were happily married to him for how many years?"

"Not so happily! We had our moments. Maybe I threw him out a few times."

Anthony asked me if I knew this. I said, "Um, Charles recently filled me in on a few nights spent on his — I hate to say it — office couch."

"Poor him," said Margot. "Poor, unloved perv."

"Just when I was going to say that he paid his debt to society, I think I won't. I'm buttoning my lip," said Anthony.

"It's very simple," said Margot. "I hate him for what he did: illegal, immoral, unethical, creepy, whatever you want to call it. It doesn't matter. He can make speeches and pay his debt to society until the cows come home, but to me, to a wife" — her voice rose — "to a devoted wife who sometimes sat in the outer office, deaf and blind, filling in for his receptionist! It's unforgivable."

Was Margot crying? Her voice got thick on the last two words so

I stepped in. "If Charles had been a politician, Margot would *not* have been standing next to him at the press conference where he announced that he was taking full responsibility for his own actions."

"We hate that!" Margot cried. "He wanted me to do something along those lines: go to court, sit behind him, look sympathetic in a matronly suit. I refused! His lawyer begged me. His mother and sister begged me. The politest answer I gave was 'Yeah, you'll see me in court, all right! Divorce court!'"

Anthony said, "So I, who am the resident expert on the trial of Charles W. Pierrepont, MD, won't get to meet or lay eyes on him, despite his living twelve floors away from his ex-wife and ex-favorite-sister-in-law?"

"Go knock on his door for all I care," said Margot. "Bring a notebook. Bring him cupcakes. Ghostwrite his autobiography. Just don't give him our regards."

It may not have been that exact night when the intercom buzzed, but it was soon enough, and in the middle of another discussion re Charles as unfortunate neighbor. I answered and heard our night doorman saying, "Dr. P asking me if Miz Considine home."

"Why?" I asked.

"To visit, I think."

Without consulting Margot—I surely knew what her answer would be—I said, "Absolutely not."

"She's out?" asked he who knew all our comings and goings.

"Actually, no. But she doesn't want to see him."

"He live here. He free to get on elevator."

I heard in the background, unmistakably Charles, "Is she home?"

I told Rafael it was an awkward situation. *Delicado.*

Margot called from the table, "What's the big discussion out there?"

"It's Rafael asking if Charles can come up."

"Maybe he has the first alimony check," said Anthony.

I asked Rafael if Charles was holding an envelope. He was not. I said, "Please tell him that he should e-mail Margot and tell her what this is about."

After another brief exchange, Rafael said, "He no has computer."

Anthony said, "Oh, let him up. It'll be interesting."

"What about the ankle bracelet?" I asked. "He can't just wander around the building."

"I made that up," said Margot.

Anthony was now on his feet and stacking our dirty plates. "Aren't you dying to know what he looks like after how many months in prison? Ten, twelve, fifteen? He probably worked out in the prison gym."

"Or maybe *you're* dying to get a look at him," said Margot.

And suddenly it was Charles's voice on the intercom. "Margot?"

I flinched, backed away, then came back to say, "No. It's Gwen."

"Look. Let's be adults here. I have something for her. It isn't a social visit."

I covered the receiver and whispered "I think he has a check" as loudly as I dared.

Margot said, "Tell him he can come up, but not inside. I'll be in my room. Yell when he's gone. And don't feed him."

"You look fine," I told her.

"You think I'm worried how I look to this piece of criminal shit? Because I could not care less! I'm hiding because I don't want to see or talk to him — not because I have to refresh my lipstick."

I said, "Rafael, tell Dr. Pierrepont he can come up."

"He probably there already," he said.

11

No Hug?

EVEN BEFORE HE materialized, Charles offended by rapping twice on our front door, opening it unbidden, and calling, "Hullo! Don't you lock the door?"

I sent Anthony out to the foyer because he was wearing a cropped, sleeveless T-shirt and sweatpants, abs and biceps exposed formidably.

"May I help you?" I heard him ask in the tone one uses with an intruder.

"Do I have the right apartment?" Charles asked.

Anthony said, "And how would I know that?"

"I'm Charles Pierrepont. Is this Margot's apartment?"

"And mine. May I help you?"

Next he tried "Is Gwen here?"

Anthony hesitated. We hadn't discussed whether I was or wasn't at home in terms of our reception strategy.

I joined them from the dining room, and from a still-safe distance, I pronounced in an onstage, drawing-room fashion, "Why, hello, Charles." He was thinner everywhere and pale. I realized that he must have dyed his hair in civilian life because it was now completely gray. He was wearing erratically bleached jeans, a plaid shirt that looked starched and ironed, loafers, and slouchy white socks.

"No hug?" he asked.

"Sorry," I said, and backed up a step.

"It's good to see you, Gwen," he said. "And I want to thank you for accepting my calls from upstate."

Anthony said, "You told Rafael that you had something to deliver?"

"And you are . . . ?"

"Anthony Sarno. I'm the roommate."

"Interesting," said Charles.

"What is?" I asked.

"'Roommate.' I didn't know the Batavia allowed its owners to rent rooms to unrelated parties."

Anthony said, "Oh, really? You might want to check the bylaws. It's just above the one that says parolees can sublet studios."

I could see that Charles understood: A fine specimen with an Italian surname wasn't going to brook any threats from a scrawny ex-con.

Charles said, "Look. I think I got off on the wrong foot here. Anybody want to offer a thirsty neighbor a cup of tea or a shot of whiskey?"

Anthony and I exchanged glances. I shrugged.

Charles reached into his shirt pocket and removed a folded white envelope. "A step toward . . . if I may, restitution."

"I'll bring it to her," I said. "She's the one who should decide if you can stay for a drink."

Charles called to me as I headed down the hallway. "Make sure she reads the note!"

Margot was lying on her bed, fully dressed, tuned to the Food Network where a southern cook was discoursing on okra and its properties.

"He's here," I announced, and handed her the envelope. She opened it, peeked in, put it down, and said, "Not a bad start."

"He said to make sure you read the note."

She slipped two reluctant fingers into the envelope and extracted a folded piece of lined paper as if it were contaminated. She read it, shrugged, and handed it to me.

> Margot: My accountant is setting up a payment schedule whereby you'll be getting these once a month by U.S. mail. In other words, I won't be bothering you.
>   C.

"Nothing inappropriate about that," I said.

"Except that he's bothering us now! And excuse me, but when was the last time you could believe anything he said?"

I hitched a shoulder in the direction of the door behind me. "Want to get it over with?"

She knew what I meant. She raised the remote control, clicked the TV off, but made no other move.

I said, "I'm supposed to be asking you if it's okay if he stays for a cup of tea or a drink."

"Was that Anthony's idea?"

"No! You'd have been proud of him. He's playing macho gatekeeper. I haven't seen him like this before."

"Yes, you have — with Olivia. The big brother in action." She tilted her body to one side, checking herself in the framed wall mirror.

"You look fine."

"I'm not primping, if that's what you think. I don't care how I look. I'll never forgive him for humiliating me. Has there ever been anyone cuckolded in a more disgusting fashion?"

I was saved from confirming or debating this by Anthony's calling, "Coming out anytime soon? Anyone?"

"I am. Margot hasn't decided."

"Can I come in?"

As I opened the door, Anthony entered the room with one long stride. "Someone has to relieve me. I've now heard twice that he hates himself and did I think he'll have the chance to tell you in person."

"Tell *me?*" asked Margot.

"You! Her! Me, for chrissake."

"All of this came up while you were standing around in the foyer?" I asked.

"There was this awkward silence while you two were caucusing, and suddenly he said, 'You're probably wondering what this is all about . . .' I could've said, um, dude? No need. I've read every word of the transcript."

"Is he still out there?" I asked.

"He'll be back! He went downstairs to get a bottle of champagne."

I turned back toward the bed so Margot and I could exchange open-mouthed gapes of astonished ill will.

Anthony said, "What? Is that so bad? He's a free man now. I don't think it's to toast anything major."

"Champagne? After all he did? And with all that it symbolizes?" I asked.

Anthony said, "What else do we do around here for entertainment? C'mon. Maybe I got it wrong. Maybe I misunderstood. Maybe he said chardonnay."

I said to Margot, "It doesn't have to mean we're making friends with him if we have a glass of his champagne, you know. You love champagne."

Anthony asked, "How long has it been?"

"Since what?" Margot asked.

"Since you were in the same room with him?"

"At least two and a half — no, almost three years."

"*Two* years," I corrected.

"It'll be three years in May when he was arrested —"

To my surprise, my voice faltered as I said, "It was, no question, two years. He came to Edwin's funeral. Which couldn't have been easy for him under the circumstances, which is to say, while on trial."

Something changed in Margot's expression. It wasn't a tempering of marital fury and it surely wasn't forgiveness or clemency. What I was seeing was sisterly devotion: Margot awarding points to Charles

69

based on the single criterion by which I measured friendship since Edwin's death.

I rinsed out four dusty champagne flutes and found cocktail napkins from the previous occupants' Christmas parties. We discussed nothing substantive, not his crimes, nor prison, nor money, nor his mother, nor his bastard child. We sat in the living room, under paintings and on loveseats that once decorated their marital home. During an awkward silence, Anthony volunteered that Margot and I had taken him in and adopted him.

"Literally?" Charles asked.

"Why, yes," Margot cut in, with a new, broad smile. "Quite literally. In court! And he's now the beneficiary on all my wills, trusts, bank accounts, stocks, bonds, and, of course, my various real estate holdings. I don't think I ever told you that I had a son out of wedlock before I met you, and we were reunited through the Internet."

"Facebook to be specific," said Anthony. "Isn't it amazing?"

"It's not technically adoption," Margot said. "More like we're his guardians."

Charles refilled his glass, lips pursed. Finally, he said, raising his flute, etched with an intertwined M and C, "Touché."

"Touché? Why the hell 'touché'?" Margot sputtered.

"You're right. 'Touché' doesn't apply. I take that back. What I should have said was 'Is it possible that bankruptcy has given you a sense of the ridiculous?'"

"Margot didn't declare bankruptcy," I said.

Charles said, "Ah, Gwen. I see you haven't changed." And to Anthony. "I've always known Gwen to be . . . quite precise."

Anthony said, "A household needs precise. She's like the big sister I never had."

"So this" — Charles waved his hand around our circle — "is all very . . . *fraternal?*"

Margot said, "Don't be a douche bag, Charles. He's half our age."

"And queer, thank you," said Anthony.

Margot, the new Margot, the champagned Margot, said, "And you, Doc, could use some etiquette lessons. Someone with your track record shouldn't be seeing sex in every situation."

Charles said, "This is good. I need this. I know you're right and I'm going to try harder. I want to start over. I need to be seen as normal and healthy. I have to go slow, glacier slow. I made that promise to myself and to my social worker at Otisville in my exit interview. Everything that happened, *everything,* was all about my father! I know that now. I'm determined to start so fucking slow that if I'm lucky enough to ever have a woman in my life, I'll be like a church boy on a first date."

"Words," said Margot. "Nothing but words."

Anthony said, "Dude, I'm not so sure you can tell the difference between appropriate and inappropriate. I mean, give me a break — turning our living situation into a ménage à trois?"

"A feeble attempt . . . " Charles began. He reached into his jeans pocket, fished out an oversize handkerchief, and wiped his eyes, which were suddenly and genuinely wet. "I swear," he began again. "I swear . . . I know you'd expect me to say prison changed me. But *I* changed me. I was showing off a minute ago. I'm nervous. It took all my courage to knock on your door. I hope I can prove myself by . . . I don't know . . . would 'walking the straight and narrow' be the proper characterization? 'Acting my age'? 'Giving back'? 'Starting over'? 'Settling down'? All in hopes of reversing my . . . misfortune."

"Misfortune!" Margot yelped. "Ha!"

"What do you mean by settling down?" I asked.

"With a woman. A mature woman. And when I find her, I intend to court her like a gentleman from another century."

All three of us visibly sat up straighter. I wouldn't have said it. I wouldn't have opened the door myself. But Anthony looked at me and conveyed a whole speech without words. *Why the hell not? He's practically written your founding charter for you.* He asked Charles if he knew about the little start-up, the brilliantly conceived Chaste Dates — the exact social network his therapist would approve of, big-time.

"Not online, I hope. I have certain restrictions."

"No! In person. Real people, in the flesh, women who are also . . . how would we describe it?"

"Taking it slow," I said.

I noticed Margot wasn't contributing to this pitch.

"Gwen?" Anthony prompted.

"I'm not sure," I said. "It's a delicate situation." *Not to mention an imaginary enterprise.*

"May I ask what this service costs?" Charles asked.

"A hundred bucks per date," said Anthony.

Charles thought this over. I prepared to negotiate.

"I can do that," he said.

12

Q and A

NEIGHBORLY RELATIONS EVOLVED. A better-behaved Charles, a Charles on a probation of our design, started taking meals with us twice a week, due mostly to geography and happenstance. The first move in that direction was his, engineered the night of a raging blizzard. The phone rang in late afternoon and Margot answered. We heard her say, "*Nothing?* Not even a can of soup? That's hard to believe." Then, "What about delivery?" And finally, "Okay. But you'll take it to go."

The switch from a sandwich handoff to a meal plan began with a turkey, allegedly won by Charles in a raffle at the local D'Agostino's. He called upstairs and said he had a fourteen-pound, grass-fed, free-range bird — dressed, trussed, and oven ready, except that he didn't have an oven. It was ours if we wanted it.

As it was roasting and caramelizing aromatically, and as I peeled potatoes and Anthony simmered fresh cranberries, we acknowledged that the decent thing to do was to share our feast with its donor. Margot, not thrilled, grumbled, "As long as he doesn't think that all he has to do is supply the main course and it's instant guest of honor."

"It's okay with Margot?" Charles asked when I called downstairs. Before I could reply, he added, "I have a great pinot noir here. I'll bring it. I'm sure my brother-in-law would want me to drink anything he left behind."

Next time it was flounder, a gift from another paroled white-collar criminal, vacationing and apparently winter fishing off Shelter Island. His driver delivered a Styrofoam cooler, fish already filleted. "He was my cellmate for three months. Quite a decent guy," Charles explained, "and obviously he remembered that one of the things I missed at Otisville was fresh fish."

Margot turned that gift into what she called a poor man's bouillabaisse, adding a handful of shrimp and calamari rings from Trader Joe's freezer section. Again Anthony and I debated: How do we *not* invite the person who supplied the main ingredient?

"It's easy," said Margot, "when he's your ex and you despise him. And what do you think he's up to with these gifts and the expensive bottles of wine? His goal, I assure you, is to make us his restaurant."

"But the food," I said. "Don't we love these gifts he gets that he can't cook himself?"

"A suspicious amount of gifting going on in this world if you ask me," said Margot.

Over bouillabaisse that night, napkin tucked into his collar, our grateful guest noted that what Margot had established was a twenty-first-century boarding house. Accordingly, would she ever, *ever*, consider another paying guest? Board only. He'd eat and run, and certainly not seven nights a week. And was it possible that she'd been to culinary school since the . . . legal unpleasantness?

A fruit basket arrived the following weekend, another regift, this one allegedly from a still-grateful and obviously clueless patient celebrating the eighteenth birthday of the child she never thought she'd bear. Besides the exotic fruit, the basket contained dark chocolate from Belgium, marzipan from Spain, and Margot's favorite, macaroons.

We e-mailed Charles a set of rules: Arrival time, 6:25. Dinner at 6:30. He'd eat, clear his place, and leave promptly. No cocktail hour or *Nightly News* beforehand, and no Netflix after. Tuesday and Thursday nights were enough. And don't expect an even number around the table because Margot herself would often be absent due to social obligations.

Why did we do this, aside from the twenty-five dollars per meal he paid that covered the cost of protein for four? None of us relished Charles's company, but how often does one get to discuss crime and punishment with someone who has experienced both? Margot coped by retreating to her room whenever she felt the old hatred coming on. And on at least one of his scheduled nights she ventured out — for a walk, to a gallery, for coffee, to window-shop, to blog at the library, or to dine with a friend, finally accepting the invitations she'd been deferring as dutiful sister and chef.

The silver lining to Margot's absences — at least from Anthony's point of view — was the opportunity to quiz Charles in prosecutorial fashion. It surprised me how frank Charles was about the commission of his crimes. Anthony and I discussed this over breakfast after a particularly candid exchange the night before. Was it simply that a good guest doesn't plead the Fifth at his hosts' table? Or did he enjoy revisiting — under the guise of clarifying and edifying — his worst impulses?

Anthony broke the ice one Margot-less night with "Charles, do you mind if I ask whether the whaddyacallits, the inseminations, in your office were premeditated? I mean were they by appointment or just an urge?"

Charles looked at me. I said, "Go ahead. I'm glad someone has the nerve to ask."

I should have taped the rest of the conversation in case Margot needed it for her blog or memoir or roman à clef. A reconstructed transcript would read approximately like this:

Charles: "I may have presented the situation as an emergency — that her first-choice donor didn't show, so it was now or never; now or wait another month, based on the patient's — to put it in layman's terms — cycle. I'm not proud to say that that was how I framed it. Still, the majority of my work for years was A.I."

Me: "A.I.?"

Charles: "Sorry. Artificial insemination."

Me (and now I'm angry): "When did the 'artificial' part stop? One day you're using a turkey baster and the next day it's your dick? And has anyone brought up the fact that you could've given Margot a sexually transmitted disease, or worse!"

Charles: "I can assure you that Margot did."

Anthony (I'm now in the kitchen, recovering, and theoretically out of earshot): "But no bullshit, dude — who got picked to join you on the couch? Only the hot ones?"

Charles (loud enough so his ex-sister-in-law *could* hear): "I refuse to dignify that with an answer."

When I returned, Charles said, "Gwen? I forget. Were you present for any of my testimony on the witness stand?"

I said no. I didn't attend the trial. Couldn't.

"Of course," he said. "Forgive me — Edwin."

"And she didn't want her presence to be seen as moral support, I believe," Anthony said.

"I went to prison for fraud. Not for my personal failings." Charles leaned back, tipping his chair away from the table in an overconfident, swashbuckling fashion. "What do you do again?" he asked Anthony. "For work. Remind me."

Anthony said, "I was in finance."

"Every day he sends out résumés and tries to get appointments with headhunters and checks every job site," I testified.

"Since?"

"Since what?" Anthony asked.

"I meant how long have you been out of work?"

"Since my company went under."

"*Your* company? As in you *owned* it?"

"Hardly. It was Lehman Brothers."

Charles raised his eyebrows. "Wasn't Lehman Brothers saved at the brink?"

"You're misinformed," said Anthony.

"Still, that was a long time ago. Any prospects now that the recession has been officially declared over?" Charles asked.

"I'd rather not discuss it. I don't want to jinx anything."

That answer was uncharacteristically tight-lipped for Anthony. He stood up and asked, rather pointedly, "Gwen? Tea?"

"Anyone else want that last slice of pot roast?" asked Charles, as I began to clear the meat platter and gravy boat.

Originally, dessert was going to be a selection of three flavors of ice cream, but Anthony came back with only vanilla — to shorten the dessert course, I guessed. He looked at his watch and widened his eyes in what I recognized as theatrical disbelief. "Seven twenty-five already! Hope it's not too late to send out more résumés and network with my employed friends."

Charles said, "I didn't mean to sound judgmental."

"Good," said Anthony. "Because I haven't noticed you out there in the world of work, either."

"Presumably you don't have to explain two prejudicial and fatal words in the course of an interview."

"Okay," said Anthony. "Hit me."

"They are, as you might guess: On. Parole."

"Bummer," said Anthony.

I walked Charles halfway to the front door, an approximation of hostess etiquette. Returning to the kitchen, I found Anthony loading the dishwasher. "Do you think he notices that he's eating off his own wedding china?" he asked.

"What is it that you don't want to jinx?" I asked in return.

"Let's have tea. Earl Grey or green?"

"Is there a big announcement coming?"

"Not yet."

"Do you have a job?"

"I have an *interview*. On Monday. With a hedge fund, as a research associate. I made the first cut."

"Does Margot know?"

"There's nothing to know unless I get it."

I realized then, utterly unexpectedly, that despite his clutter — of weights, dumbbells, and muffin tins — despite the near tic of his constant chinning up in the kitchen doorway and his often-unsolicited professional and wardrobe advice, I didn't want Anthony to abandon us.

"Are you upset?" he asked.

I thought it was enough to say "If you got this job, I guess you'd be able to swing your own place."

"One thing at a time."

"Does it pay a lot?"

"What's a lot?"

I didn't want to admit what was "a lot" to me, the freelancer without assignments, collecting a public school teacher's pension. I said, "High five figures?"

"At least . . . I know that amount is obnoxious and crazy when the word 'associate' is part of the title," Anthony said.

"It's not crazy if you can get it. And it's not crazy compared to the millions of dollars you hear about. The bonuses. Even now."

He smiled. "But haven't you heard? The recession is officially over." He opened the refrigerator to get milk for our tea, and even that caused a little pinch in my heart. Would there soon be no battalion of jewel-colored vitamin waters lining our door?

"I suppose you'd like to live with people your own age," I said.

"Let's not jump the gun. I don't know how many candidates were called back. My chances could be way lower than fifty-fifty."

What was wrong with me that I was getting choked up about an unrelated, unemployed, overequipped roommate moving out? I knew what a shrink would say, what anyone who'd ever met me would say. *Gwen hates separations. The scar tissue has not yet grown over her previous major loss.* Some might adopt the other popular psychoanalytic theory: *Son substitute. Son surrogate. Son period.*

78

13

Professional Updates

1. Margot

Having Googled the phrase "what publishers want," Margot reports the answer is "a platform," and she has one, big-time: the thirteen thousand Madoff victims plus millions of regular Americans living below the poverty line. Wouldn't every one of them be a potential buyer for her memoir/guidebook?

"Have you written any of it yet?" Anthony asked. We were waiting for the popcorn to pop before we started our ladies'-choice DVD night, which was to say *Bridget Jones: The Edge of Reason*. Margot said that all she had so far were a few notes, but this much she knew: The book should be small and adorable to catch people's eye at the cash register; it had to be cheap because her target audience was broke; it would give tips on surviving hard times, cutting corners, finding free everything—openings, museums, readings, concerts, hors d'oeuvres at happy hours. There would be chapters called "Grow Your Own," "Bake Your Own," and "Shop Your Closet," and lots of recipes throughout using cheap cuts of meat and beans in bulk. Most of all, it needed an irresistible title that would work in several languages.

"Let's not get ahead of ourselves," said Anthony.

"It's going to take a lot of work and research," I said.

Without prompting or apparent rumination, Margot recited, "Tip number one: Sell your car so you aren't paying for a garage, gas, insurance, inspections, detailing, tune-ups, tolls, you name it. If you're leaving the city, rent a car — or stay home. Two: Do your own manicures and pedicures. Three: Get your hair colored at a cheap salon or at a beauty school instead of by someone famous. Four: Buy all cosmetics, creams, makeup, et cetera at Duane Reade or CVS. Five: Go to the library. Six: Buy a whole chicken and cut it up yourself and learn to love thighs."

After a short, diplomatic pause, Anthony asked, "You're kidding, right?"

"About which one?"

"About all of them!"

Margot said, "In that list alone, a person could save hundreds a month."

I said, "The problem is, people on budgets already know these tips."

"Not to mention, they're totally New York–centric," said Anthony. "Do small towns even *have* different tiers of hair colorists?"

"And, no offense," I said, "but advising someone to go to the library instead of buying books has pretty much been a well-known custom for hundreds of years."

"Penny-pinching one-o-one," Anthony grumbled.

"Not a bad title," Margot said. "Penny-pinching à la Ponzi."

"Don't you dare," said Anthony.

Margot, ever unflappable, said, "Hold your fire. I'll get the popcorn. And my secret weapon."

We could hear the opening and closing of kitchen drawers that were not associated with bowls, salt, or napkins. When she rejoined us, she was waving a yellowed magazine, which on inspection turned out to be *Great Ground-Beef Recipes*, a Family Circle publication marked ninety-five cents. "Copyright nineteen sixty-five!" Margot exclaimed. "A treasure trove left behind by our predecessors. Presto: my entrées."

I said, "You can't use someone else's recipes. They're copyrighted."

"I've already thought of that. I'll throw in a line saying that many were inspired by concoctions from a simpler time, blah, blah, blah . . . *Merci beaucoup, Family Circle.*" She turned to her first bookmark, a strip of wax paper, and read, "Chapter one: What *would* we do without ground beef, exclamation point." Smiling happily, she turned to another marked page. "Meat Balls — two words — Stroganoff . . . Meat Balls Veronique . . . Persian Spoonburgers . . . Meat-loaf — hyphenated — Reubens."

Anthony sighed and announced that he was going to skip *Bridget Jones* the sequel and opt for a workout.

"Is it the ground beef that's making you both so mopey, or is it the whole project?" Margot asked.

"I can't speak for Gwen," Anthony said, "but I don't love the idea of recipes from the nineteen sixties."

"You don't think the message is 'I'm no snob. I used to buy porterhouse, but I'm happy with hamburger now'?"

I said, "I suppose . . ."

"It's role-modeling. It's saying 'Keep your chin up.' And I think I'm good at that."

"I think I'll go to the gym," said Anthony.

"What about yours?" she asked him.

"My what?"

"Your recipes! Just our favorites. The gingerbread chocolate chunk, the Scarlett O'Haras, the Mixed Marriage, the PB and Js . . . five or six of the showstoppers. You'd get your own chapter. 'Anthony's Famous Cupcakes.'" She winked at me. "Illustrated with photos of our pastry chef."

"Do you have these recipes written down?" I asked him.

"Of course I do."

"It could be my ticket," Margot said.

"Or mine," said Anthony.

2. Me

I didn't fix Charles up with any of my female acquaintances. Follow-through wasn't my strong suit, anyway, and Charles didn't mention it again. Margot did, but only to scold Anthony for suggesting that Charles was even a remotely appropriate blind date for an unsuspecting woman. She insisted that he didn't deserve companionship, especially if it led to sexual gratification. Could I promise her I was out of the matchmaking business, especially where it involved an ex-brother-in-law? I said, for about the fifth time, "Yes, I promise."

Recently, I posted signs in our building's laundry room, advertising my skills in grammar and punctuation, diagramming sentences, and tutoring in the above disciplines. I check every day to see if any of the vertical tear-off tabs bearing my phone number are missing, but so far all are intact.

3. Anthony

He didn't get the job at Lewiston Capital, but the company's HR department invited him to apply for the job vacated by the successful in-house candidate. Although it pays less, Junior Financial Analyst was described as a "foot-in-the-door opportunity providing direct access to upper management who will help facilitate professional growth."

He said he'd be embarrassed if he doesn't get this one since it's entry-level and has been practically handed to him. Margot and I tell him to put our names down as references, and we will rave about every aspect of him that could conceivably pertain to employment.

Present that same evening, Charles asked Anthony if he had a police record. When I rushed in to take offense on his behalf, Anthony said calmly, "He means my green-card fiasco. And the answer is no; my lawyer got me off."

"How did you know about that?" I asked Charles.

Charles smiled. "We have conversations while you're in the kitchen putting the finishing touches on your delicious stand-in meals." He meant the more and more frequent substituting I'd been doing for the often-absent Margot. I had to say thank you. That very night was one of mine: cabbage soup with meatballs with a crusty *boule* on the side. Who would believe that a day-old loaf of bread could cost five dollars?

4. Olivia

There is another Sarno under our roof temporarily, on the parlor couch. Olivia's two-week notice has expired, and her boyfriend-boss hasn't yet found the one-bedroom apartment where they'll live after he extricates himself from his marital home. None of us have met Noel, but we offer to go along on their dates so it looks more like friendship than alienation of affection. Noel's wife, Davida, is not a divorce attorney, but her firm has a famously litigious and unforgiving family law unit. Without Davida's unlovability and frigidity factored in, the potential screaming headline — MAN FALLS FOR NANNY — has the entire division licking its chops.

Like her brother, Olivia is handy and considerate around the house. We didn't know she was a licensed bartender, but now we have gin and vodka in the freezer and cocktails of every hue. It's a good guest indeed who empties a load of clean dishes without being asked and without interviewing the hosts as to where every bowl and pan are housed. Besides supplying the booze, she has assumed my cleaning responsibilities in lieu of paying rent, making us, in almost every sense, a cooperative. It all evens out, each of us contributing our own talents. As a big fan of Louisa May Alcott, and after my second Blue Lagoon, I expounded one night on Bronson Alcott's utopian commune. Eventually, I had to renege after looking up Fruitlands, because we weren't vegans or transcendentalists or farmers. In fact, I have stopped using "commune" even jokingly because Charles, being Charles, hears a note of promiscuity in that word.

Olivia loves children and misses the baby dreadfully, but she probably won't be able to continue in the au pair field, having undone one employer's marriage. Accordingly, the agency has her situation under advisement.

14

Say Anything

AFTER A TEN-WEEK absence, I forced myself to attend my widows' support group to work on what my sisters call my "stasis." My visit was ill timed. Valentine's Day was approaching, inspiring our group leader to pronounce — in the manner of a decorating-happy classroom teacher — that love and romance were this week's theme. Her suggestion was that we go around the circle and answer the question, "What am I afraid of?"

We coughed into our elbows and attended to the vital work of silencing our phones. Katherine Glazer, MSW, tried, "Let's start with one-word answers. Don't overthink it. Say the first thing that comes to mind. For example . . ." She looked around, snapped her fingers as if she hadn't chosen the noun the night before, and called out, "Intimacy!"

None of us, with our grocery bags and knapsacks at our sensibly shod feet, looked like we had anything to confess along those lines.

"I am afraid of . . . fill in the blank," Katherine prompted.

"Does it have to be something personal?" I asked. "Or can it be a general fear, like death or heights or snakes?"

She reached over and squeezed my left hand. Was that dismay in her glance, at finding my rings still there? "Let me clarify," she said. "I want us to discuss what fears keep us from pursuing — what will be our code word for love and romance today? How about just L and R?"

A hand went up. It was Joanna, one of our most bedraggled members, who wore her grungy orange parka throughout every meeting. "I worry about a prenup," she told us.

We waited. Our leader, her features admirably composed, repeated, "A prenup?"

Joanna asked, "Am I the only one who thinks, *What if I got involved with someone who wants to get married?* He'd have to sign a prenuptial agreement. So when I picture that conversation and how angry he could get, it just makes me want to stay home and watch TV."

"As opposed to what?" asked Hildy, mother of two grown sons who still lived at home. "I mean as opposed to what activity? Going out to parties? Clubbing?"

"Clubbing means going out to bars and, of course, clubs," our leader explained.

Joanna said, "I have my volunteer jobs . . . my subscription to the Philharmonic. I meet people. Some are men. One invited me out for coffee, but I declined."

"For the reason stated?" Katherine asked.

"I didn't know him," said Joanna. "And the person who gave him my e-mail address didn't even know him that well."

"It's called a blind date," said Katherine, glancing up at the wall clock.

Hildy said, "One more question for Joanna. Not that I'm into fashion, but my boys give me the once-over before I leave. Sometimes they say, 'You're not going out like *that,* are you?' I trust them, so I change into something else."

"Your question?" Katherine prompted.

"Right. My question is, let's say you were going out. What coat would you wear?"

Before Joanna could answer or take offense, our one attorney-member said, "May I speak as someone who's negotiated any number of prenups?"

"Please," Katherine said.

"Cross that bridge when you come to it. I haven't seen one engagement broken because of it."

"Find yourself a rich guy with a prenup of his own!" said Rose, who at eighty-six was reliably nostalgic and pragmatic.

"Cross that bridge when you come to it is good advice for everything," said our leader. "Who else? Let's go around the circle."

I was in the folding chair to her right. "Gwen? It's been a while."

"Pass."

Several members booed. Wasn't that unkind enough to earn a reprimand? But all Katherine said was "C'mon. *Anything* related to L and R."

"If I have to, I'll go with intimacy."

"Already been used," said Rose.

"That's okay," said Katherine. "Gwen is allowed to say she's afraid of intimacy. She doesn't have to come up with a synonym. But let's ask her to elaborate." She turned ninety full degrees in her chair. "Gwen?"

How to amplify without actually admitting anything? I decided on "I wasn't very good at jumping into bed with men back in my single days . . ."

I thought that was enough, but Katherine the voyeur needed an autobiography.

I said, "So I guess I'd be even worse at it now."

"Why?" asked Katherine.

Was she punishing me for my poor attendance record? For my failure to evolve under her tutelage?

I said, "Let's give someone else a chance."

Hildy said, "I know what Gwen is getting at. I'm wondering how I'd ever get into bed with someone who wasn't my boys' father."

"Because of your sons?" asked Lisa, our youngest member, widowed while separated. "You need their approval? Or because of the sex?"

Hildy said, "I meant doing it with a whole other guy. I'm not a bathing beauty. I have veins where I never used to."

87

I said, "You can always undress under the covers."

When this produced baffled and unsatisfied looks, I added, "If it got to that, you could shut off the lights first and maybe undress down to your slip and then finish under the covers. For privacy."

"What if you wanted to see *him?*" asked Lisa.

I hadn't thought that far ahead. I said, "It would depend. He might be modest, too. Not everybody likes to parade around naked. He might be just as nervous. Maybe he hasn't done it in a long time."

Katherine appeared to like this new direction. "How many of you feel like virgins?" she asked eagerly.

One by one our hands went up except for Lisa's. "Don't tell me I'm the only one who's actually had a sleepover?" she asked, looking left and right.

Katherine said, "Gwen? Your hand shot up first."

"So?"

Lisa, suddenly deputized, asked me, "How long has it been?"

"Two years and two months."

"Not since your husband died. I meant since you hooked up with someone."

"Two years and two months," I snapped. What was to be gained from this interrogation, and why had I returned? I surveyed the faces around the circle in search of the equally offended.

Hildy said, "You've been absent for months. We were hoping you met someone."

"Well, I haven't. When I get the urge to have sex outside my marriage, I'll let you know."

This was not the right answer. Katherine had my hand again, a pity squeeze. "Gwen? He's gone. You're a widow. Edwin would *want* you to meet someone."

That old cliché. How did any of them know what Edwin would want? Or what I wanted, for that matter. Finally, to signal I was living not only in the present but in the moment, I said, "If you must know, the last time I had sex with Edwin was the night before he died" —

88

a declaration I immediately regretted, lest anyone think I'd caused the fibrillation that killed him.

Rose said, "You're so lucky. I wish I'd had sex with Morty the night before he died. I can't even remember if we kissed good night . . ." Her chin wobbled. She managed a whispered postscript. "All those things we'd have done if only we'd known."

Such moments tend to be contagious. The institutional box of tissues went around the circle. Did that stop Katherine? "Who wants to share what plans she has for Valentine's Day?" she asked brightly.

I stood up and yanked my coat off the back of my chair. I don't know whether it was the teeth of my metal zipper or one of my antler toggle buttons that hit Katherine's lip, but something did, and she was bleeding. I said I was sorry. It was an accident. Here — have my tissue. I had a bus to catch.

15

No Yes No Yes

OLIVIA BROUGHT US wonderful news and all the details! Despite her banishment to the "Dead and Disgraced" file of NanniesNY, she had popped into mind when a new client called the agency, describing herself as desperate. She was custom-made for Olivia: a single mother, a CEO with a maternity leave screeching to a halt and no man on site to fuel any dalliances.

"Let me meet her," said the broad-minded Stephanie Bradford, who gave more weight to Olivia's prescandal evaluations ("cheerful, competent, kind, college educated") than to her exit reference ("too pretty for her own good" and "lock up your husband"). The interview took place in Ms. Bradford's all-white apartment, its furniture oversize, its *objets* of the breakable, knockoverable variety. She spoke plainly: Every previous candidate had diagnosed the décor, the colicky baby, the yappy Yorkie, and no visible television as symptomatic of a difficult and clueless boss.

Yet here was Olivia, expression melting and pupils dilating at the sight of seven-week-old Maude. "May I?" she asked. The baby studied Olivia's face, seemingly feature by feature, and then raised one side of her mouth into a drooly smile. "It didn't hurt that I was wearing a hot pink sweater and a necklace made of ribbons and feathers," Olivia later reported. "If I say so myself, Maude was in love."

Perusing notes in a folder, Ms. Bradford asked, "So you and your boss screwed around. Is he still in the picture?"

"Yes, thank you for letting me explain," Olivia said. "You see, it wasn't a random affair. We're in love. We're unofficially engaged, which would *not* take up any of my workday. He hasn't extricated himself from the marriage due to custody and real estate concerns. I would not entertain him at my employer's residence if I was lucky enough to be hired. Does Maude respond to music? Because I play the flute."

"I have a good feeling about you," said the new mother. "And I'm not that interested in my employees' love lives. We should get along fine."

Olivia said, gesturing around the living room, "It's immaculate. I don't see any . . . baby stuff . . . any toys."

"I hate clutter," said Ms. Bradford. "I don't have one thing on my desk at work, not even a blotter." But then her voice changed to a worried whisper. "I think to myself: When I get back to work, do I keep pictures of Maudie on my desk? I might not be able to look at her without crying because I'll miss her so much." She involuntarily touched one breast, a gesture that any experienced nanny knew meant *I'll pump at work. But it won't be the same.*

From her white ruffled bassinette, Maude began fretting and thrusting her legs fitfully.

"Have you tried eliminating milk products from your diet?" Olivia asked. "That could help with her colic. And this . . ." She sat down on a white leather ottoman, reached for Maude, placed her belly-down across her knees, and made circles on her back with two expert fingers. The baby's eyes closed. Olivia said, "If you offer me the job, I'll take it."

"I do offer you the job," said Stephanie Bradford. "I'll call the agency. I was one week away from setting up a crib in my office."

"One more thing," said Olivia. "Would you feel better if you met Noel, my last employer? He can vouch for me. And you'll see that he isn't a creep."

"And the wife?"

Without hesitation, Olivia said, "I signed a confidentiality agreement so I can't answer that."

"Well done," said Stephanie. "But do answer this: Are you going to run off and get married just as Maudie's stranger anxiety sets in?"

"I'll sign a contract," said Olivia. She smiled to soften the qualifier that was ahead. "I stay for one full year, minimum, as long as you're fair and reasonable."

"I like you," said Stephanie. She then volunteered that Maude had been her paternal great-grandmother's name. She'd arrived in steerage from England, worked on Beacon Hill as a governess, married the boss's bachelor brother, had five sons, the youngest of whom grew up to be Stephanie's grandfather. No scandal. Maude was beautiful, educated, and to Boston ears sounded like nobility. They stayed married for fifty-something years. "So you see where I'm coming from," Stephanie confided.

Olivia did. This boss held no bias against household shenanigans based on love.

A jubilant Anthony organized a celebration. We had to invite Charles after he spotted the bottles of prosecco on the kitchen counter and wanted to know what was on the calendar. When I told Margot that I felt obliged to include him, she said, "Well, there goes any good time I might have had." I offered to disinvite him, but she said it would probably be fine because the actuality of Charles was often better than the prospect. Bolstering his case: the spiral-cut ham he offered to supply.

Besides Charles, Margot, Anthony, and me, the guests were a man named Douglas, nattily dressed in a silvery striped tie, who looked starched and polished and fresh from the gym where he'd met Anthony, too soon to be called "boyfriend" but getting there. We had Olivia's college roommate from Philadelphia, now in law school. Noel the paramour (very brave — we hadn't met him); new boss Stephanie, who was rushing over between feedings. We had our grouchy across-the-hall neighbors, Jacques and Solange, who spoke only French in the elevator and never to us.

Charles arrived fifteen minutes early. Why? Because he believed —he actually *believed!*—that it would be a good time to tell his ex-wife and her sister that he'd met, in person, the son named Charles, aka Chaz, the ill-gotten offspring Charles had elected never to claim or know. Oh, and by the way? Chaz was downstairs in his biological father's pied-à-terre, perfectly happy to wait until the party was over, but also happy to drop by since the host was his Facebook friend Anthony Sarno.

In the few minutes remaining before the desired guests arrived, Margot and I pushed Anthony into the kitchen and demanded that he explain. It took rewording and repetition of simple declarative sentences before we understood, so shocked were we that he, our defender, confidante, and advisor in all things practical, had undertaken something as hugely presumptuous as digging up a son no one asked for. With a swat to his closest bicep, I said, "I know you found him online, but Jesus! That wasn't enough? You had to put him in touch with Charles? Have you ever heard the term 'Pandora's box'?"

"I think the outrage should be Charles's, and he was pretty cool about it," Anthony answered.

Charles, on cue from the foyer, called in the direction of the summit, "Everything okay in there? I'm fine with whatever you decide."

Margot, now with both shoulder blades pressed against a far wall, muttered, "Beyond, beyond belief."

"Are you taking a vote?" Charles asked.

"No we are *not* taking a vote, you asshole!" she yelled.

Anthony said, "May I say something?" He closed his eyes as if silently counting down to the opening of a prayerful oration, then finally said, "Look. I'm sorry. Obviously I didn't know he'd pull something like this. But I can't help thinking what this is like for the kid. He's not a runaway. He isn't needy. He goes to FIT. And he's majoring in hat-making."

At this point, we sisters would surely have ranted about the un-timeliness, the arrogance, the selfishness, the cluelessness of bringing the bastard child of a philandering ex-husband to his wounded ex-wife's party. But what we both sputtered instead was *"Hat-making?"*

"He has a website," said Anthony. "I think he's really good. And if you're worrying about how to engage him, he loves to talk about his work."

Now Olivia appeared, the first time Margot or I had seen her in a dress, a champagne-colored gauzy affair with a brown velvet ribbon at her waist. "Everything okay in here?" she asked.

"It certainly is not!" said Margot. "Charles wants to bring his out-of-wedlock child to your party, and I want to kill him."

"You can say no," Anthony pointed out.

Olivia said, "Please! Noel will be here any minute. And Stephanie. It's not a good night for drama."

"Or bad karma," Anthony added.

"You started this," Margot told him. "I thought you knew how the world worked, that long-lost children show up when they need love or money—"

"Or closure," Anthony said quietly.

"Closure? Where's *my* closure? I divorce him and he not only moves into my building, but he thinks I'm a caterer and brings his little bastard as a plus-one to the only party I've given in three years!"

"I think it's a tribute to you," Anthony said.

"Oh, really?" she said. "Exactly how is it a tribute to me?"

"It's a tribute to you because Charles knows that, in the end, you al-ways do the right thing. The gracious thing. The kid is downstairs—"

"Where he's probably trashing the apartment or looking for cuff links to pawn!"

"I am quite sure that's not the case," said Anthony.

"Is this some sort of gay support thing?" asked Margot. "Like that hotline for troubled teenagers?"

Anthony's expression changed, not to one of anger but of incomprehension. He glanced my way for clarification and then back to Margot. "I'm confused," he said.

"Duh! He wants to design *hats* when he grows up!"

"He has a girlfriend. Who's also majoring in hats."

"Did you friend her, too?" Margot asked.

Anthony said, "I understand your sarcasm. But this has now reached another stage. There's an eighteen-year-old kid downstairs wondering how this touchy situation is going to resolve itself."

Margot yelled, "Charles! Get in here!"

While I wouldn't describe her lunge in his direction as a physical attack, we all moved out of her way. "Why tonight?" she cried. "Was this the only night Junior could come meet his mother's sperm donor — note the sanitized term! — and you couldn't call us and say, 'Sorry, something's come up'? You think we'd *care* if you couldn't make it? You think we couldn't have a party without you?"

Charles said, "I wanted to help Olivia celebrate. I thought of just bringing him and introducing him as a young friend, but I thought you'd find that strange."

"I'm speechless!" Margot cried. "If I were some weakling instead of me, I'd be in the bathroom now, retching my guts out."

"Does he know who we are?" I asked Charles. "So we can't just pretend we're some random neighbors?"

"I haven't whitewashed anything. He knows I inseminated his mother fraudulently. She was married . . . I was married . . . to the lady giving the party upstairs. He knows I served time and am on parole. Happily, he is a *very* open-minded and forgiving young man. I'd like to think that in some small biological way, I contributed to that."

Margot turned to me, and I knew the expression well: incredulity and stupefaction, yes. But now there was a flicker of what I recognized as grudging amusement at that which often stunned us: Charles's award-winning narcissism.

She really was remarkable, my sister. I could see the turn. I knew at that moment that she was going to say "Okay. Bring him up."

16

Chaz with a Z

Here's noel!" olivia called from halfway across the room. "He came!"

This required a reload of the image in our heads. The actual Noel was not the lonely yet smoldering father — a Captain von Trapp or a Mr. Rochester — that I had fashioned in my mind's eye. He was a be-spectacled, pot-bellied man with a receding hairline, who was smiling so fondly at Olivia that I'd taken him for a party-crashing uncle. Until he kissed her on the lips, hungrily.

"Welcome!" Margot called. "We're so glad, totally delighted" — I felt the nudge of her elbow — "that we finally get to meet the famous Noel."

He shook Margot's hand and then mine. "I'm so grateful that Olivia landed here during this difficult period," he said.

"You should thank Anthony," Margot said. "He has to be the most devoted big brother on God's green earth. We just get credit for the couch and the afghan."

"Anthony's new boyfriend is coming," Olivia told Noel. "We're supposed to be very cool about it, though."

Noel said with a wry smile, his eyes an unremarkable blue behind his rimless glasses, "Am I ever anything *but* cool?"

An answer in the form of another lingering kiss finally terminated when Olivia pulled back to say, "Stephanie was able to get a sitter so she's not bringing Maude."

"The baby's how old?" Noel asked.

"Weeks! Almost seven."

"My little girl will be a year in March," Noel told us.

I said we knew that because Olivia talked about her all the time.

That made Olivia's features gather into such a sweet, wistful pout that Noel touched her cheek and said, "It'll be fine, babe."

Olivia said, "Noel is asking for joint custody."

The doorbell rang again and Margot said, "I can't. It might be Charles. Gwen? Would you? I'll be under a blanket somewhere."

It was only the malignant Solange and Jacques, coatless, purseless, giftless, protesting that they were dropping in for only a minute. We didn't think they would come at all because we had the unresolved issue of the copper umbrella stand of undetermined ownership halfway between our two front doors. A week earlier they had left a curt message on engraved, monogrammed notepaper stating that we were taking up more than our share of the "*palier*."

Later Anthony would report that they seemed baffled as to the party's raison d'être. *An au pair's finding employment? Why would that be of interest to anyone of their station?*

New employer Stephanie was next, attractive in an intense, nubby-suited, CEO kind of way, hair expensively streaked and well coiffed, not one to smile easily as she studied new acquaintances a few seconds too long.

Olivia introduced her new employer to the old, who exclaimed, "She's the best!"

"I reached that conclusion myself," Stephanie said. "Obviously, I wasn't troubled by your ex-wife's condemnation. I'm much more interested in her caretaking than her private life."

"Not officially my ex," he said. "That takes time. None of it was Olivia's fault. I know you'll be very happy with your new hire."

"Maude took to her immediately, blob that she is. And I had to get back to work, like, yesterday."

Olivia volunteered that the feeling was mutual. Maude was adorable. And named after her great-grandmother.

"Great-*great*-grandmother," Stephanie corrected.

"Who was a nanny!" said Olivia.

"A governess," said Stephanie.

Though the doorbell didn't ring, the front door opened and in came Charles with the very stranger whose arrival Margot had been dodging.

He was dark and slight. A teenager in a vintage tweed overcoat. His eyes were large and brown, and his face had the bones and planes of an ethnicity more interesting than Charles's. Even within the wool and herringbone folds, he looked as if he might dance on Broadway or model in Milan. And hard to miss: a hat that his new father figure would soon describe as an insouciant bowler — dark forest green, studded with brass grommets.

Before approaching either, I watched them at the buffet table. It was Charles in his paternal role, working stubborn precut slices of ham away from the bone. With his chin and elbow, he seemed to be pointing out the two kinds of mustard and various kinds of bread. I waited until he'd constructed his own sandwich before I approached. The young man didn't quite smile and seemed uncertain what the name Gwen-Laura Schmidt connoted.

"Margot's sister," I explained.

Charles said, "As you probably surmised, this is Chaz —"

"With a Z," said the young man.

"Hats by Chaz," said Charles. "Not a bad name for a line."

"I'm working on a certificate in millinery techniques," Chaz explained.

I then voiced the backup sentence I'd been saving should follow-up be required. "I understand hats have made a comeback."

"It's true. I like to think I saw the trend coming. They certainly did at FIT. Which is where I'm studying."

Charles said, "He started off in shoe design, but he switched majors almost immediately."

I was able to deliver only an unenthusiastic "oh" due to my greater fondness for footwear than headgear.

Chaz helped, conversationally, by saying, "Wow. Nice place. I mean, like, maybe the nicest apartment I ever saw."

"He thought all the apartments in the building would be the same size. Like mine," said Charles.

"Like a dorm," said Chaz.

I thanked him and said that it was my sister's. Margot, of course.

"Hope she's not too freaked out about this," said Chaz.

There it was, the acknowledgment of adultery, paternity, fraud, and home wrecking.

I said, "I know none of this is your fault —"

Chaz said, "I didn't think it was such a cool thing to do, but Doc said you were all pretty good friends and sooner or later —"

"We came up with 'Doc,'" Charles explained. "What do you think? It's less formal than Dr. Pierrepont without being overly familiar." He winked at Chaz. "For now."

By "not his fault," I hadn't meant Chaz's attendance at the party, but his very existence. I let his misapprehension — uninvited guest — stand. I asked Charles if he could hack off another piece of ham for me and pass the seven-grain rolls.

Charles said, "Sure. It's a little salty. But that's because it's a genuine Smithfield." Then, prone as always to introduce awkward topics at improper junctures, he said, "Chaz, tell Gwen how your legal father has dealt with all of this."

Chaz took several long swallows of the beer he seemed to be sharing with Charles, then sputtered, "He freaked! And walked out. I mean, like, the minute he heard it. Like he was waiting for some excuse. Which sucks because even if Doc got my mother pregnant, it was for medical reasons, and Dad is my . . . dad."

I hadn't expected this: the other side of the story. I said, "I'm sorry. I hope he hasn't abandoned you, too."

"Do you believe that someone would be so pissed off at his wife that he'd walk out on his kid, too?" Charles demanded.

I murmured, "I'm sure he'll be back. I'm sure it'll take a little time."

I saw that Charles's expression didn't quite match his indignant words. He looked smugly victorious. Finally, someone could view him as the honorable guy and better dad. He was gazing so fondly at Chaz that it made me forget how this boy had come about. He was, tonight, the Moses who'd been placed in the bullrushes, raised by strangers, and found his way back to his people.

I thought of issuing something like a warning to Charles, reminding him that he was vulnerable in his little hole of an apartment without friends except for his fellow released inmates and parolees. He saved me that awkwardness by reading my mind.

"Gwen is worried that this is too much too soon. That you and I, Chaz, should be taking it very slowly."

"I thought it might be kind of weird to meet the wife and everything," said Chaz.

I said, "It's okay. Margot's very . . . what's the right word . . . ?"

"Resilient," said Charles. "Famously so. Not very much throws her."

"I figured that," said Chaz. "Anthony told me that she lost all of her money to that guy who's in jail for, like, life."

I hesitated: confirm or ignore? Chaz must have sensed my reluctance to elaborate because he said, "Whoops. Sorry. I forced that out of Anthony. I was wondering why a bunch of you were living together, so that's how I found out she was broke."

I asked, "So you met Anthony before you met Dr. Pierrepont?"

After chewing and swallowing a large bite of his sandwich, Chaz said, "He friended me. After my mother outed us."

"He means on the witness stand," said Charles.

"Did she tell you in advance that she was going to do that?" I asked.

Chaz said, "No. I mean I know she got one of those things where the guy knocks on your door —"

"Subpoena," said Charles.

"And she told me like a hundred times after my dad left why he was angry and bailing."

Charles said, with another revoltingly proud smile, "Chaz's theory,

100

and Anthony's, too, I might add, is that his mother, a single divorcée, may have wanted to identify herself" — and here he paused with faux humility, a bite of the lip — "so that I could find her."

"And hook up with her," Chaz stated. "And I know this for a fact. Way before the trial, she tried to friend him."

Charles said, "I think he means *be*friend."

I said, too stunned to comment on anything but the etymology, "While you were out of circulation, 'friend' became a verb."

Chaz asked me, with what looked to be a hopeful smile, "Are you on Facebook?"

I said, "No, not yet . . ."

Charles said, "I can see the question that's on the tip of your tongue, Gwen. And the answer is no, I have not yet reached out to Chaz's mother. She lives in New Jersey and you know that my social life is limited to the borough of Manhattan for a while."

Would I remember Charles's statement so I could repeat it verbatim to my roommates? Luckily, the doorbell rang: more strangers arriving. I rushed through a farewell — we have Coke and Diet Coke and apple cider at the bar. And cupcakes later. We are a very cupcake-oriented household. Nice to meet you, Chaz.

He surprised me with one of those hugs, the new substitute handshake, his ear barely grazing mine. When it knocked his green hat askew, Charles righted it.

17

Your Public Awaits

MARGOT WAS NOT under a blanket but at the kitchen sink, in a lab coat I'd never seen before, furiously scrubbing a Pyrex casserole's baked-on stains.

"He's pretty easy to talk to," I told her.

"I can't," she said.

I reminded her that she was always comfortable socially, always poised, charming even, never at a loss for words. I tried again with "If I can do it, so can you."

She shut the water off, turned toward me, and said, "I don't see any resemblance."

I laughed. Translation and footnote: Chaz is handsome and these days I can't stand the sight of Charles. I said, "So you *did* peek."

"Of course! And if you can laugh, you don't understand how annoyed — no, how *traumatized* — I am having this kid in my living room."

I, who rarely took a scolding tone with my older sister, said, "It's Olivia's party, but you're still the host." I waited. What would constitute a helpful prompt and good psychology at this moment? "He designs hats," I told her. "Expensive ones, I think."

A pause, then a quiet "For men or women?"

I didn't know, but volunteered that anyone studying millinery techniques at FIT surely would be interested in hats for every orientation.

She didn't agree aloud to anything. But she did slip off the lab coat and devote too much time to its conscientious folding.

"C'mon," I said. "It'll be fine. He knows about you —"

"Knows what?"

"Everything. That you were married to Charles. That you divorced him because of his crimes."

My crusade ended there when we heard male voices. Accompanying a jaunty few knocks was Anthony calling, "Where is she? Margot? Your public awaits."

"Fuck my public," she called back. "I'm in a very bad mood."

Anthony and Douglas entered the kitchen, brandishing a bottle of prosecco and an empty glass. "We'll fix that bad mood," said Anthony. "Douglas has some compliments for you."

"Gorgeous place," Douglas said. "Whom did you use?"

Penthouse pride was just the right note to sound. Margot said, "I bought it as is. I didn't change one wall color. The furniture came from my house." She sent a smirk my way, adding, " . . . my former marital abode."

I could always count on Anthony for just the right conversation expander. He glided to Margot's side, lowered his voice, and said, "Did you meet Noel? Olivia's love? *Quelle surprise.*"

"How come we didn't know this before?" she asked.

I pointed out that Noel's appearance and physique were testimonials to Olivia's depth of character.

Margot said, "Thank you, Mother Theresa. Thank you for that little life lesson."

Douglas said, "Whom are we talking about?"

Anthony said, "Olivia's paramour. The short chubby fellow."

"I had a nice chat with him," said Douglas. "He doesn't take his eyes off your sister."

"It's very sweet," I said. "You don't have to be around them very long to see that they're in love."

103

Margot announced, "It's hard to get down and dirty around Gwen. She doesn't like to gossip."

I protested that she wasn't being fair. I could be critical and gossipy if the occasion warranted it. When did I ever hold back about Charles, for example?

Anthony said, "This is why we need Gwen-Laura. She steers us back onto the path of goodness and mercy when we get snarky."

"Thank you," I said.

"She was a live-in for this guy, right?" Douglas asked.

"He didn't fill you in on that headline story?" Margot asked. "Daddy falls for nanny?"

Anthony said, "I've been busy with my bartending and cohost duties."

I said, "You're serving minors."

Anthony said, "I saw you and the long-lost son having quite the cozy conversation. Do tell."

"Not now. We're being very rude. I came in here to drag Margot away from the sink."

"Isn't that a dishwasher?" Douglas asked.

"Yes! Nothing needed washing. She was hiding out in here."

Margot said, "I find washing dishes soothing. It's all about the hot soapy water."

"The kitchen . . ." Douglas began, running a hand along our white Formica counter, "Nineteen seventies is my guess."

Margot said, "The listing said 'meticulously maintained,' which is real estate for 'can't remember when it was last updated.'"

We heard something: not exactly a crash, but a loud thud. Anthony was the first one out of the kitchen. Douglas held the swinging door open for Margot and me, and it was on that threshold where we froze at the sight before us: Charles, on the floor, possibly dead. The utterly competent and CPR-certified Olivia was kneeling beside him, taking his pulse, calling for aspirin, and ordering her brother to dial 911.

I pulled Margot into the semicircle around the supine Charles, who was drained of color but now murmuring, "I'm okay. I'm okay. Don't call anyone."

Olivia asked, "Are you having chest pains?"

He said, "It's not a heart attack. I just fainted."

"You can't be sure," I said. "It can be other symptoms. It can be silent. People die in their sleep."

Margot said, "He's a doctor. He'd probably know if he was having a heart attack."

"Are you nauseated?" Olivia asked him.

Charles propped himself partway up on his elbows. "I'm just embarrassed. I'm sure it was a vasovagal reaction." And being Charles, who had already brought the party to a dramatic standstill, he had to make a speech. "Please . . . as you were. You've already given me your kind attentions. I think most of you know that tonight is something of a watershed moment for me. I've become a father after a lifetime of being childless—"

Margot sent a prod into his rib cage with the sharp point of her lizard pump. "Shut up," she hissed. "Just do us all a favor and shut up."

"Should I call 911 or not?" Anthony asked.

Charles said, "No, don't. It was the excitement, the anxiety, and probably the martinis. I've fainted before. Please, can we get on with the business of this party? Has everyone met Chaz?"

Poor Chaz. His nose was running and his mouth was in a droop so miserable that I reached around Anthony to pat his tweed arm and say, "He's a doctor. If he says he's fine, then he is."

Margot was scowling, and I could guess the complaints and suspicions she'd rail about later. *He always has to be the center of attention. He's trying to evoke the sympathy of every guest and possibly attract a sexual partner. He faked it.*

The law-student friend of Olivia's made her way over to Chaz and said, "My father faints all the time and it's nothing."

"Really?"

"I'm Julie," she said.

I was just standing there, an awkward eavesdropper, when the young woman turned to me and repeated "I'm Julie" in the tone one uses when the hoverer is an unwelcome third party. I almost warned, "He's barely eighteen, you know," but instead introduced myself as Chaz's biological father's ex-sister-in-law, Gwen.

"Biological father? Are you adopted?" Julie asked her new friend.

Chaz said "No! No way. I only met him today."

"You looked so upset when he fainted," Julie said.

"I wasn't. I was, like, *what the fuck?*"

Julie said, "It was scary. He could have hit his head and died from that alone. I thought it was very sweet that you got upset."

"He just kind of slipped to the floor. I should've caught him."

Julie patted his arm. He smiled and told her that her hair was an unusual color, like, pale peach. He saw a lot of hair in his profession, but not like hers.

"Do you work in a salon?" she asked.

"I don't. Actually, I'm a designer." He tapped the brim of his bowler.

Why was I still standing there? I looked around for Margot and spotted her, one room away, on her tufted periwinkle velveteen sofa, next to Charles. His color was returning, and they were talking in a manner that appeared to be amicable.

I retreated to the dining room where I saw Stephanie, Olivia, and Noel, a complete conversational unit, undoubtedly in child-care talk, so I didn't join them, either. Anthony and Douglas were tête-à-tête over the Smithfield ham, patting slices onto each other's bread. Solange and Jacques? Gone. Chaz's hat was now perched prettily on Julie's head.

Although the guest list had contained an even number, I was clearly the odd person out. I poured myself the last dribble of martini from the pitcher, added a shot of gin, and took it to the kitchen. The casserole dish was submerged and soaking. A quick probe showed me that the baked-on stains still needed work. I added a few squirts of soap, which didn't help with the scrubbing, but did ease the underwater transfer of my stubborn wedding ring from left hand to right. With my glass next to the sink, I ran hot water until rubber gloves were required.

It was still early, but I knew this night was not going to widen my social circle or yield new friends. It was then that I decided I would venture outside the building. Maybe such outreach would prove fruitful; maybe in this vast city of allegedly lonely people there was someone waiting for the Gwen-Laura I used to be.

18

My Devoted and Monogamous Self

I TOLD ANTHONY, JUST him alone at breakfast, that I had had something like an epiphany. No, "epiphany" was too strong; what I'd experienced was an attitude adjustment.

"I don't even know what you're going to say, but I bet my response is going to be 'It's about time.'"

I explained: "I looked around last night and thought to myself, *The world is coupled.* When I take Edwin out of the equation, I'm an outsider. Maybe the other half of me could move into the future and not just live in the past."

Anthony said, "Sweetie? Edwin hasn't been in the equation for quite a while. You do realize that, right?"

I said that what I'd meant by "not in the equation" was a sense that dating now would not violate the customs, the mores, the widow's code of behavior; that you were allowed to be unfaithful once the person had been dead for a decent interval.

"Unfaithful? Seriously? You've been a nun!"

I said—automatically and falsely—"Not true."

"Well, what do I know? Maybe you had lovers before I moved in. Maybe you've always had lovers on the side."

Luckily, he said that with a smile and a nudge, saving me from delivering a testimonial to my devoted and monogamous self.

He asked if I'd told Margot yet about last night's near epiphany.

I told him no. I'd tell her today. She'd be happy and she'd have some ideas.

"So what can *I* do to advance the cause?" he asked.

"Nothing right now. Last night in bed I was thinking, *What would help prepare me and possibly inspire me*? And I thought, *I know: a marathon of romantic comedies.*"

He said — and this is why we loved having Anthony around — "I'll watch with you! Where do we start? With the classics? *Dirty Dancing*? *Moonstruck*?"

"I was thinking of something quiet. Maybe about two shy people, one or both widowed, who meet at a dance. Or on a bridge."

"I saw that one. He works at a post office in Australia. She takes care of her elderly father. Next!"

"Maybe *Sleepless in Seattle*?"

"No. I don't mean next in our Netflix queue. I meant in real life — a move that takes you out of the house and into the streets of New York. A date with a proper stranger? Maybe an early dinner in a well-lit restaurant?"

I said, "I know everyone thinks I'm socially retarded. But I think I'm normal for a woman my age who's suffered the irreversible loss of a husband."

Unfortunately, this statement flew into the ear of Margot, who was entering the kitchen, red kimono sliding this way and that. I motioned *Close that up before your breasts fall out.*

"Normal?" she repeated. "I don't even know in what context you're using that word, but if it's the widow thing, I'll have to disagree."

Anthony said, "You're wrong! A new day has dawned."

Yawning, Margot poured herself coffee, black, and didn't ask for elaboration.

"Gwen has decided she's ready to go out on a date," he continued.

"Now you're talking," said Margot. "Do we have a candidate?"

"It's only in the theoretical stages right now," I said. I held up my hands for her inspection.

She squinted in my direction. "What are you pantomiming? 'I surrender?' To what?"

I said, "No. I switched my wedding and engagement rings to my right hand. That's an announcement. And a metaphor."

"Some people might take them off altogether," she said.

Anthony said, "One thing at a time. It's a step in the right direction."

"A baby step," said Margot. "And before you get mad at me, let me say that I'm not judging you. I'm employing tough love."

Did I overreact? Maybe. I said, "Tough love? Because I'm breaking laws? Harming myself and others? Wreaking havoc on the household? Or has it been just me staying home and getting used to Edwin being dead? What about you? You're always trying to whip me into shape, but I don't see you taking too many steps forward."

She was at the open refrigerator, excavating shreds of ham from last night's main course and collecting them on a paper towel. "What do you think I do on Tuesdays and Thursdays besides avoiding Charles? I go out! With men. I've done it on the QT so no one feels left behind."

"You go out with men plural?" I asked. "Or a man?"

Margot brought her coffee and shredded ham to the table. "My life, as you have seen with your own two eyes, is complicated. Very. I have an ex-husband virtually under the same roof, who fainted on my dining-room floor so I could start worrying about him. Which I hate."

"Worrying about what, specifically?" I asked.

Margot did a full-body shift in her chair so she was facing me with intervention intensity. "Gwen? Are you a robot? Didn't we both think for a few seconds that Charles was dead?"

I said, "Sorry. Yes, but ten seconds later he was sitting up and talking."

"It was visceral on my part. It *is* visceral. And here's why. I didn't hate him when I was married to him, so making the hate retroactive is not as easy as you'd think. Some part of my brain is nagging me to nag *him* to go to the doctor and get whatever you get after you faint. A CAT scan? An EKG?"

Anthony had left the table and was rummaging around the shelves of his flour/sugar/ baking powder/spice cupboard. Margot asked what he was looking for, and he said, "I had some pancake mix back here. Maybe I used it all. By the way?" He cocked his head toward his room and his bed. "Douglas stayed over. Do we have a serving tray and a little pitcher for the syrup?"

Margot said, "The ever-growing population of penthouse B. Why don't you make him French toast with last night's bread?"

I don't know what made me ask, maybe my new social activism; maybe I felt that Margot was patronizing me by hiding her dating life. I was suddenly wondering aloud, "We're not going to hear that Charles stayed over, too, are we?"

"Puh-lease! He is not now, nor will he ever be, staying over here unless he faints and we leave him where he fell. I can't believe you'd think that! Trust me, I have not gone soft on Charles."

Anthony weighed in with "Sometimes we can have a little fling of the meaningless variety. No love or romance involved."

"You boys are famous for that. Women are different," Margot said. She looked down at her chest and pulled her kimono tighter. "Women want love and romance. And I'm not saying that I've found that, but I have been seeing someone. Which I can now announce since my sister has gone to lavender."

Anthony and I both said, "Huh? Lavender?"

"You don't remember Mom saying that about Rita Collins next door? It meant she stopped wearing black after the first year of widowhood."

Anthony said, "Very *Masterpiece Theatre* of you, Margot. I love it."

I said, "I didn't wear black after the first month."

"And we're off topic," said Anthony. "Gwen and I need to know who your paramour is."

"Guess," said Margot.

I said, "It has to be the guy from your website, the one selling the Girl Scout cookies."

"Bingo."

"Do we know his name?" asked Anthony.

"Roy."

"What was his screen name that we all liked so much?"

"I forget."

"No, you don't. It had a sexual connotation, as I recall," said Anthony.

"It did not! It happens to be HardUp, which is purely financial."

Anthony said, "Ha! I'm sure."

I asked how often she saw him.

"Once or twice a week."

"His joint-custody, night-off kind of thing?" Anthony asked.

Margot said, "More like a Charles's-nights-here kind of thing."

"How old is he?" I asked.

"Young."

Anthony said, "Young like a boy toy or just younger than you?"

"Ten years younger than the age I told him I was."

"Love it," said Anthony.

"What do you do on these dates?" I asked.

Margot said, "I'm worried that you're asking that prescriptively, as in 'What do a man and a woman do on a date?'"

"No! I meant what can two people who met in the PoorHouse chat room afford to do on a date?"

"Fair question," said Anthony.

"Okay, then: We talk. We go to free nights at museums and free events — his bible is *Time Out New York* — or to readings or poetry slams in clubs without covers, and before or after, we get some ethnic food." She smiled, cupped both hands around her coffee mug, and leaned forward as if testifying outrageously before a congressional panel. "Then, typically, we go to his place."

Was I obliged to ask for details? Luckily, Anthony said, "We got off track. A new day has dawned. Gwen is ready for some social outreach. Let's toast new things and new friends."

I lifted my mug. "To new friends. Whatever that means."

"It means real dates," said Anthony, "as opposed to chaste ones."

"Where do we start?" I asked. I meant with candidates and venues, but Margot did not. She reached over and repositioned one lock of my hair from its usual resting place to what was, presumably, a more flattering one. Eyebrows arched, she consulted Anthony, whose lips twisted unhappily to one side.

"I haven't even combed it today," I protested. "If I'd known you were going to judge me by this" — I pointed to my hair, my naked face, and my stained bathrobe with the pajama cuffs protruding from its sleeves — "I'd have come all gussied up —"

"In lavender," said Anthony. "I am not letting that image go."

Margot said, "Stop worrying. You have an excellent team behind you. And you know what? I think Edwin would be cheering us on."

I shouldn't have winced, but I did.

"What? What did I say?"

From the sideboard, whisk in hand, Anthony supplied, "I'm not sure waving that particular flag helps Gwen move forward."

Margot raised her eyes to the ceiling. "Edwin? Are you there? Do you mind if I pull your widow off your funeral pyre? She's made her point. Enough is enough."

Anthony laughed.

"He loves my metaphors," Margot said.

19

December

Something happened in the outside world, something terrible enough to change the tenor inside penthouse B and expose a layer of previously unimaginable sympathy for our Public Enemy Number One.

The day after Madoff's elder son committed suicide, Charles came calling, ostensibly to inform us that our phones were out of order.

"They're not," I told him at our front door, having thrown a raincoat over my nightgown. "We let the machine pick up."

"Is your sister home?"

"Yes, but she's busy. As you can imagine, there's been a ton of traffic on her website."

"Are you going to stand guard or may I come in?"

I told him I was just about to take a nap—

"At one in the afternoon? That's not a good sign."

Because he was wearing some version of a motorcycle jacket over a black turtleneck sweater, I asked where he was going dressed so fashionably.

He smiled. "Fashion! Precisely! I'm here with an invitation."

I waited.

"I thought Margot might enjoy a student-faculty exhibition at FIT."

I said no on her behalf. She was still in her bathrobe and hadn't eaten all day. She'd have to shower, fix her hair, get dressed . . . all too much.

"I don't mind waiting. The opening is from two to five. I sense depression has fallen on the population here. Where's Anthony?"

"Still sleeping."

"Someone has to play activities director."

Margot must have heard every word because she yelled that she was busy, too busy. Her chat room, for the first time in months, had a quorum.

"Madoff's son," I told Charles. "I'm sure you heard. He hanged himself while his baby was asleep in the next room. She's been online since she got the news yesterday."

"That's why I came up. I *know* her. I knew this news would cause some recalibration and possibly some soul-searching."

I didn't like that. Charles had lost any right, marital or diagnostic, to use the term "soul-searching," especially when applied to the paragon of empathy that was his ex-wife.

He lowered his voice. "Correct me if I'm wrong, but I wondered if the Madoff family tragedy might in some way soften Margot's attitude toward Chaz."

I asked him how he'd made that particular leap.

"It's not a leap. The sons weren't speaking to the parents, and look how it ended, estrangement and heartbreak everywhere. Irretrievable!"

This was the new Charles speaking, the one who tried to be insightful in a way that Margot, Anthony, and I enjoyed ridiculing after he left on meal nights, the postprison Charles who spoke from a psychosensitivity phrasebook. "Do you think it's fair that you're making the final decision about a possible outing?" he continued.

I said I'd ask. Margot did like fashion trends and fashionistas. This wasn't just about hats, was it?

He patted a few jacket pockets until he brought forth a pink postcard. "The show is called 'Head, Shoulders, Knees and Toes.' So I'd say definitely more than hats. Also refreshments. Admission: free." He handed it to me and added, "It's the first piece of mail I've ever received from him."

I motioned *Come inside*. And once over the threshold, *Stay there*. I didn't tell him that Margot was at her laptop only a few yards away, probably listening to everything we were saying. Proof came with her yelling, "What's he doing here on a Sunday?"

Charles said, "Margot, for chrissake! I came as a Good Samaritan. I called several times and no one picked up. You could have all been dead in your beds."

"Lame!" she shot back.

"The machine didn't pick up, either."

"Oh, boo-hoo."

"May I?" he asked, gesturing in her direction. "Preferably alone."

Several minutes passed. Who knew what old times or current events he evoked, but when he returned to the foyer, he said, "She'll come. I'll wait in the parlor while you two get ready."

"Me?"

"It was a condition of her saying yes. You and dinner later at the restaurant of her choice."

We dressed better than usual, in leather boots, winter coats, and the scarves we thought would please the eyes of the fashion conscious. Charles, Margot, and I were descending in the Batavia's beautiful brass-and-mahogany elevator when its doors opened at the eighth floor and a young woman squeezed her way on with a twin stroller. Ordinarily, one of us might have cooed, but the homeliness of both babies seemed to render us mute. The new passenger said, after the doors finally closed, "I'm Vanessa. I'm staying with my parents for a week while our floors are being refinished. In Westchester."

And after a few more floors in silence, she asked, "Are you residents of the building?"

"We are," Margot said, "but on different floors. She and I are sisters and he's my ex." After a pause she added, "It looks amicable, but it's not."

"And you can see why," said Charles.

"She's had a challenging weekend," I said.

Luckily, we had reached the lobby. I said, "I hope you have a nice visit with your parents."

Backing the stroller out expertly, Vanessa said, "I'll try."

"Can I help with that?" Charles asked.

"I've got it," she said.

At the front door, I told Margot and Charles that I was thinking of sitting this one out. "You two go," I said. "I'm already not enjoying myself."

"We insist," said Charles. "Someone's got to apologize for your sister after each of her tactless remarks."

"Shall we cab it?" Margot asked.

He led the way out the door, beyond our awning to the sidewalk. After a fleet of off-duty yellow taxis passed by, an empty one swerved to a stop. "Twenty-seventh between Seventh and Eighth," Charles told the driver. "Fashion Institute of Technology, I'm pleased to say."

"He doesn't know why we're going there," said Margot, "so you don't have to sound so tickled."

"Seat belts," I said.

"Am I going to hate this?" Margot asked.

"You love accessories," I reminded her.

Charles jumped in to proclaim that it was a juried show and a high honor to have any design at all included, let alone two, let alone the work of a first-year student.

"What kid knows at eighteen that he wants to design hats for a living?" Margot grumbled.

Charles, now staring glumly out the window in the opposite direction of his fellow passengers, said, "Gwen? Please tell your sister that her peevishness is wearing thin."

"It's curious," Margot said. "It's like I took truth serum and I'm blurting out whatever comes to mind. No tact needed. It's quite liberating."

"It's about Madoff's son," I told her. "You never know how a death will hit you, even a stranger's."

Our driver, who'd been chatting on his Bluetooth, asked, "Twenty-seventh Street where?"

Charles repeated, "Between Seventh and Eighth avenues. Do you need the exact number? It's FIT."

"Where his newly discovered son is in a show," Margot offered.

"I have a new son myself," said the driver. "Finally, after three girls!"

"Actually, he's nineteen, and it's an exhibition of his millinery work," said Charles.

The man said, in an accent I guessed to be Jamaican, "I hear a proud daddy talking!"

"Of course he's proud," Margot offered. "A son in fashion who's straight? He's cock of the walk!"

I gave her a look that was half *What's wrong with you?* and half *Knock it off.*

Our driver volunteered in the loveliest lilt that his grandmother used to wear hats to church, then switched to mantillas when Mrs. Jacqueline Kennedy was the First Lady of the United States, but that she had recently started wearing hats again, big ones, in every color of the rainbow.

Margot said, "I can picture that. I sometimes go to church in Harlem, and it's largely for the ladies' headgear."

"You do?" I asked.

"Do? Did? What's the difference? I went to a wedding up there once and then another time just for fun because of the choir."

"Here we are!" announced our driver. Margot and I slid out as Charles studied the taxi's credit-card machine.

Alone on the sidewalk, I said, "Truth serum or not, it's wearing thin. It's like I'm out with a stranger."

"I can't help it. He wants us to be pals. Everyone. Me and him. Me and Chaz. Me and the taxi driver."

Charles called, "Do either of you have money? This good man prefers cash. I'll pay you back."

Margot yelled back, "He has to take your card. And, no, we don't have any cash."

After settling up, and with a gentlemanly hand on the small of both our backs, Charles guided us toward the front door. It reminded me of my spinster days, going out with my married sister and her still-gallant husband, who was good at pretending that both of us were his dates.

Chaz, more than I remembered from the first sight of him at our party or from his Facebook pictures, was so striking, so smooth of olive skin, so shiny of dark hair and straight of teeth that Margot and I were struck a little mute. He was wearing a white shirt that looked buccaneerish, as if it would billow in the wind. His jeans were black and his high-top sneakers lime green. "I'm so glad you came!" he told us. "Do you want to see my stuff? Do you want some cider? There are some totally sick cookies, too — frosted hats and purses."

Charles asked, "Are any members of the millinery faculty here? Because I'd like to meet them."

"As what?" Margot asked. "Don't make him do that."

The pleasant, hospitable expression on Chaz's face faded. "Oh shit," he said. "Excuse me. Gotta see someone."

We watched him meet a new arrival, a dark-haired, pretty woman, maybe late forties, dressed in a black velvet coat suitable for opera-going. Neither Margot nor Charles nor I had to state aloud who the visitor was. Her stunning hat, worthy of a noir film star, might as well have been a neon sign that said MOTHER OF CHAZ ADAM HICKS.

"Oh, Jesus," Charles muttered. "Why didn't he tell me?"

We watched Chaz plant the kind of kiss that looked obligatory, then lead his guest into an alcove where, presumably, his creations were on display.

Margot said, "Who's coming with me?"

I said, "We can't leave without seeing his work—"

"Or signing his guestbook," said Charles.

"Who said anything about leaving?" Margot asked, heading not toward the exit but toward Chaz.

I hung back with Charles, unwilling to witness whatever scene was going to unfold. "Why didn't it occur to me that he'd invite his own mother!" he moaned. "Oh, God. Do you think it was a trap? Do you think she crashed? I should have my head examined! Of course, he'd invite every friend and relative. What was I thinking?"

I said, "Stay here. I'll get us something to drink" with a dual goal of cider and spying. At the refreshment table, I had a full view into the alcove where two colorful hats were perched on the limbs of a shiny papier-mâché cactus. Though Margot's back was to me, I knew her musculature well enough to know she was not in a fight. Chaz, standing between the two women, was pointing to a vinyl beanie, tracing a seam with one finger and looking pained. I returned to Charles and reported that from my vantage point all looked strangely peaceful. Here's your cider, and hold mine. I'd be right back.

A cluster of young women had moved in on Chaz. One by one they were trying on both the beanie and the other creation, whose description read A PLAYFUL VERSION OF A BIRETTA, A SQUARE CAP WITH THREE OR FOUR PEAKS WORN BY ROMAN CATHOLIC AND SOME ANGLICAN AND LUTHERAN CLERGY. Margot noted my arrival with a quick but neutral glance. I widened my eyes, silently inquiring as to what the hell this sudden armistice was all about.

"Nice to be a guy at FIT, obviously" was all Margot said. Chaz's mother turned to me and said, "I'm the proud mom."

"Kathleen Hicks," Margot supplied.

We shook hands. Kathleen wondered aloud if we'd ever met before.

I asked, "Where would I have ever met you?"

"At the office?"

Margot said, "She means at Charles's practice. Mrs. Hicks remembered that I sometimes filled in for the receptionist. And since we were a mom-and-pop operation, a sister-in-law might have helped out, too. Or came by for lunch."

What? This degree of civility seemed inconceivable. All I could manage was "No, I didn't help out. Maybe I should have."

Kathleen next offered the opinion that working in an obstetrical office, helping doctors bring babies into the world, must be a most rewarding mission.

"Charles didn't deliver babies," Margot said. "His specialty was helping women conceive them." Then I knew. She *was* acting. For whatever reason — and I hoped it was for Chaz — she was playing the grudgeless ex-wife. Further proof: the slight, ironic tilt of her head when she said, "Let's get Charles. I know he wants to see Chaz's work. And I assume you two haven't seen each other since you took the witness stand."

Kathleen said, "I saw him after that. I visited him up at Ossining."

"Otisville," said Margot. "That was nice of you."

"I needed to explain my reasons for testifying," she said. "Also I wanted to tell him more about our son."

Our. Son. There were two words that a home-wrecking witness for the prosecution probably shouldn't use to describe her love child.

Margot said, "My understanding is that your husband's name is on your son's birth certificate. Wouldn't that make *him* the father?"

Kathleen said, "Legally."

"Are you still married to him?" Margot asked.

"We're divorced. It was final in October."

"And you were married how long?"

"A long time by today's standards. Five and a half years before Chaz was born."

"*Then* what?" I asked.

Kathleen said, "I think we all know that answer. When Chaz was sixteen, I read in the newspaper that Dr. Pierrepont had been arrested for fraud. Of course, I had to find out about my own child's paternity."

Margot asked, "Really? You had no inkling before that?"

"Not a clue," said Kathleen.

I said, "I'm sorry, but our other sister was at the trial every day. I believe you testified that the transfer of DNA was accomplished" — I looked around, lowered my voice — "directly. Person to person."

What were we expecting? A confession? An apology? What we heard instead was "Are you and Dr. Pierrepont reunited? Because Chazzy seems to have that impression."

Margot said, "Dr. Pierrepont and I live in the same building. We can't help running into each other, and since we're both civilized people, we occasionally eat at the same table."

"That's what I'm asking. Is it an amicable divorce or is it dating?"

I blurted out, "Amicable or not, it's obvious to everyone that Charles will always be in love with my sister!"

Kathleen jumped back as if I'd taken a swing at her. And Margot? She touched my arm, sovereign to subject. "Really, Gwen," she scolded. "That was uncalled for." And then, grandly, to Kathleen. "Charles and I are *not* dating. The coast is clear. Or should I say the *couch* is?"

Then Chaz was calling. "Mom? Wanna meet Sophie? She made the chenille cloche."

Quite politely, considering the climate and the united sister front, Kathleen said, "You ladies will excuse me. Sophie, I believe, is the new girlfriend. And for your information, I'm seeing someone, and I'm quite certain that we have an understanding."

"Still, I'm sure you want to say hello to your former doctor. He's here. On parole. Should I send him over?" Margot asked.

All was well. My sister was back. I found a bench, a handsome one made of brambles and stuffed birds that might have been part of the exhibition, and sat down. Unlike Margot, I was exhausted.

20

Were You Speaking to Me?

WE WERE OUT ON the town, at a deli on Sixth Avenue that served its hot beverages in old-fashioned ceramic mugs, treating ourselves to cappuccinos. Our purpose: crafting the all-important, proactive personal ad that I was going to submit to an undecided classified advertising medium under WOMEN SEEKING MEN. We were of three minds in terms of tone and terminology. I wanted truthful. Anthony wanted attention-getting. Margot wanted naughty.

We couldn't even agree on the headline. I nominated YOUNGISH WIDOW, but as soon as the last two syllables were out my mouth, Margot said, "Do you want me to leave? I thought we'd agreed that that word had been banished."

Anthony said, "Not so fast. 'Widow' says 'I wasn't dumped. I'm someone who was desirable or attractive enough to snag a guy in the first place.' It says 'It's not my fault that I'm single.'"

Margot conceded that he might have a point; she had been speaking as the sister-roommate who had OD'd on that particular reference to my marital status.

Anthony asked me, "If there was one adjective or noun, other than the w-word that described you or your . . . I don't know . . . romantic outlook? What would it be?"

I said, perhaps too quickly, "Chicken."

"Oh, great," said Margot. She angled Anthony's laptop toward her and with a few quick strokes had Craigslist personals on the screen. With one finger busy on the track pad, she read descriptions at random: "Tigress . . . temptress . . . adventuress . . . pussycat . . . playmate . . . *gatita* . . . mischief maker . . . let's get freaky . . . discreet lunchtime fun."

Anthony said, "No. No. No." Then, quietly, "I sometimes wonder if you two share any DNA."

I said, "May I now argue the case for an honest ad?"

"Proceed," said Anthony.

"First, let me point out that the typical person I'd like to meet is someone who isn't a regular. Maybe he's never answered an ad before and is nervous, too. He isn't ready to try online dating, so this is his first step."

Anthony said, "Still, I'm not crazy about 'chicken.' I don't think it's the most attractive image one could project out of the starting blocks."

"No kidding," said Margot. "You want something that says 'Hey, mister. Read me. Write me. Call me. You won't be sorry.'"

Anthony countered with "Gwen isn't looking for sex —"

"Are we back to Chaste Dates?" she asked. "Because if we are, I give up. I'll walk around the block a few times until you two have your perfect little G-rated ad."

I said, "Do I want someone who's so superficial that he judges a candidate by one word? And by the way, I don't think 'chicken' is so bad. Who doesn't like chicken?"

Anthony said, "Let's move ahead. Margot, sit down. And let's go with 'chicken' for now. Maybe Gwen's right. Maybe it would be seen as appealing — like she's a newbie and not a barracuda."

Margot muttered, "Scrawny. Loud. Squawking. Quite the unattractive bird."

"Jesus! It's not supposed to be a physical description," I said. "It's about a state of mind. It says 'I'm new at this.' Or 'I'm not a woman of the world. I'm nervous about this, and I admit it.'"

"How about 'coward' instead of 'chicken'?" Anthony tried.

Margot said she was switching to decaf. Anyone else? Anthony took back his laptop, and I asked him to peruse the MEN SEEKING WOMEN ads on the screen. When she returned, Margot announced, "I'm coming around. I think 'chicken' could have some appeal to a certain type of man with a rescue complex. And it's certainly modest. It says 'I'm not threatening. I won't scare you. You're safe with me.'"

"That was a quick about-face," I said.

"I asked the guy behind the counter."

"Does he speak English?" I asked.

"I think he got the gist. I used *pollo.*"

"We want eye-catching," said Anthony. "And I do think that word would set Gwen apart."

"Settled then," I said.

"Only if what follows is a really strong pitch," said Anthony. He tapped the open notebook in front of me.

"You'd actually let me write it by myself?"

"Try it. A first draft."

Margot said, "Just don't make it pathetic."

"We can revise," Anthony told her. "Nothing's set in stone. Let her do her thing."

I said I wouldn't mind if they moved to another table while I worked on the first draft. Or went home.

Margot said, "Okay if I blog about this? I'll be unbelievably discreet. I won't even say it's my sister who's ready to date. I'll say it's a friend."

Anthony shrugged. "What harm?"

"What *point?*" I asked.

"None! Words on the page. I'm sick of Madoff and me . . . my empty bank account and me. I'm developing a new persona, pretending that life is more interesting for me and my posse." She smiled. "Poetic license. Besides, I'm pretending that you, whom I identify only as a female roommate who helps defray expenses, and our male roommate have a little thing going on. I've given you names: Violet and Christopher."

Anthony asked, "Are we sleeping together or just flirting?"

"I'm dragging it out. You're attracted to each other, but you're resisting it. You haven't even kissed yet. It's fun. I'm getting comments. Everyone's rooting for you two."

I asked if our story was a metaphor for what was happening between her and Roy.

Margot said, "I think Roy and I are a few installments ahead of Violet and Christopher." With that, she took a final swig of decaf, fished out a dollar for a tip, and advised us to do the same.

Anthony said, "I just want to go over a few important points."

I don't know what possessed me, but I turned to the nearest patron and asked, "What have I done to make these people think I'm not capable of writing a few sentences on my own?"

I was immediately embarrassed, especially when he looked up and then immediately back down at his laptop as if he didn't know where the noise was coming from.

Margot said, "It's not that we think you're incapable. It's just that it's so much fun to compose a personal ad. We want the vicarious thrill —"

"Which I won't be providing. Nor will I be doing anything reportable on these alleged dates."

"Just being on the sidelines will be fun for us, seeing who answers and then helping you cherry-pick."

She seemed so happy at that prospect that I didn't want to say anything tinged with pessimism. I opted to continue in my newly independent vein. "Go! Coffee's on me. I'll be back in time to peel the potatoes."

Anthony finally stood. Margot said no hurry and no help needed; we were having hot dogs and beans.

"In that case, I'll see you both . . . eventually."

"Do you have plans?" she asked.

I said, "Oh, who knows? I may just walk this straight over to the classified department at the *Voice*. And then I might go clubbing."

"The *Voice*? Who said the *Voice*?" said Margot. "You'll get an old lefty who doesn't have Wi-Fi."

"Who goes clubbing at five p.m.?" Anthony asked.

"Then maybe I'll go to a hotel bar and treat myself to a Cosmopolitan."

"What's gotten into her?" Margot asked.

I accomplished this much: My headline in boldface was NERVOUS. Below that: "This ad has less 2 do w/me wanting 2 find love & more 2 do w/pushing myself out the door with a polite man, 40–50, for . . ."

What noun or participles came next? "For conversation"? "Companionship"? "Early dinners"? I didn't know. I tried again. "I was widowed 2+ years ago & have been sitting on the sidelines of my own life. This ad has less 2 do w/me wanting 2 find love & more 2 do w/pushing myself out the door. Looking for kind M 40–60 with similar ambivalences."

Was I reading this aloud? Maybe I was, in a mumble, because the man at the next table, previously intent on his laptop, murmured, "Your friends won't like it."

Let me describe this interloper. He was, I guessed, fiftyish, with a broad, clean-shaven face. He was the only person in the deli wearing a tie, its knot visible just above the neck of a brown V-necked pullover sweater. Was I imagining that he looked like a secondary-school teacher? Next to his laptop was a pot of tea; the saucer under his cup was holding a dissolving biscotti. He had not lost his hair, which was that shade of gray that announced he'd started off blond.

Knowing full well the answer, I asked anyway. "Were you speaking to me?"

"I was."

"Was I reading aloud?"

"Almost."

I said, "I'm composing a personal ad."

"Got that."

Quite bravely, if not aggressively, I asked him if he was a reader of personal ads.

He said, "Oh, who doesn't read the occasional personal ad, even for pure entertainment value?"

And more boldly: "Are you married?"

"I once was."

"Not a widower, by any chance?"

"Sorry. No."

"Divorced?"

"Unfortunately, yes."

"Recently?"

"No. Long ago."

I was not the best judge of where polite conversation left off and badgering began. I said, "Sorry if I'm interrogating you."

"I'm Mitchell," he said, and reached across the gap to offer his hand.

"I'm Gwen."

He said, "I was married when I was twenty-two and divorced before I was thirty. So I barely remember what went wrong."

"I guess you overheard my whole story."

"I did. You're a recent widow who hasn't ventured out yet." He paused, the way all polite people do upon pronouncing or hearing that word, and said, "I'm sorry for your loss."

"Not so very recent, but thank you."

"Just be careful," he said. "I'm sure you've heard about the crazies who find their victims through Craigslist."

I said, pointing to the scratched-out lines in my notebook, "I thought I'd start with an ad in a newspaper or magazine."

He was shaking his head with what appeared to be conviction.

"No?"

"No longer. These days it's all online."

I said, "I thought a print ad would be more . . . I don't know . . . dig-nified? Or maybe attract people who were readers."

"My girlfriend and I met through OkCupid."

Had I imagined we were conducting a mild flirtation? Yes, I had. This confirmed what I already knew: that every man was unavailable, and what seemed like friendly attention was two sentences away from a call across the room, to the effect of *Honey! Come over here. I want you to meet — sorry, your name again?*

I said, wanly, "You certainly see online dating services mentioned in every other marriage announcement in the *Times*."

My new nonfriend answered with "I wish you luck. I think you'll get lots of winks."

Really? Winks? As if I'd been the beneficiary of such things my whole life through. I thanked him. I hunched over my notebook and pretended to be working hard on an irresistible advertisement for a desirable me.

"I really shouldn't be pressing you one way or the other about how to get back into circulation," I heard. "My girlfriend tells me lots of people try it and aren't so lucky."

Did he think I wanted to hear a quote from his smug girlfriend? I did not. I said, "Lucky? *My* luck ran out when my husband died."

Good thing Margot wasn't there to hear that answer. I didn't like it so much myself. Poor Mitchell. He meant well. So why did he have to add, "One more piece of advice: If you upload a photo, make sure it's up-to-date."

I must have looked perplexed because he said, "No. Wait. That came out wrong. Some people post an old picture because they don't look so good now. I just meant . . . you'll be fine. You have nothing to hide. A headshot. Not you in a group or at a distance."

Maybe we *were* flirting after all. I said, "Okay, then. New headshot, a close-up."

"Gwen, is it?" he asked.

I told him that it's officially Gwen-Laura, hyphenated; named after two actresses my parents had seen on Broadway during their legend-arily rapturous honeymoon.

"Rapturous" must have sounded racy. He said he had to run along. Renee was waiting. Best of luck to me in finding someone, no matter where I went fishing.

21

Is My Life Not My Own?

NEWS TRAVELS FAST. Two minutes after I'd left the deli, my sister Betsy texted me to say *Congrats*, necessitating a callback from me to ask "On what exactly?"

I was window-shopping at a cupcake boutique just off Sixth Avenue, staring not out of hunger but because I was thinking that Anthony's wares were prettier than these standard-issue chocolates and vanillas with sprinkles. Betsy said, "I heard you're working on a personal ad. Will you let me vet it before you send it in?"

"Margot called you already?"

"Of course! It's big news. Overdue, I might add."

I said thanks, but I could handle this myself. I reminded her that of the three sisters, I was the one who'd been the actual writer. Not a blogger like Margot, not a writer of corporate memos to fellow bankers, but someone who'd been a professional wordsmith, thank you very much.

"A wordsmith for utility companies, as I recall. This is different. This is an invitation. This is an advertisement. Margot said yours was too self-effacing. Besides, it's fun for us, a vicarious thrill!"

"So I've heard. And editing my ad will give you that?"

"The results will! The answers, the e-mails, the potential dates. I hope to have a front-row seat."

As I switched the phone to my other ear, I missed the beginning of a sentence that was now ending in ". . . but she didn't go into detail."

I seized the opportunity to insert a new vein of vicariousness. "Are we talking about Margot's new paramour?" I asked.

Betsy didn't allow herself a telltale gasp, but there was a distinct and abrupt pause. I knew her and her silences. Wasn't *she* supposed to be Margot's number one confidante when it came to matters involving romance?

"His name's Roy," I continued. "And I think he's around forty. I can fill you in. I know a lot."

"I was away," said Betsy. "And I have a job that doesn't allow for lingering over breakfast, lunch, and dinner."

"Like us, you mean? Your slacker sisters?"

"I didn't say that. I just meant you two are under the same roof so, of course, you'd have the inside track."

"You're jealous that I knew before you."

"Just fill me in," she said. "We're not children."

I said, "Okay. Here's what I know: They met in the PoorHouse chat room, where he's a regular."

"I know all the regulars! What's his username?"

"How do you know all the regulars?"

"Visitors are allowed. I sometimes log on late at night."

"As a chaperone?"

"No! So she won't be the only one in there. She has no idea it's me."

I said, "That's actually very sweet of you."

"Just tell me it's not HardUp."

I said, yes, sorry — though not sorry at all and quite enjoying my one-upmanship — it was indeed HardUp.

"I'm speechless. She's actually met him and *dated* him?"

"More than that," I said.

I hadn't realized how long I must've been standing at the bakeshop window until a young woman, wearing a chef's apron, her hair in braids, her hands in disposable gloves, came outside with a pink-on-pink cupcake cradled in a napkin. She said, "You were out here so

132

long, and we saw you staring at the display. We don't keep our stuff overnight. We thought you might like to take one home."

Oh dear. I must have been looking like a hungry waif. I said, "I was talking to my sister. I didn't realize I was looking needy." And added as proof of my own solvency: "In fact, the sister I'm talking to is a banker."

"Please. It's what we do around this time every night. We close at six and give away what we don't sell."

I accepted the cupcake as Betsy was squawking my name. I thanked the baker and said into my phone, "This is a nice city, you know. I don't get out enough to appreciate that. I just got a free cupcake."

Betsy was giving directions — which corner of which intersection she wanted, presumably from the back seat of a taxi. Then to me, contradicting my Manhattan testimonial, "Give me a sec. I'm paying with a credit card and he's arguing about the tip!" Then to him, "Buddy! Get real! It's not up for negotiation!"

I waited. The pink, I decided, was only food coloring. It didn't suggest the cotton-candiness of Anthony's. From what must have been her lobby, Betsy returned to the subject of HardUp. What was Margot thinking — rewarding a blatant flirtation that all the world could see?

"She's happy," I said. "It gets her out of the house." I stopped there because I couldn't remember if we had told Betsy that Margot felt the need to escape because Charles was on a two-nights-a-week meal plan chez nous.

Betsy said, "You sound . . . I don't know . . . different. Like you're fine with this HardUp, like you don't disapprove of her dating a penniless and possibly homeless predator."

"It started off as coffee in broad daylight. And then only because he was selling Girl Scout cookies for his daughter and Margot ordered three boxes."

"Are we sure he's not married?"

I said, "You're quizzing *me* because you two never pry into each other's personal lives?"

133

"Never mind. I got sidetracked. I'm about to get into the elevator. E-mail me your ad before you run it. I'll have Andrew look at it, too."

I couldn't say "But Andrew isn't the guy I'm looking for," so I said instead: "It'll be its own test. If I only hear from creeps or no one, I'll revise."

"Gotta run. Where's the ad going?"

"To be determined. I started out thinking the *Village Voice,* but —"

"Why not everywhere? Why not a blitz? Why not cast the widest net? In print, online, a matchmaker? I was thinking of giving you one of those private matchmaker consultations for your next birthday."

I had turned onto West Tenth and I was sick of the topic. I caused my own voice to produce a faux cell-phone skip. "Bets . . . have to . . . a quart of . . ." Then I added for good measure: "You're break—" I snapped my phone shut and slowed down to a leisurely stroll. It was warm for March. And it was fun eating a cupcake on the streets of New York. People smiled at me for that reason. If I was ruining my appetite for dinner, who would care?

We weren't supposed to be feeding Charles on a Wednesday, but Margot had been more flexible and indulgent since his fainting spell. I found them in the kitchen, Margot making a salad and Charles watching. Because they went silent when I arrived, I guessed she had told him about our afternoon's project. "Where's Anthony?" I asked.

"Gym. Then out with Douglas."

"So this isn't just a series of one-nighters," Charles observed.

To avoid the inevitable sarcastic remark by Margot about Charles's being the documented expert on meaningless sex, I asked him, "How's Chaz?"

Charles's face manifested instant paternal pride. "He's great, isn't he?" he enthused. "I was petrified. And wary! And then this solid young man walks into my life and asks for nothing except a meeting, a handshake, an interview about my family tree and medical history. I don't deserve it. I'm a little overwhelmed, obviously."

Though Margot was across the room, vigorously chopping garlic with her sharpest knife, I knew she was listening intently.

I asked when he was seeing Chaz again, but before he could answer, Margot threw out, "Before you get too attached, maybe you should have a DNA test."

Charles turned slowly, a theatrical pivot in her direction. "I think you forget that during the trial you couldn't bring yourself to attend—you who once pledged 'for better or for worse'—the question of paternity was resolved on the basis of DNA testing of anyone suspected to be my issue. And as you occasionally need reminding, I was punished in ways matrimonial, financial, professional, and every which way. The government and most of my friends think I paid my debt to society."

She was now chopping so fiercely that the garlic had gone from minced to macerated. "To society," she muttered. "Society! Whatever that means. Total strangers and taxpayers who weren't hurt by any of your crimes against humanity."

I said, "Please. Let's stipulate that Chaz is Charles's true son. Okay? No need to discuss further."

"Thank you, Gwen," said Charles. "Maybe we can switch to a much more pleasant topic."

I waited. I took three plates from a cupboard and three napkins from a drawer.

Charles continued, with a broad, condescending smile, "*I* heard something quite intriguing today."

Before I could ask what, he said, "I hear you're dipping your toe into classified waters. Brava!"

If Margot weren't already grumbling to herself, I might have pleaded, "Is my life not my own? Is there *anything* I do or say that is off the record?"

Charles said, "Not to worry. Your sister told me in confidence. I won't tell a soul."

Margot said, "I did *not* tell you in confidence. The point was to get the word out. Direct your loyal, forgiving, noncriminal friends

— maybe some fellow doctors or one of your legions of lawyers — to Gwen's upcoming ad."

"Which I'd love to see in advance," he added.

I said, "You and every person I've ever met. For the hundredth time: No, thank you. If nobody answers, I'll start over."

Charles said, "No, no. You misunderstand. I peruse the personal ads myself. I wouldn't want to answer your entreaty by mistake."

Was he kidding? *I* thought so. But Margot slapped the knife down with a bang. "Do you have no boundaries? Is there *anything* you wouldn't say in front of your ex-wife! What's next? 'Oh, did I tell you that I answered an ad for an ovulating woman looking for a sperm donor shooting blanks? She didn't get pregnant, but it was fun just the same.'"

"Margot —" he began. "Honey —"

"I wanted babies! I never *didn't* want them. But who had the last word? *Mister Zero Population Growth. Mister It Would Cramp Our Style.*" Her voice lowered to a mocking impression of his. "'You and I don't need children to be happy, darling. Marriages fall apart because of children!' How ironic was that little argument? How evil and untrue? And who's the proud, happy papa now?"

I didn't expect to see what happened next: Charles strode across the kitchen and put his arms around Margot.

More surprising — she let him.

22

What's the Worst
That Could Happen?

AFTER DUE DILIGENCE, and despite the pressure to go modern, I decided against Craigslist. Its personal ads were very much by and for the young, many of whose "pics" unabashedly exhibited not faces but erect penises. Anthony's three-pronged argument (my ad would stand out; I had nothing to lose; look at all the youngsters advertising for older chicks) did not convince me.

Before taking another leap, I analyzed two weeks' worth of classifieds in the *Village Voice,* in search of somewhat older gentlemen who weren't blatantly seeking sex. Anthony sat at my elbow, urging me to click on ads that had a 40 or higher in parentheses, indicating the poster's age. Exactly zero posts moved me to answer. Among those run by my contemporaries:

- Wanna watch me with my stepdaughter?? — 47
- Submissive guy at your service — 45
- Looking for Mother — 50
- Get paid to have breakfast with me Monday — 46

By week's end, I was doubting the whole enterprise and hating everyone who had composed an ad with any cheesy intention. Thus my ad ran in the *New York Review of Books*, word for word, the one I'd composed at the deli, with NERVOUS as my boldface headline. No photo needed, though I was prepared for that request. If there were any inquiries, I had a brand-new one of me, makeup by Margot, with my hair blowing in the wind above our rooftop terrace.

A day passed, then two, then a week. No one answered, and I knew why. The competition in that highbrow publication were women aiming for a man with books on his shelf, art on his walls, smoked salmon in his refrigerator, and tenure. I was at a distinct disadvantage, lost among ads posted by Ivy Leaguers with advanced degrees in Masculine Preferences. What man would ignore "Tall, sophisticated, stunning, affectionate, and irreverent. Easy laugh, warm heart. Smart as a whip. Just plain fun to be around." Or below that: "Sparkles with natural charm, no games, positive approach to life. Curious/avid traveler, doesn't complain when the AC is on full blast or the music is loud. Former runway model. Graceful, easygoing, cosmopolitan. Bakes her own bread." Or, following the adjectives describing the next perfect woman's beauteousness and svelteness: "Self-deprecating humor, adventurous streak. Will learn to fly plane but draws line at skiing when it's 20 below. Tennis devotee. Loves 'no agenda' vacation days; well, maybe a little snorkeling & Jet Skiing. Loves red wine & rare red meat — give me a thick, juicy burger any day."

See what I mean? Mine might as well have said, "Mouse seeks same for not much at all. Very ambivalent about this whole thing. References upon request. Hope you don't want sex."

To keep the in-house harassment to a minimum, I didn't raise the topic of my advertising failures with my team, but, of course, they were following my nonadventures independently, quizzing me at every juncture. As more and more nothingness happened, Margot said that this was only one avenue. A person could get out, do things, mingle.

It was shortly afterward, on an afternoon of browsing in Soho, that she came up with a terrible idea that she viewed as brilliant. We were looking at silk-screened T-shirts displayed outdoors on Prince Street when she clutched my forearm. "Remember when you wanted a piano?" she asked.

"Yes. So?"

"And Mom was reading the classifieds, looking for a secondhand one?"

"Vaguely."

"Well, someone else had placed a 'piano wanted' ad in the classifieds. Mom called and said that if he got more responses than needed, would he share the info. In which case, she'd be happy to split the cost of the ad!"

"And this relates to what?"

"That's how she got our upright! Maybe you could e-mail these dames who post the come-hither ads, offer to contribute to the cost, and see if they have any guys to spare."

I didn't realize that this entire conversation was taking place with an audience, the artist whose T-shirts were before us. He looked about twenty-five, and was eating tabouli from a plastic container.

"Whoa," he said.

I turned around.

"I'm getting the picture," he said.

I asked what picture that would be.

"Love," he answered. "As in looking for it." He took two business cards from a small stack on his table. "My girlfriend is a psychic. She's the real thing. She actually makes a living at it. I mean, it's spooky. She told one woman to get an EKG, and a week later she needed a triple bypass. Her husband came back to thank Serena. She's like five minutes from here, on Mott. Mention Adam, and she'll give you a discount. All of her reviews on Yelp give her five stars."

I could see that Margot took the cards with a little too much enthusiasm. "Mott Street," she said to me. "C'mon."

We thanked Adam, me insincerely because I had no intention of availing myself of Serena's palm, tea-leaf, or tarot-card readings. I trotted after Margot, who was already hustling east. When she turned onto Mott, I stopped and called ahead, "No way."

"You *are* a chicken. C'mon. Maybe I'll get a vibe, too, and that'll decide it."

I checked Serena's business card. No fee mentioned. "It could cost a hundred dollars, for all you know."

Margot stopped, faced me, and said as if she were mustering all her patience for the upcoming life lesson: "We'll ask her fee, Gwen. Then I'll make a counteroffer, and after we've agreed on a price, I'll mention our discount, courtesy of Adam."

We walked up two more blocks of shops and restaurants before we spotted a blue neon sign flashing in an upstairs window: CLAIRVOYANT and in red, OPEN.

"If I have to drag you there, I will," said Margot. "We have to be more spontaneous."

Up two flights and down a dark hallway, Margot stopped at a heavy door, its dark brown paint reptilian after many coats. The knocker was a brass mermaid. The nameplate read SONDRA APPLEBAUM. We checked the business card again, matched its 3-G with the symbols on the door. We knocked. A voice called, "Who is it?"

Margot asked, "Are you Serena?"

"Just a moment, please," the voice sang out.

It was a whole minute before the door opened onto one room, painted a nervy sapphire blue. Serena was wearing a red and gold sari, not the colors I'd have chosen with her orange hair. "Have you come for a consultation?" she asked.

Margot said yes and pointed to me. Suddenly I wished I'd worn my good camel coat instead of my parka, my chocolate beret instead of my earmuffs. Serena asked what service we needed her to render. She pointed to a cardboard sign, painted in the same hand as Adam's T-shirt slogans.

Quick Palm Read . . . $10
Full Palm Read . . . $20
Tarot-Card Reading . . . $25
Psychic Consultation . . . $60
Tea-Leaf Reading . . . $12 (includes tea)

Margot and I stepped away and conferred. I said, "I wouldn't mind the psychic consultation, but, yikes, sixty dollars. Forget it."

Margot asked Serena, "Do you look for what's ahead, or would you say it's more about the past and the present?"

Serena said, "It varies from person to person. If I see something, I say it, and sometimes it's already happened and very often it's still ahead. What my mind's eye produces doesn't have a timeline."

Margot handed her the business card. "We were referred by Adam. He said we'd get a discount."

Serena frowned.

"Not good?" I asked.

"We broke up," she said.

Margot said, "It seems to me that only a nice guy, and maybe someone still carrying a torch, would be promoting his ex-girlfriend's business."

Serena said, "I didn't break up with him. His referrals? They're guilt."

"Was it another woman?" Margot asked.

"You probably met her, at his side, selling her pot holders."

Margot said, "Tell me he didn't leave you for someone who makes pot holders."

"They're only pot holders in the ironic sense. She means them to be quote-unquote kitchen art."

I asked, "Are you still honoring his discounts?"

"I can do five dollars off the psychic consultation. One dollar off everything else."

"How about forty?" Margot countered. And to me, "I'll go halvsies."

Serena closed her eyes. I sensed it was forbearance mixed with math. "Forty-eight," she said. "Final offer. And please don't tell anyone I gave you that price."

"We promise," said Margot.

Serena instructed Margot to please wait in her kitchen, through that door. She and I would be in her reading center.

Margot asked if she could observe.

Serena and I said no. She pointed to the kitchen door. "Make yourself at home. There are magazines on top of the microwave."

I followed Serena into what must have once been a closet, with a fringed overhead ceiling fixture and two chairs facing each other. As soon as we sat, she took my left hand in her right and stared down at it, frowning.

"I opted for the psychic consultation," I reminded her.

"Just a quick look," she said. "On the house. Every hand I study increases my — for lack of a better term — database. It's an ongoing learning process."

She returned my hand to my lap. With her eyes half shut, she said, "I sense a sadness beneath your smile."

"Do you want me to confirm or deny each statement?" I asked.

She shook her head. "You think you put on a brave front," she continued, "but actually you don't. You like people to know that something bad happened. You like putting that forward. It's your calling card."

From the open kitchen door, Margot called out, "Bingo!"

"No running commentary," I yelled back.

Serena left our little room to close the kitchen door, then returned. "Someone very close to you died," she said. "A man."

"Did she tell you that?"

"Of course not!"

I waited.

"A loved one. A lover."

"My husband," I said.

Serena seemed to go smaller and grayer and she slumped in her chair. "I need a minute," she managed to say. "Please forgive me."

When she recovered, she asked if that was my wedding ring and could she hold it. I said, yes, sure, here it is. And my engagement ring, too.

Squeezing both in a closed fist, she asked, "Cancer?"

"No, it was his heart."

"Sudden! Before his time. No one knew."

I said I certainly hoped it *was* sudden because I'd slept through it. A hole in his heart that no one knew about.

"I'm sorry," she said. "The shock is still with you. It was only last year, wasn't it?"

Oh dear. Instead of correcting that impression, I asked, "How am I doing?"

"Your friends aren't letting you grieve. They're impatient." She closed her eyes and opened them quickly. "I see a circle of women. Many women. Is it a book group?"

"A support group, so-called. I've stopped going. It wasn't any help. I hated our leader. She didn't like us looking back. Only forward. Do you think that's how a widows' support group should be led?"

Serena said, "No, I do not. And why don't I see any men in that circle?"

I said, "It was supposed to be coed, but no widowers signed up."

Squinting into the air a few inches above my head, she asked after a long pause, "Who's the man with the dark hair and dark eyes? Not too tall. Young."

"Anthony? Our roommate?"

"He's smiling," she said. "He brings sunshine into your home. He's very fond of you."

I knew she was thinking "fond" in a meaningful, optimistic way, so I said, "He is fond of me, but he's not even thirty. And he's gay."

"I knew that," she said.

I didn't want to appear inappropriately and prematurely boy crazy, but I finally whispered, "Do you see any other men?"

With a slow, meaningful nod, she said, "This is important. I wanted to build up to this. There's a man standing behind you. He's been there the whole time. He's saying, 'You think I'm very far away, but I'm not.'"

I asked what he looked like and what he was wearing because Edwin wore button-down shirts and ties bearing musical instruments to work, and that tended to be the snapshot I called up.

Serena said, "He's a little chubby. But not in an unattractive way."

143

I didn't correct her; didn't announce that Edwin had never been chubby except in his baby pictures, that he had thinned down without trying in ninth grade.

"I know what you're thinking, that I got that wrong. But it's not your husband. I'm not sure if you've even met him yet."

"Did he answer my personal ad?" I asked.

"It's possible. His name begins with . . . a D. Daniel or David. Maybe Donald. Or Dennis."

I said, "Anthony's boyfriend is Douglas. That's not causing any interference, is it?"

"No," she said. "You'll find out soon enough. Derrick? Diego? I definitely see a D."

"What else?"

She returned to my hand. "See the shape? It's oval. You're empathic. But"—and now she was tracing some horizontal line—"cautious. You tend to overanalyze people rather than trusting your instincts." She added, "This? Your head line? It shows me that you're a late bloomer." Serena looked up. "Which fits, don't you think?"

Something in my expression must have launched a whole new psychic subspecialty. "May I say something personal?" she asked.

"Of course."

"Your sister—that was your sister, correct?—may have been the prom queen or voted Most Popular or had the lead in *Grease*. I can tell. She has that confidence and gives off that energy. You give off a reverse energy. It says: I'm the lesser sister."

I told her I was the studious one. The middle sister. The shy one. But I'd been secretary-treasurer of the photography club and a soloist in my high school chorus, and I'd gone to the senior prom with a handsome tenor.

"Did your mother or your father or your sisters ever tell you that you were pretty, too? Because, believe me, that family stuff can do a job on you. We're all given labels in the family—the pretty one, the smart one, the wild one—and it sticks!"

"I had a happy childhood. There were three of us, and my parents didn't play favorites."

"I'll tell you why I'm saying this," Serena continued. "Because I don't think you're aware, fully aware, that you're a very pretty woman. Maybe you weren't a pretty child so that's how you still see yourself. If this seems outside my job description, I say 'Screw that.' I want people to leave my center feeling better about themselves. Sometimes it's coming from another dimension. But sometimes it's factual and in this world. Like the face in front of me."

I tried to arrange my features into a tranquil, pleasant expression infused with a little sexual oomph that lived up to her characterization. She leaned closer and said, "So I'm giving you homework. I want you to carry yourself like the desirable and attractive woman that you are."

I said, "Okay. I'll try. Is our time up?"

"It is. But I hope you'll come back. We still have work to do."

"I know. I hear that every day."

"Your sister loves you," she said. "It's so clear. I can feel it from here." She gestured around the closet, then patted a breast. "And from here."

I thanked her and offered my hand. She reminded me: the fee? Did I have cash? I said I did. I added a tip. Margot's footsteps sounded outside our little compartment as if she'd been summoned, as if she'd heard every word.

"All good?" she called to us.

I wasn't sure if I should sum up my hidden and future life so succinctly, but Serena did. Tucking my bills into the top of her sari, she answered, "*Very* all good."

I knew her by now, my new shrink and life coach. Her reply hadn't been a reflex or a nicety. It was an order.

23

The Way of the World

DUE TO THE BUST that was my print ad, and because every wedding anyone attended in this century celebrated the union of people who met in cyberspace, I was finally persuaded to sign up for a three-hour seminar titled Fine, I'll Go Online.

Might I have paid better attention to the course description? It advised those of us who were "online-dating virgins" to hold off until our workshop, and those who were already "initiated" to bring copies of their profiles. Laptops mandatory. Digital photos encouraged, ready for uploading.

I was pleasantly surprised to find that the course had been limited to twelve and that our leader, Franny Bagby, had been married for the first time at the age of forty-seven to a divorced man she'd met on Match.com. Also helpful: her southern accent, which promoted fraternization, and her memorizing our names within the first ten minutes. "I know y'all are slightly embarrassed to be here, right? I would've been, too, before this" — and up on her PowerPoint screen appeared the smiling face of her first example, presumably a *no,* a pot-bellied man whose bolo tie and handlebar moustache could not have been the lures he had hoped them to be.

"See?" she said. "Not much, am I right?" And then the arrow danced over to what she called the candidate's "turnoffs." There were more than I had noticed at first glance. The pine paneling behind him indicating an ugly rec room. The digital camera at his navel indicating this was a self-photo in a mirror. "Like he didn't have a single friend he could call on to take a decent pitcha," Franny said.

And still more red flags appeared in the parade of his photos: his arm around two young women in matching dresses. "Why?" Franny pleaded with this image. "Is this to signal that you got yourself a date? Captions, please!" Next photo: him nuzzling a large Persian cat. Next: him toasting the camera with a giant Teutonic beer stein. Next: him, sweaty, at a finish line, arms raised in a most unappetizing fashion. The last of his five photos: him wearing an Elvis T-shirt and fanny pack in front of what was surely Graceland.

Just as we're feeling squeamish about exploiting this embarrassing profile, Franny squealed, "Ahm not as mean as y'all think! This is the doll-baby ah married!"

What could one say? A smattering of applause helped fill the void.

Smiling fondly, she continued. "This is to demonstrate two thangs: Y'all have to dig deeper. And y'all have to go beyond the goofy words, the bad pictures, and the bad taste. The motorcycle? Borrowed! The two slutty-lookin' bridesmaids? His daughters! Yup, y'all know what ahm sayin'! Y'all are nodding. Y'all get it. It's a process. Y'all have to kiss some frogs!"

I looked around. We were ten women and two men, one of whom was hunched over his keyboard, head down, typing nonstop. And just when I was feeling relieved that we didn't have to tell our life stories or confess what relationship failures had brought us to this moment, Franny passed out paper and pencils, and asked for our ten favorite foods.

"Not sayin' why, yet," she said. "Y'all are just going to have to trust me."

There was a lot of staring off into space and pursing of lips, but not by me. I wrote quickly. "Chicken, olives, artichokes, capers, chocolate, raspberries, cauliflower, coffee, clam chowder, salmon." Then, as a fallback, I added hazelnut gelato in case beverages didn't count.

With time to spare and in Anthony's honor, I added, "Red velvet cup-cakes."

I assumed the assignment had to do with likes and dislikes — that which would be attractive to the similarly inclined. But that wasn't our objective. Franny wanted us to appeal to the senses. Food as usernames sent a subliminal message of comfort and deliciousness. And not to brag, but her username had been — the next slide went up — DeepDishApplePie — with her own photo, hair color, and style different than today's. "Notice," she said, arrow circling her face, "A close-up. No group shots. Not me a mile away, posing in front of the Taj Mahal or Fort Sumter. Ahm smiling. Ah look open and wel-come if ah say so myself. Now can we discuss why DeepDishApplePie worked?"

When no one volunteered, she asked, "Are y'all thinkin' *No way!* 'Apple pie' says 'date your mama'? Because that's not always the worst association for some guys . . . the lonely ones . . . boys who loved their mamas and on some level want to crawl back into their laps. And 'dish'? Don't make me say why that got some friendly inquiries."

Another classmate asked if Franny's husband chose her because of her food name. And, by the way, what was his?

"Ahm glad y'all asked because his was *awful.* Gentlemen take note! It was LuvMeTender69 — and y'all know where he got *that.* Ah do not recommend y'all use your username to suggest you're lookin' for sex. A Franny Bagby no-no."

This was the juncture at which I started to worry that our entire curriculum was based on the star-crossed profiles of LuvMeTender and DeepDish.

"Food favorites?" she persisted. "William?" This classmate was wearing a crisp Izod shirt in tangerine, collar upturned, hair jelled, jeans pressed. I guessed midthirties. Without prompting, he recited, "Nutella, spanakopita, Cobb salad, mangoes, smoothies, arctic char, bacon, champagne, osso bucco, goat cheese."

"Easy!" crowed Franny. Then to us: "What if y'all went online and saw this handsome fella and his username was ChampagneAndMangoes!" Would you ladies not e-mail him on that alone? And you know why? Because the champagne says *I can afford it,* and the mangoes say *Ripe, juicy, and sweet.*"

William said, "Um, sorry, ladies, but not looking on your side of the aisle."

That seemed momentarily to confuse Franny. She recovered quickly and said, "Then we're still talkin' about appealing to men! We are on the same page! Ah *love* your side of the aisle! And ahm stickin' with ChampagneAndMangoes!"

There was nowhere else to turn for a male opinion but to Joel, the bearded, ardent notetaker. Every classmate must have been thinking the same thing: *Just the person we don't want to meet online. Just the man, after five minutes over drinks, you'd be plotting your escape route from.*

"Joel?" prompted Franny.

He finally looked up, and after a tug or two that loosened some beard hairs, he answered. "You really think 'mangoes' appeal to guys? Because I don't get 'juicy and delicious' from that. I get 'tropical fruit,' no offense. And it's kinda anatomical. I don't want to get graphic in front of the ladies, but it's not a great image."

Franny asked, "Can you tell us what kind of username you'd respond to?"

He said, "I don't care about usernames. I look at the pictures."

William said, "I totally agree with Joel. If the guy is hot, I don't care if he calls himself Attila the Hun."

Clearly sold on her own formula, Franny was not expecting blowback. She asked us to humor her on usernames, then asked for another volunteer. I didn't raise my hand, but she called on me anyway, noting how fast I'd finished the assignment. I said, "I understand what you're going for, so I'm leaving out cauliflower and salmon. I'll just cut to hazelnut gelato and red velvet cupcakes — not that I see myself in either of those."

"RedVelvetCupcake!" Franny exclaimed. "Bingo! Two down! Who else?"

Another woman, who was typing with only one hand due to a heavily autographed cast on the other, asked if there was a study — a reliable, scientific one based on a large sample — that showed what worked and what didn't.

Franny said, "Ah know this much. Be positive! Upbeat! Don't be Debbie Downer!"

We nodded politely. I was already worried about the course evaluation I'd have to fill out and how honest I should be.

The same classmate asked, "What I was thinking of specifically was how much do you have to hint about being a willing sex partner? Because isn't that really what men want, bottom line?"

Whom to turn to but Joel and William? We waited. William said, "I think Joel would be better for your boy-girl stuff."

"Could you repeat the question?" Joel asked.

The woman in the cast said, "Like in real life, aren't men looking for sex, even though the request is in code?"

Franny pressed a button, and a new slide appeared. Gesturing toward the screen she announced, "Ah did my own survey of words that send a wink in that area. Here we go. 'Passionate' and 'affectionate' — those are easy. And these phrases: 'loves to cuddle' . . . 'hold hands' . . . 'moonlit walks on the beach' . . . 'I'm great at back rubs and foot rubs' . . . 'massage your scalp,' which came up a few times . . . 'great kisser.' And there's one that should only be used if you want sex on the first date: 'high-octane hormones and high-touch sensuality.' That's a direct quote from a JDate profile."

I must have *eeeyewed* loud enough to catch Franny's attention because she turned squarely to me and pointed.

I wished I'd kept my groans internal. I asked as pleasantly as I could, "Isn't it a little slutty to call yourself 'passionate' or 'craves intimacy' online for all the world to see? Isn't that what Craigslist is for? Isn't that using a dating site as an escort service?" I felt compelled to explain that I was a widow, and even though I was ready to date . . . well, none of this was coming easy.

Franny said, "First of all, God bless. Second of all, you're here!

You came! That's the headline: Gwen is ready! Everyone? Gwen. Is. Ready!"

When no one echoed her slogan, she tried, "We're *all* ready! And y'all know what that means? We're ready to write our profiles! Get out your pencils and your keyboards."

A gray-haired woman who hadn't yet said a word asked, "If you make a joke, should you write LOL after it so they know you have a sense of humor?" Her follow-up: "Should I describe my politics as 'middle of the road' so I cast the widest net possible?" Others asked if they should mention their children, their salaries, their allergies.

Oh, it was tedious, twelve people trying to sound appealing but not desperate, trying to appear intelligent, witty, healthy, toned, and open to romantic love and its inevitable activities.

I didn't employ "passionate," "affectionate," or even "friendly." I announced in three different ways that I was new to this, that I was a widow after a long, faithful marriage. That I was nervous. That friendship would be a good and comfortable place to start.

When it was my turn to share, my short paragraph earned a literal and figurative thumbs-down from everyone except William. I sounded sad was the main complaint. I sounded unready. "Frankly, kinda pathetic," said Susannah, a recent college grad. "Reluctant," said another. "Like someone put a gun to your head," said Joel.

"Make stuff up," said Franny. "After my first profile got no hits, I added 'I love to cuddle by a blazing fire and bury my face in your shoulder during a scary movie' and that same day I got three e-mails."

I didn't say "No, thanks" or "Over my dead body." I conceded that I would tinker a bit and leave out the widowed part since it was already noted under "relationship."

Franny insisted my profile had to be romance-ready today, now, before I left. No stallin'. No procrastinatin'. So I tried again, describing myself as loyal, creative, smart, independent, honest, dependable, low-maintenance, grammatical, and punctual. Franny wanted me to add "fun" and "have a silly, girlish side," which would suggest romantic potential.

I compromised. I added "good company" and "quite presentable."

By noon, everyone else had produced a credit card and membership in at least two websites. I whispered to William across the aisle that I knew someone great for him in real life, then pantomimed pen to paper. *Contact info, please.*

Franny asked me if I cared to share with the class what I'd just exchanged with William. I said sure, no problem. I'd just told him that I couldn't officially register for online matchmaking today. Unfortunately, my screen was frozen and I'd left my wallet at home.

24

I Take Action

WILL THIS MAKE you happy?" I asked my harassers at breakfast the morning after the workshop I regretted taking. "I'll join Match dot com while the pointers are fresh in my mind. I'll use my advertising copywriting skills. I'll exaggerate a little. I'll brag. I'll post handsome photos even if they're ancient. I'll throw some words into my profile with double meanings that horny men will hear as my having urges. I'll join all of the sites, in fact. Why not? 'In for a penny, in for a pound.' That's what Franny Bagby told us."

I waited for my sarcasm to register.

"Do it," said Margot. "What have you got to lose?"

Anthony held out his arms and wriggled his fingers in an exaggerated, get-me-to-a-keyboard fashion.

I said, "Not again?"

"Not again what?" Margot asked.

"You two stepping in to ghostwrite."

Anthony said, "It's only when it comes to men that I put in my two cents. And who better than I?"

Still pretending to be on task, I said, "I'm doing this in private. In my room. I know what to look for, especially now, fresh from the seminar." I stood up, took my coffee with me after adding more to my mug, straight black, for fortification.

What an unappetizing task — advertising oneself like a picture bride. I looked around my room, at what Margot called my "shrine": photos of our parents; of Edwin; of my two favorite childhood dogs; Betsy and me with Margot in her bedroom, we three barefoot in crinoline slips — maid of honor, bridesmaid, and bride — hair in rollers, an hour before her lavish hotel wedding.

Had I not noticed before that everything on display was expired in one way or another?

Maybe I'd start small, but only because my roommates would be asking me every morning what datable strangers had winked at me overnight. I remembered the unappetizing candidate Franny had settled for and the admonition that I'd have to kiss a few frogs before finding . . . what? Someone tolerable? I was supposed to look past the tattoos and the toupees, the fanny packs, the gold chains, the double chins. I remembered to look for, as recommended, nouns that meant something to me, bonus words that added stars to my ratings: Widowers, teachers, nonsmokers, good spellers.

I chose my membership duration (one month, the minimum). Next, the username I would be hiding behind. I wasn't sold on the food formula, but what if Franny was right? I experimented with her concept, hoping to find an unused fruity appellation. AppleTurnover was taken. So was AppleCrisp, AppleKuchen, LemonMeringue, PeachesAndCream. I rejected GrannySmith and CantElope without even submitting.

Why did I care? I didn't want to be Franny and I surely didn't want to attract a LuvMeTender69. And what if appealing to a man's senses backfired? Suggestions of smell and taste could attract the sexually ambitious. I decided on something that was accurate and autobiographical without being revealing, mysterious without being coy. I typed in "MiddleSister" and pressed RETURN. Unclaimed!

Next hurdle: uploading photos from my computer. The best one had been taken by the artist in our extended family, Chaz, at his FIT exhibition, and e-mailed to me with the subject line "Nice!" With my head cocked as I studied his hat display, I thought I looked both pleasant and contemplative.

More photos! I heard Franny call to me from her happily married home. I uploaded the head-and-shoulders shot that I used in my freelancing days: in a black sweater and pearls, with the suggestion of a smile and excellent work habits. Also the recent windblown one on the roof. And one more, a flattering picture of me in the bleachers among faculty, in sunglasses, at a varsity baseball game, Edwin next to me, his school's team in some playoff. I hated to do it, but I had to crop him out. A bit of his shoulder remained, which I thought could be either good luck or bad. I often studied this picture, marveling at how unaware I was that June day of what was just around the corner.

As soon as I had one foot in and one out — a username, three photos, no profile — I lost my nerve. Margot knocked on my door as I stared at my screen. "How's it going?" she called.

I said, "Okay. Not done yet."

"What's the holdup?"

Me, I thought. *I am.*

"Gwen?" she tried again.

"I'm embarrassed! Okay?"

"Embarrassed just sitting in front of your computer? Can I come in?"

I said no. Maybe. Yes. But not if she was going to force my hand.

"I get it," she said, still outside my door. "Hard to take that final step. Maybe you need a break? No guy with a job is going to be trolling for dates at ten a.m. anyway. Let's do something. Let's take a sandwich up on the roof. It's nice out."

I said it was too early for lunch. I wasn't hungry.

"Then coffee! C'mon. We'll enjoy the view. I need it. You'll be doing *me* a favor."

"Are you using psychology on me?"

Finally, she opened the door. "It's for me. I'm trying to be nice to myself. I wouldn't expect anyone else to remember, but Charles was arrested three years ago today. I have 'meal on terrace' on my low-cost bucket list."

"Can't we do better than that? Like a movie? Like a concert in some park? What would you really like to do, even if it's not low cost?"

She didn't hesitate. She said, "I'd love to get dressed up and have dinner at the nicest restaurant I've ever been to."

"Which is what?"

"I didn't mean a specific one. I meant one that I might have been to if my life hadn't fallen in on several sides. Just a great restaurant in general. That category. But, hon — you're not doing that. I won't let you."

I said, "Me? Uh-uh. Not me. I'm going to the source. I'm asking Charles to take you out for the most elegant dinner you've had in three years. It's the least he can do."

"Won't he think you're playing Cupid? Like I've confided in you that I don't hate him anymore?"

I said, "I will make it absolutely clear that this is purely — what should I call it? — compensatory. Not a date. Not the passing of a peace pipe. You've been deprived. But for his crimes, you'd be enjoying delicious meals with good wine, good service, tablecloths . . ."

"Dover sole?" she asked.

"Dover sole and the chocolate soufflé that requires advance notice."

She said, "For someone who won't get matched up, you're quite the operator."

I shooed her away and e-mailed Charles, more of an order than a question. *I very seriously recommend that you take Margot out to dinner tonight. It's not a date. It's the third anniversary of the worst day of her life.*

He wrote back. *You sure she wants to commemorate that?*

This time I picked up the phone. "That's not the point," I told him. "The point is to do something exceptionally nice for her on a day that will live in marital infamy. And make sure it's a restaurant that earned at least two Michelin stars."

"Your naïveté is showing," he snapped. "No restaurant of that caliber will have a free table tonight, regardless of the hour."

"Try. They get cancellations. Put yourself on waiting lists. Make a backup reservation at the best place that *does* have an opening. Use your powers of persuasion. Use your fellow big-shot white-collar parolees who have connections."

There was a long, unreadable pause. "What's gotten into you?" he finally asked, but it wasn't with his usual disdain. It was friendly. In fact, it might have contained a note of admiration.

"You in?" I asked.

He said he was in. I told him to start calling restaurants and get back to me as soon as possible.

While I was at it, flexing other people's social muscles, I pasted my Franny-approved profile into the appropriate sign-up box. I did ponder for a minute the embarrassment factor: putting my face into the catalog of lonely women seeking lonely men.

Did I think I was above it all? Maybe I was, or maybe I had been. I closed my eyes, clicked, and a reckless woman named MiddleSister was launched.

25

I Am She

W AS THAT AN EXULTANT "What the fuck!" from the kitchen, or was Anthony in distress? Margot and I both jumped up from the sofa where we were watching *Earth Girls Are Easy* and ran to his side. We knew as soon as we saw him, at his laptop, an amused smile on his face.

"Something good?" Margot asked.

"Something very interesting," he answered.

"A job?"

"Not a job," he said. "Not in that section. Not about me." He then asked, "Are either of you familiar with Missed Connections?"

Margot said, "All too often."

"No, not in real life. On Craigslist."

I said, "In the personals?"

"A section unto itself," Anthony said, "which I read every day. For example"—his fingers traced lines on the screen—"Gyro shop on Ave A Mon. around 7, U R about 5' 6", female, pretty, & u had on black tights w. glitter."

"Okay," I said. "So?"

He read another. "Dr. Goldfarb's office, New Hyde Park, blond woman. You were in the waiting room. I was the guy reading *Wired*.

We exchanged smiles. Why didn't I get your number?" He repeated to us rookies, "It's called Missed Connections. You notice someone, maybe check each other out, but don't meet, and now you're sorry so you advertise. There are dozens every day."

"Is someone looking for you?" I asked.

Ever-generous Anthony said, "Better than that."

"Must be about Charles," said Margot. "Or *by* him."

Grinning, Anthony said, "Hold on to your hats. You ready? . . . 'Two weeks ago you were at Sammy's Deli on Sixth at Waverly around four p.m. You are a widow with two first names. I left too abruptly. How are you?'"

"You think that's for me?" I asked a little hoarsely.

"Read it again," Margot commanded.

Anthony said, "I don't have to. Sammy's on Sixth? At fucking *Waverly*? Two weeks ago. *Widow*? C'mon. It might as well say 'Dear Gwen-Laura Schmidt.'"

I did admit that I had talked to the man at the next table and he had left a little abruptly.

"What now?" asked Margot. "Is there a number she calls?"

Anthony said, "Easy. You click on REPLY TO THIS POST."

I said, "He has a girlfriend. He's only asking how I am."

Anthony said, "Even *you* don't believe that."

"Obviously, he broke up with his girlfriend and now he's rooting around," Margot said.

"Or he's just trading up," said Anthony.

"Was he cute?" Margot asked.

"He was okay."

"How old?"

"I didn't ask."

"I don't mean his date of birth! I mean young? Old? Thirty? Forty? Seventy?"

"Maybe forty-something? You were there. The guy at the next table who was ignoring us?"

Anthony raised his hand, and with his index finger traced a figure eight through the air, a diving glider, until it was poised on the REPLY button. "Ladies?" he asked.

"Do it," said Margot.

Without waiting for my okay, he clicked. An e-mail form appeared, its address a string of numbers, anonymized. Anthony's ten fingers wriggled above the keyboard, awaiting inspiration or dictation.

I said, "Really? You think it's me?"

"A thousand percent," said Margot. "If you don't tell him what to write, I will."

The truth is, I was a little thrilled. Something that could be considered an actual social development had just flown in the window — unsolicited, positive, flattering. I said, "Okay. Write this: 'Is your name Mitchell? My roommate saw your posting on Craigslist, and I might be the person you described. Thank you for your inquiry. How are you, and how is Renee?'"

I smiled, proud of my nerve. I noticed, though, that Anthony wasn't typing.

"Not there yet," he explained when I asked what was wrong.

I said, "We all have to agree? Maybe you need to get Betsy on the phone. I'm sure she and Andrew would like to join the Gwen-Laura ghostwriting team."

This caused a moment or two of what looked like remorse. Margot said, "Okay. Maybe you know what you're doing. Maybe we're being too bossy."

Thus Anthony typed *Are you Mitchell?* but stopped there. He asked, "What came after that?"

I said, "I forget. But I think it was something like 'If the person you are looking for was named Gwen-Laura, then I am she.' Then add: 'I am well, thank you. Has your situation changed?'"

"Getting there," said Margot. "I like the direct approach. And if he's still with Renee, maybe he has a friend he could introduce you to."

160

As Anthony typed, I asked, "If he was interested in dating me, wouldn't he have tracked down my ad and answered it?"

"In the *New York Review of Books*?" asked Anthony. "Not so much."

Margot said, "His 'How are you?' is code for 'Can we get something going?' I'm guessing he's a polite guy. He knew he wasn't going to get your attention with 'Wanna hook up?'"

Anthony looked down at his work. "Wait. Wrong. He'll be writing back to *my* e-mail address. Okay, new plan. Gwen, go to Missed Connections, find his little love note, and write back."

I said, "I will. On my own. The Ghostwriting and Intervention Team will have to trust me."

"We don't care what you write, as long as you press SEND" said Margot.

I composed a longer e-letter than I had intended. I told the possible Mitchell that my personal ad had run, but without results, due largely to my misjudging the target audience and the keen competition. I had very recently, twenty-four hours ago, taken his advice and joined Match.com. After a cursory read-through, I closed my eyes and sent.

How long did it take before I heard back? How long does it take a woman to walk to the nearest toilet, pee, wash her hands, consider herself in the mirror, run a brush through her hair, and shrug? Three to four minutes? That's how long it took for me to find a return e-mail from mdavidson@mitchelldavidson.com in my in-box.

> Glad you saw my "missed connection." Thanks for writing back. Would you send your tel. number?
>> Sincerely,
>> Mitch

This was not the degree of relief and delight I was anticipating from someone hitting his mark. His reply had the flavor of an e-mail from the Good Samaritan who had found a wallet and then its luckless owner.

Why are all men obtuse? I wrote back. *That's it?*

He answered immediately. *I'm sorry. I thought it would be nice to talk.*

I felt something unfamiliar in the nerve impulses running between my brain and my fingers: power. I wrote back. *1) I know your name, but who are you? And 2) Why did you want to find me?*

His answer took longer than the first round led me to predict. After about five minutes, I walked back to the study where both Margot and Anthony were watching *The Real Housewives of New York City*. I said, "I answered and then he answered."

"Forward them to us!" cried Margot.

I said, "I may have stopped him in his tracks."

"No!" Margot said. "Why? How?"

"He wrote back very blandly. Like 'Thanks for writing. Please send your phone number.' So I wrote back and said, 'That's it?'"

"We *love* it!" said Anthony.

Margot silenced the television and turned toward him. "We do?"

"Yes! Translation: Why aren't you overjoyed? What are the odds that I'd ever see your lame post?"

"Did he answer?" Margot asked.

"Not yet."

"You're suddenly playing hard to get?"

I said, "Yes. I guess I am."

"Keep it up!" said ally Anthony.

I returned to my room. More minutes elapsed. I spent them sitting at my computer, waiting for Mitchell's statement of intent. I cleaned my screen. I experimented with the various sounds announcing new mail and changed mine from ping to frog to pop.

Then it came.

Dear Gwen Laura (hyphenated or not?):

I'm not sure what I was hoping to accomplish. I do know that you have been in my thoughts since we "met." I think I was rude (telling you the odds are bad, don't post an old photo, etc.) so let me apologize for that. I looked for your ad online but didn't find it. Also I may have overstated when I called Renee my girlfriend. We don't have an exclusive relationship. She lives in New Jersey and I live in Forest Hills. I am in the process of taking over my parents' dry cleaning business (also in Forest Hills) at the same time I'm studying for my real estate license. I have a bachelor's degree from Saint John's. Did I tell you I was divorced? It was a long time ago. My ex is remarried and lives in FL. I guess you don't like talking on the phone. Would you like to meet for a drink? If so, please suggest a day & time & place.

Sincerely,

Mitchell T. Davidson

How soon should I answer? What kind of waiting period does the person in the driver's seat observe? I didn't forward his e-mail to Anthony or Margot, but texted both of them. *Heard back. Will meet for a drink.*

Anthony would know a bar with flattering light and reasonable prices. In a week, it might be warmer and I could wear my floral-print dress with the sweetheart neckline. Also the red strappy heels I almost returned. While brushing and flossing, I decided to answer in the morning. Ten hours felt like the proper interval between invitation and acceptance for a woman practicing nonchalance.

26

Doesn't Sound Like You

B ECAUSE I WAS familiar with Margot's entire professional team —her internist, gynecologist, dermatologist, ophthalmologist, lawyer, and dentist—I knew that a Dr. Sadler (Post-it reminder of a 3:45 appointment on our bathroom mirror) was an addition to the lineup.

"You're seeing a doctor today?" I asked, as we passed in the hallway, a towel draped over her arm and a turban covering her hair.

She stopped. Didn't answer.

"A Dr. Sadler?" I prompted.

"Oh, him! That's right. This afternoon."

"Everything okay?"

"He's a shrink," she said. "What are you up to today?"

"The usual. Laundry. Fiddling with my résumé. A perusal of the classifieds."

"Good. We both could use a job. Even if it's at McDonald's."

I agreed: yes, that was true, because we said the same thing every morning. The topic of her shrink appointment receded until she was standing in the kitchen, waiting for her bagel to toast. "Dr. Sadler is a couples counselor," she announced. "And I don't want you to think it's about getting back together. It's about being more amicably divorced."

"You're going with *Charles?*"

"I have to. This guy only sees the couple together. I said I'd go once."

I said, "Boy, are you nice."

Now at the open refrigerator, with her back to me, she shrugged. "It's fifty minutes out of my fairly pointless existence. He's paying, and then he's taking me to lunch at the restaurant of my choice."

"Toward what end?" I asked.

Margot said, "Maybe I'd be easier to live with."

I had her repeat that sentence before I managed to ask, "Are you considering living with Charles?"

"No! Easier for *you* to live with! You and Anthony! Don't you think I've turned into an angry, sarcastic shrew since Charles moved into the building?"

"No," I said. "I most certainly do not. When you rant and rave about Charles, Anthony and I know it's about *him*. We don't take it personally." In truth, we may even have enjoyed it. An angry Margot was a sight to behold. Anthony had discovered that laughing during her fuming encouraged her to ratchet up her performance.

This seemed to give Margot pause. Had her anger *not* leeched into the atmosphere of penthouse B? And had she been sold a bill of goods by the very object and subject of her occasional ill humor?

I said, "To me, there are clear signs that Charles wants you back — the wine, the ham, the fish? It doesn't take a marriage counselor to see that all those gifts were stand-ins for the long-stemmed red roses he wanted to send."

Margot didn't argue back. She said, "People change." And then volunteered: "The guy's subspecialty is sexual addiction."

Fortunately or unfortunately, she pronounced those two words just as Anthony of the acute hearing opened the door to his room.

"Did I hear 'sexual addiction'?" he asked, accompanied by a quick swing and dismount from his chin-up bar. "It's not even eight a.m. and you've already made my day. I pray it's someone I know."

"It's Gwen," said Margot, causing both to laugh a little too heartily.

I said, "The correct answer is that she and Charles are seeing a marriage counselor today —"

"Who happens to list sexual addiction therapy on his website, period. I never said that's why Charles picked him," Margot told us.

Anthony, as he palpated the lumpy bag of bagels defrosting next to the toaster, noted, "I don't believe our friend's legal problems were ever pinned on sexual addiction. Not even by his defense team."

Was that a derisive "Ha!" coming from Margot, now seated at the kitchen island?

"Do tell," said Anthony. "Is he actually tomcatting around or just bragging about it?"

Margot said, "No comment."

"Rather nice of you to accompany him," said Anthony.

"One time only. And the office is a block away from Le Cirque."

Anthony asked if they had had counseling the last time.

"Last time, meaning when I threw him out?"

"Correct."

"No! I refused."

"That doesn't sound like you," I said.

"How could it ever have been fixed? Did we have *issues?* Did we need help *communicating?* Was the problem fifty-fifty, his and mine, or was it one hundred per cent Charles in the headlines for screwing his patients? Who needed bullshit marriage counseling? I didn't even want to be in the same room with him."

"But now it seems doable?" Anthony asked.

"He wore me down. I'm not going because I want us to get back together."

We waited, but she didn't explain further. "Then why *are* you doing it?" I asked. "It can't be all about an expensive lunch."

"So he'd stop nagging me. I said no ten times before I said yes."

"Addiction or no addiction, wouldn't a guy want to speak privately to a counselor about his sex life?" I asked.

Margot said, "We're not going for that. We're going supposedly to find" — air quotes — "peace and harmony. And you know what would help? If the guy hypnotizes me so I leave with marital amnesia."

"Wanna know what I think?" asked Anthony.

166

"I know what you think," said Margot.

"I don't," I said.

Anthony patted my hand. "It's my belief that Charles is looking for peace and harmony, all right . . . in his ex-wife's bed."

Margot rose. Did she look offended? Not at all. She yawned and stretched rather grandly. Body language translation? *You might be correct.*

I reminded her, on what we were calling our daily constitutional now that the weather had inched into the sixties, that she was still dating Roy.

"Roy? Here's the trouble with Roy: He doesn't have a red cent. It's no longer cute."

"But you've known that from the start. And it's not as if you have much in the way of disposable income, either."

"I know! But I have the apartment. And my alimony. And my fabulous boarders. I don't feel as poor as I actually am."

I said, "I've never thought of you as someone who needed a rich boyfriend."

"Rich? I didn't say rich. I don't need rich." We were passing a market with fruit and vegetables displayed outside. An aproned young man was tossing out the old, the yellowed, and the overripe. "But would I like to stop picking up every check for two cups of coffee and two glasses of wine? Yes."

"I guess the question is, do you like him anyway?"

Instead of answering, she asked the vegetable guy in pantomime if she could have the cabbage leaves he was paring off and presumably discarding. He handed her a plastic bag with a wave of the hand that said *Help yourself.*

She said with a grin, "*Sopa, sí?*"

"*Sopa,*" he answered with an instant grin indicating some happy recovered soup memory.

That was so Margot. You could call it good manners or friendliness, but really it was charm. "*Cómo se llama?*" she asked him.

"Mañuel."

"*Gracias*, Mañuel."

He offered two bruised tomatoes, but she said, "*No mas! Gracias.*" I knew she had exhausted her Spanish, which was limited to the vocabulary of menus and amenities, but still she'd won a friend.

After our adioses and a few blocks in silence, I asked, "Isn't it going to be hard to break it off with Roy after you've been sleeping together?"

Margot said, "Not that hard." She nudged me with her elbow. "Especially since I haven't heard from him in a while. Tomorrow it'll be two weeks."

"Does that hiatus have something to do with Charles?"

"I am not admitting any interest in Charles. Nada."

And then the question I'd been waiting for an opportune moment to ask: "How did it go today with Dr. Sadler?"

She headed for a bus-stop bench and I followed. "I was dying for you to ask! I enjoyed every minute. It was ladies first, so Sadler asked for a little history and what brought us there today. So I had the floor for the whole time! Of course, everyone thinks that appointment number two is Charles's turn."

"But it's not?"

"I only agreed to go once, remember?"

"But wouldn't it be fair to go for one more?"

A bus had pulled up and was waiting after two passengers disembarked. Margot yelled, "We're just sitting. Thanks!" She slid closer on the bench. "You think I need to be fair?"

Reflexively, I said "No." But then, "It depends. Do you want things to get better? I don't mean a reconciliation. Just working toward . . . something more comfortable."

"Oh, it's plenty comfortable," she said. "More than I saw coming."

Should I request amplification? Betsy would. Anthony would, too. So I asked, "Have you slept with Charles since he got out of prison? You can tell me. I won't be judgmental. I know that kind of thing happens."

She said, "I've thought of it. *He's* thought of it every night for the past — as he likes to put it — ninety-nine weeks. You'd think he'd been marking days off in chalk on his cell wall."

I asked if she thought she'd have to forgive him in order to take him back into her bed.

When she didn't answer, I said, "I won't be shocked either way."

"Do I think what he did was forgivable? No. But is he sorry? Extremely sorry? Insanely sorry? Yes. Do I have flashbacks about the good times? Yes. Do I think my bed is too big for one? Often. So maybe one answer is 'Hate the sin but have sex with the sinner.'"

I didn't expect I'd react with anything but surprise and scorn, but there was something about the image of an empty bed that caused my voice to choke. Eventually, I said, "You're lucky. All you have to do is forgive Charles. Not everybody can be brought back with mere forgiveness and marital amnesia."

"I know what you're saying. I do. I worry: How would Gwen feel if one of us was able to turn back the clock. If we weren't the team we are now." An arm snaked around my shoulders. "Because you know what we are, don't you? Two eligible women in the most exciting city in the world. Two dames on the verge of . . . something."

That interpretation of us seemed to require more energy and action than merely sitting at a bus stop. We rose, and suddenly we were costars in a bygone movie — two sisters seeking their fortunes in Manhattan, cabbage leaves swinging from the elder's resourceful hand.

Were we happy? Should we be? That unspoken question made me miss a beat in our tandem high-step. But I recovered. "Do we need these old leaves?" I asked. "Haven't we had enough second-time-around cabbage soup to last a lifetime?"

"You surprise me, Gwen-Laura Schmidt."

I said, "I know. I surprise myself."

27

In Which I Go Out on a Date

WHEN I ARRIVED AT the beautiful hotel bar, dark wood everywhere, Mitchell rose from our small, votive-lit table and greeted me with a polite kiss on one cheek. He was wearing a dark suit, a starched white shirt, and a tie striped in orange and royal blue.

The waiter was there in seconds. I ordered a datelike Cosmopolitan before Mitchell chose from the bar menu a gin and tonic with grapefruit bitters and grapefruit zest, inspiring me to say, "Make that two."

The waiter said, "It's one of our signature cocktails. And a personal favorite of mine."

And then we were alone. He complimented me on my choice of venues and told me I looked nice. Did I sense that he was somewhat taken aback by the grooming improvement? I said thank you, adding that this was the first warm day of the year, hence this cotton frock.

"Quite toasty," he said. "And maybe not just the ambient temperature."

I heard myself babbling that my dress was a hand-me-down from my sister Betsy, who had decided it was too long and she had no time to get it altered. Otherwise she and I are the same size. I'm taller. I'm the middle sister. She's a banker . . . she wears suits to work . . .

"Was this the sister I saw you with at the deli?"

I told him no, that was Margot. Which led to more babbling about the population of penthouse B, i.e., Anthony Sarno, sterling roommate and excellent baker.

"How many roommates and how many bedrooms?" Mitchell asked.

I told him it was a large place. That, one by one, various undesignated spaces were being turned into sleeping chambers.

"Sounds nice," he said. "Do you have your own room?"

I said, um, yes, I did.

"Me, too."

"Do you have roommates?"

"What I have," he said, eyes closed with the burden, "is joint custody of a college-aged daughter."

I said, "I think that's nice. Where is she in school?"

"College-*aged*," he said. "Not college-enrolled. She works for my parents, which I think I told you about. We're in dry cleaning."

I asked if that meant he was inhaling dangerous fumes, and he said no, that was off-site at the plant. He did the books. "I have a bachelor's degree from Saint John's," he added.

"I know. You mentioned that before."

"And you? College?"

"Yes. Syracuse. English major."

"Syracuse," he repeated. "Do you follow basketball?"

I said sometimes, which was a stretch. Edwin was the one who had, on my behalf, adopted Syracuse, filling some vacuum, he always said, because his own alma mater, Juilliard, never made the sports pages.

"Saint John's was eliminated in the first round this year," Mitchell continued.

"That's too bad," I said, without asking first round of what.

"They lost to Gonzaga, which was seeded eleventh."

I asked if this was that thing they call "March Madness," and he said yes, exactly.

"Was Syracuse in it?" I asked.

"Not the Sweet Sixteen. They lost to Marquette."

"You know a lot," I said.

Our drinks arrived, and we concentrated on our first sips. He proposed a toast. "Thank you for joining me. What're the odds you'd have seen my 'missed connection'?"

I clinked his glass. "Slim. But you're welcome."

"I read those things all the time, but, honest to God, I never thought I'd try it myself."

I changed the subject to a more businesslike one: reminding him that when we met at the deli, he was very keen about online dating.

"Did I tell you to do it? Because it stinks! The women post pictures that are twenty-five years old. I mean — be serious! They're standing in front of a nineteen-eighty-eight Buick holding a kid in diapers!"

"Is there really a Renee?" I asked.

"There is . . ."

"But?"

Without looking up, he said, "Issues."

When nothing followed, I asked, "Would you care to elaborate?"

"I don't want to be a whiner. The major problem is that my daughter hates her."

I took what I hoped looked like an offhand sip from my drink before asking, "Because . . . ?"

"She thinks Renee acts one way in front of me, and another way when it's just the two of them."

"So they do things together, without you?"

"Once. A movie I didn't want to see. And believe you me — it was a disaster."

I said, "I'd be scared to take the daughter of a man I was dating to a movie unless I already knew she liked me."

"No kidding! And maybe you'd let her reach into your box of popcorn without asking her to first wash her hands."

"That's terrible," I said, though I could recognize the impulse.

"Renee claimed that she didn't know anything was wrong. Becca's not a sulker, either. It didn't help that when they got back to the apartment, Renee asked her if she had homework, and if so, had she finished it. Becca heard it as *Go to your room so I can be alone with your father.* And said something to the effect of 'I graduated from bleeping school two bleeping years ago.'"

"And when was this?"

Mitchell frowned. "Last Sunday. A matinee."

"Like three days ago? Or the Sunday before that?"

"Whatever. It's for the best. Are you familiar with the term 'exit relationship'?"

I said yes, of course. I'd been in a support group so I knew every term. How long after his divorce had he met Renee?

"I was still technically married. That happens. It takes a long time before a divorce becomes final." He blotted his upper lip and brow with a cocktail napkin. "Enough about Renee. She blew it. And it never was a hundred percent."

I asked what made something a hundred percent.

"Lots of things," he said. And with that, unfortunately, came a rather fond and lingering gaze into my eyes.

What would throw cold water on this sudden romantic spell? "Obviously your number one priority is — and should be — your daughter's approval," I ventured.

"No! Not number one. 'Good with kids' falls under the heading 'Bonuses.' Trust me, numbers one through three are chemistry, chemistry, and chemistry."

I made a quick downward check at my sweetheart neckline. Had it suggested to him that there was an accommodating woman across the table?

He continued: "Let's be honest, even at my age there has to be good old-fashioned animal magnetism."

I asked what his age was. "A young fifty-one," he said, winking. "But don't get me wrong. I'm careful. I'm a good dad. Becca shouldn't have to wake up to a strange woman drinking coffee at breakfast in her negligee." And then, as if I hadn't already mentally excused myself from the table: "Is it awkward — having two roommates around all the time?"

I said no. Margot and Anthony and I were most compatible and respectful.

"I didn't mean *everyday* getting along. I meant in terms of privacy. Private lives . . . as in entertaining guests."

Was this the new territory I wanted to conquer, and this its indigenous species? Another woman might have hinted that penthouse B was awash with chemistry and queen-size beds. But I didn't. I was flummoxed by his ambitious smile and felt nothing except his clammy hand on my thigh.

I looked down. I said, "I just met you."

"I know! And I like what I see."

"I meant take your hand off my leg."

He did. His smile collapsed. "I thought you were enjoying my company!" he whined. "Am I wrong?"

So this was romance; this was how a missed connection worthy of publicizing on Craigslist rewired itself on a first date. Civility abandoned me. "Yes you are," I said.

28

Hopes Up

I DIDN'T RETURN HOME immediately, but went to an unfortunate, scenery-driven indie at the Angelika. Back in penthouse B, I found Margot watching television, sharing our mother's afghan with Charles, long past his usual one-hour dinner allowance.

I averted their inquisition by saying that there were no particulars to share. The date was terrible. The chance of my ever seeing Mitchell again was zero.

Margot confessed that she'd gotten her hopes up.

"Because?"

"Am I the only one who noticed that Mitchell's last name began with a D?"

"So?"

"The clairvoyant! About the next man in your life? I thought he was fulfilling her prophecy."

"How scientific," said Charles.

"Not this D," I said. "Any leftovers?"

"I didn't cook," said Margot.

"Both of us had big lunches," said Charles. "We watched a movie instead."

The cable box said seven-forty-five. The Tuesday/Thursday visitor's schedule was dinner at six-thirty sharp.

"Anthony?"

"Out."

Were they looking a little rumpled? And had they just shimmied apart on the couch when they heard my key in the lock? I asked what movie they'd been watching. Margot looked to Charles. He said, "I forget the title, but it was one of those Tuscany ones. British woman goes abroad to find a lost love."

"Was it good?"

"It was excellent," he said. "Very evocative."

I said, "Good. I'm starved. Are either of you interested in ordering a pizza?"

"As soon as you mentioned leftovers, I realized I was starved, too," said Charles. "And you know what I have a sudden craving for? Lobster-salad sliders."

I said, "Lobster salad . . . Wow. It's been ages."

"With a delicious Sancerre," said Charles. "I have a beauty downstairs on ice."

"You'd better have some lobster on ice, too," said Margot, "because that is way above our pay grade."

He rose from the couch, but not before he folded the afghan into a mathematically perfect rectangle. "May I propose that we all go out to the closest seafood restaurant, whether it's for lobster rolls or whatever other cravings you ladies might be experiencing?"

"Give me ten minutes," Margot said. "I'm going to put on a dress, too. Doesn't she look nice? In the meantime, think of a place where we can get a table."

"I already know exactly where to go," said Charles. "It's on Mac-Dougal." He patted two pockets until he found his phone, then typed something into it. Within seconds, he announced, "Got it! Mermaid Oyster Bar."

As soon as Margot left the study, Charles sat back down. "Seriously, Gwen," he began. "One shouldn't judge a person too quickly. I learned that in prison. My time there was filled with surprises about people's characters and IQs. What I'm trying to say is if this man asks you for a second date, I think you should go."

"And you know where he wanted to go on our second date? To bed."

"And that has no appeal?"

"Not with him."

"No chemistry?" he asked, earning a groan from me. "Is that not a fair question?" he persisted.

I said, "I'm sick of chemistry. 'Chemistry' is code for 'I did not find him or her attractive enough to want to touch or be touched by this person I've known for ten minutes.'"

That triggered his explanation about attraction being so very hard to understand or discern — how one man's dream girl can be another man's maiden aunt.

"You've already forgotten: He liked me. Every sentence had a sexual accent."

"For example?"

"Okay, how about this. An example of his good parenting was not letting his live-in daughter find a scantily clad stranger at the breakfast table."

When Charles looked perplexed, I asked, "You don't think that's inappropriate and unwarranted?"

Still not looking convinced, he asked, "What is your idea of an inoffensive or even welcome come-on?"

I said, "Okay. You want to hear a really nice, sincere compliment? Edwin said it on our first real date, or maybe our second. It was this, almost word for word: 'You remind me of Teri Black.' So, of course, I asked, 'Who's Teri Black?' And he said, 'This girl I had a big crush on in high school, but never had the nerve to ask out.'"

"That worked?"

I said yes, obviously.

Charles asked if he could come across as such a guy — as sincere and harmless with unrequited crushes.

"Maybe. With a little practice."

"Isn't it a matter of taste, though? You'd like a sweet, modest guy. Dare I say another Edwin? Your sister, on the other hand . . . Wasn't she the girl in high school who sneaked out at night and had a fake ID?"

This required my admitting that yes, different overtures appealed to different women.

"And tonight's deal breaker was . . . ?"

"Bedroom this, bedroom that, do you have roommates? Do you have privacy? On and on."

Charles said, "That's not a come-on. That's a real estate inquiry."

"Not this time."

Margot called from down the hall, "Get your shoes on. I'm ready . . . Just looking for my keys. And shut off the lights behind you."

I said to him, "You two go alone. I'll make myself an omelet and get some work done. Besides, I think I interrupted something."

I noticed a slightly more complicated expression than I was used to seeing on Charles's face, possibly a layer of compassion and delicacy over his usual unwavering confidence. "We may, Margot and I, have reached a new — how do I say this? — understanding."

"Are you back together?"

"Unfortunately not."

"But something's changed."

"Certain things have, shall we say, fallen into place . . ." He patted my knee in a brotherly fashion. "I'll let Margot explain. And until she does, you're not to worry."

Were we New Yorkers unusually alert to real-estate nuances? Suddenly I was worried where I would go if Charles and Margot reconciled. My first thought was perhaps Anthony and I could be roommates elsewhere, until I remembered what a two-bedroom apartment without our friends-and-family discount would cost. I'd have to return to my own place, sublet for so many months that I'd almost forgotten its zip code.

Charles said, "Gwen? I lost you there. Where'd you go?"

I said, "Nowhere." A lie. I'd just been to West End Avenue and had watched myself entering my old apartment. And despite the reality of a possessive sublettor and belongings in storage, I was walking through the rooms alone, past our furniture, our bed, our books, our paintings, our dishes; seeing Edwin's Quaker Oats in the cupboard and his Chunky Monkey in the freezer.

Margot called, "C'mon! I'm starved."

I pointed the remote at the TV and said, "Really. You two go."

Charles asked, "Can we bring you back a slider?"

Margot, now in the doorway, dancing into her high heels, said, "No, because she's coming with us. I haven't heard word one about this alleged flop of a date. We've got work to do."

I promised we would go over everything at breakfast. Until then, I told her, I'd use my time wisely, studying the classifieds, online and on paper. I didn't say which kind.

29

Gotta Start Somewhere

LESS THAN TWO months into what looked like a relationship,
Douglas dropped out of their spinning class and stopped answering Anthony's text messages. We learned that he had not been
as pleasant as he first appeared; what's more, he was an elitist, hinting
that most of his boyfriends, even the one-nighters, had professional
degrees in this or that. Anthony was offended and annoyed, but not
heartbroken. Because we were a little in love with Anthony ourselves
(Margot's theory), we were indignant, already having sensed Douglas's disapproval of both Anthony's domestic arrangement and his joblessness. "Houseboy" was the word Douglas had used to describe the
baking and multitasking we so appreciated.

Unsolicited, he had advised Anthony to explore the field of personal assisting. "It's practically what you do now, minus the celebrity
employer," he'd observed.

True. But what nerve.

As Margot and I sat in the kitchen watching Anthony fill his muffin
tins, ingeniously using an ice cream scoop, we discussed how demeaning the term "houseboy" was. But after the oven door was closed, the
timer set, the wine poured, I remarked that "personal assistant" could
be something Anthony was stunningly suited for.

Margot said, "He *is* like a manager, an organizer, a live-in personal trainer, technical consultant, and pastry chef all rolled into one."

"Hardly—"

"Where do we start?" I asked.

He gave me a look that said, *After all these months . . . after my coaching, after I added memory to your computer and found a shout-out to you in Missed Connections, you have to ask where one searches for opportunities?*

Craigslist, I mouthed. "I know."

Margot declared that our pinot grigio had been too long in the re-frigerator and had been lousy to start with.

Anthony said, "We could always call Charles and invite him up for a glass of excellent pinot noir. BYOB."

"No, thank you," said Margot. "Tuesday's soon enough."

Anthony said, "I thought you were getting along very well. In fact, I thought you were unofficially back together."

"Who told you that?"

"No one," I said.

"A surveillance camera caught you two cupcakin' it under the same afghan," he said.

"Is that really a verb?" I asked.

"Is that what you surmised, too?" Margot asked me.

"More or less. If not back together, at least no longer enemies."

Margot said, "That much is correct. We are no longer enemies."

"So no big announcement?" Anthony asked.

"Not in that department." She took a sip from her glass. "Remind me not to buy this one again." She paused. "But I do have something to tell you. And this might be the right time."

What she then announced, her tone outsized for what followed, was "Gwen. Anthony. The time has come for me to close down the PoorHouse."

What I heard, or what I perceived, was Margot wanting to live alone. "PoorHouse," in something like an auditory panic, struck me as "penthouse." I processed her announcement as a request for us to leave.

"I don't make a red cent," she continued, "and for sure it hasn't attracted any publishers. When I don't blog, I feel guilty. And since the death of the Madoff boy, I just don't have the same fire in my belly. It's so discouraging to find my chat room empty all the time, except for the occasional sister."

I couldn't speak for Anthony, but I had long ago relegated her Poor-House.com to the inactive file. I said, "I think you're making the right decision. Time is money. And what about job satisfaction? You fired up the blog when you were aggravated."

Anthony said, "I'm going to say something harsh now. Maybe not harsh. Maybe just candid. But here goes: We have to get jobs. Real ones. We're too comfortable sitting at our laptops, pretending it's work, scraping by on lentils and ground chuck and cheap wine."

I said, "That's not harsh. It's true. I need a job. What's been stopping me from looking?"

He pointed. "You, life insurance, and probably savings, and maybe Edwin's pension. Me, unemployment compensation and savings . . . Margot, alimony and boarders. We're getting by and we're getting used to it."

Margot said, "Maybe I need to go back to school."

"In what?" I asked.

"In whatever gets a person a job. And wherever they give scholarships."

Anthony said, "Maybe you could work the Ponzi angle into your financial aid applications."

Margot said, "I'm taking a look at my divorce settlement. I think there's something in there about Charles paying for graduate school."

Anthony asked me, "You used to do — what was it? — advertising copy?"

"Freelance writer. Usually for utility companies."

Margot and he exchanged looks.

182

I said, "I know it sounds dull, but sometimes I got to write about employee heroics."

"Such as?"

"Such as the engineer who pulled a customer out of a swimming pool and gave her CPR when for all intents and purposes she had drowned! And another about an employee in a call center who talked a customer through childbirth."

"Do you have clips?" Anthony asked. "A portfolio?"

I said that my reporting didn't make for much of a portfolio since it appeared on bill inserts and in-house newsletters.

"I don't want you at the computer all day," said Margot. "We've had enough of the stationary life. I'd like to see you out in the world, in an office, in a skyscraper along with thousands of people, making friends in the cafeteria — that very thing you said you were ready for."

"I wouldn't mind that, either," said Anthony. "Out in the world again, which is another reason why personal assistant is a nonstarter, unless you're a twenty-two-year-old girl."

"Not so fast," said Margot. "You could design a job yourself, some kind of hybrid. Does Craigslist have position-wanted ads? Because Gwen and I could write it for you." She drummed her fingers on the kitchen island and stared out over his shoulder. "Okay. Like this: 'Do you need someone fabulous to run your life? We have the ideal candidate — smart and talented, energetic and personable . . .' You'd write it, of course. But it would be in the third person, from our point of view, so we can rave."

"Maybe," said Anthony, clearly meaning *No way*. "But what about Miss Margot? Remind me what you did in your working life."

This was more than a sore subject. "What did I *do?*" she asked. "You know the answer. I was a deaf and blind part-time receptionist, filling in for my husband's office staff on their sick days. So what should my résumé say? 'Hostess? Homemaker? Clueless Frau Doktor'?"

I winced. Anthony, however, said, "Okay. I get it. But isn't there something to mine there? Office skills? You probably had to deal with Medicare and insurance and all that, right? And answer the phones and — what else? — call people to remind them they had upcoming appointments."

"So?"

"I'm saying this: I think you'd be a dynamite receptionist in the right kind of office."

"And for sure Charles would give you a glowing reference," I said.

Anthony said, "I'm getting my laptop. Don't go away."

For the ninety seconds Anthony was out of the room, Margot tossed questions at me, all in the same vein. *How many receptionists have a degree in art history? How many are my age and haven't held a full-time job since* The Mitch and Mike Show?

Anthony was back with his laptop, already open and almost humming. "Okay! I'm on Craigslist and I'm clicking on, here we go — admin slash office jobs." He slid onto the empty stool, skimming, evaluating, mumbling. "Nope, nope, nope, lame, intern, intern, audition — ha, good luck with that . . . Here's one."

"For whom?" Margot asked.

"*You* tell *me*. The headline says PLASTIC SURGERY RECEPTIONIST, MIDTOWN EAST. And the description reads 'A prominent plastic surgeon has an opening for a well-spoken and poised front-office person. This is a high-profile position. The successful candidate should be well-presented with good phone skills and excellent interpersonal skills.'"

"Not interested," Margot said.

"Why?" I asked.

"The patients."

"Because they'd all be women?" I asked.

"Vain women! They'll be impossible — matrons wanting their faces peeled and their wrinkles Botoxed. Women with enough money to have their breasts enlarged and their belly fat sucked out. You think they're going to be nice to the woman answering the phone? And what kind of horse's ass calls himself a prominent plastic surgeon?"

I said some of those procedures were done in a dermatologist's office, and besides, didn't she care about her appearance? Didn't she give herself facials — ?

"With tomatoes! And rotten papayas! That's hardly the same thing. If it sounds so great, you go work there."

Anthony said, "Ladies, please. I once got very good advice from my dad, which was 'Never turn down a job before you've been offered it.'"

I said, "And how do you know this isn't a practice where the partners are reconstructing faces of disfigured children in Africa and Latin America?"

"East Side of New York," she said. "That's how."

Anthony said, "We are sending them a CV and an unbelievably convincing if not charming cover letter, are we not?"

"Gotta start somewhere," I said.

Margot poured the rest of the inferior wine into her glass, along with a crumb of cork she didn't seem to notice. And then, quietly from behind her glass: "Besides, things are happening. Charles can practice again in three months."

"Practice *medicine?*" I asked. "I thought they took his license away."

"It was only a suspension. And he can't do infertility work, or *fertility*, as the case may be. He'll find a clinic. Or set one up. Only for OB and gynecology. If a patient can't get pregnant, she'll get sent to another doctor."

"Wow," said Anthony. "I had no idea."

I said, "I'm surprised they're letting him practice down there at all —"

"And by 'down there' she doesn't mean Tribeca," said Anthony.

"Of course, there's a ton of work to do — office space, furnishing, staffing, permits. It could be months before he hangs out the proverbial shingle."

I could tell that there was another layer of news, another admission we hadn't dislodged. "Has Charles asked you to help him in some way? Has he promised you a job?" I asked.

"In a manner of speaking. But I've turned him down."

185

The oven timer buzzed. Anthony, as usual, didn't have to test for doneness, but brought forth two dozen beautiful red cupcakes, distracting Margot but not me. "He better not think you're going to be his receptionist! That'll be the day. Imagine having to tell Betsy that you were going to help Charles in his new office, filling in for his 'girl' on her sick days and vacations . . ."

Anthony said, "I bet that's not the position he's offering. I'd put money on it."

Margot said, "I haven't accepted. And I probably never will."

"Should I leave a few unfrosted?" he asked.

"No," said Margot.

"What position did he offer?" I asked.

"I think we can both guess," said Anthony.

Was I deaf or blind or addle-brained or all three? "I don't care what he's offering," I railed. "I don't care about salary or benefits or hours —"

Anthony was opening a new package of cream cheese as he informed me that I was on the wrong track. "Think romantic, not professional. Take a stab at it. What would be the offer on the table?"

Was I in denial? Was the idea of romantic forward motion for my partner in singlehood so alien that I couldn't summon the obvious?

Margot said, "You know he never wanted the divorce. Is it so unthinkable that Charles would propose?"

I tried to look as if such a thing were extremely thinkable and on the tip of my tongue.

"You don't have to look so glum. I turned him down. I mean, why would I say yes?"

Anthony said, "Not so fast. Frau Doktors can have very nice lifestyles. And it could trickle down. We could afford protein at every meal. We might even get rib eye and sushi-grade tuna on occasion."

"No, we wouldn't!" I cried. "If she married him, he'd move in and we'd have to move out."

There. I'd said it. Margot was protesting that she'd never be happy without her posse, but I couldn't hear a word. It wasn't Charles per se. It was our nuclear family. It was Margot and Anthony and I in penthouse B, with Olivia occasionally on the couch. As of that day, it was the only portrait I could paint of the widow Gwen-Laura Schmidt where she was neither lonely nor alone.

From StanByMe to MiddleSister: I'm a high educated. My friends say Im sincere, cheerful with good sense of humor & friendly. Women consider myself handsome. I like to do things such as sport, specially swim, listen good music, give & get affection, eat out, read tech journals. I look younger then u think.

30

SWWF Seeking No One

REUPPED WITH MATCH.COM by accident, an automatic renewal I forgot to nip in the bud. When invited out, I tended to accept. Thus there was the date with the man who said he was a cultural anthropologist, but whose actual job was driving a double-decker sightseeing bus. There was the ex-academic who, after being denied tenure, spent his days pounding out op-ed rants, unpublished, on a manual typewriter. Civilization, he advised me, was going to end sooner than I realized.

There was the date who proudly counted Weight Watchers points —not just on his plate but on mine. There was one who said he didn't eat salad because it gave him gas. There was the first and last date with the handsome ex–baseball player who stuck his Nicorette gum under his chair when the appetizers arrived. There was the dentist who excused himself after pecan-toffee pie to floss in the men's room.

And finally, a fix-up arranged by Olivia's boss. He was her next-door neighbor, and his name was Geoffrey, the spelling of which suggested good breeding and a whiff of the British Isles. The scouting report by Olivia: *I've seen him in the elevator. We've never talked. I think the baby makes him nervous. Nice-enough looking. I can't tell his age. I'm not good at that. Fifty? Midfifties? No bums live in this building, that's for sure. What have you got to lose?*

His overture came in the form of a voice-mail message. He'd chosen the restaurant, one of his favorites. Seven-thirty on Monday. He'd swing by and get me at seven-fifteen.

"No 'Looking forward to meeting you,'" I noted to Margot.

"He's a guy, probably a businessman. They're all like that. He's making an appointment."

When I expressed something less than optimism, Margot said what she always said. "But this could be the one. Call him back and accept. Sound enthusiastic. He may not be your cup of tea, but maybe he has friends."

Monday was six days away. And I confess that by the time that evening arrived, Olivia's bland description of the stranger/neighbor had upgraded itself to "attractive, child-friendly, and kind." Margot agreed on my wardrobe choice: the cute black cocktail dress I chose for those occasions I faced without foreboding or a sinking heart.

As ever, I timed my ablutions so I'd be at my freshest and best arranged, made up and blown dry very close to the departure time. So when the phone rang at approximately six p.m., I had just stepped out of the shower. It was Geoffrey, and he was neither confirming nor canceling. He was waiting downstairs.

I stammered something close to an apology. Had I misunderstood that our reservation was at seven-thirty and that he'd be picking me up at seven-fifteen?

No, I had not misunderstood. But he'd called to change the time and unfortunately I hadn't picked up.

"When?"

"I don't know! Fifteen minutes ago? Ten? I left a message. I have a car and a driver. My daughter wants it later. I had to move us up."

Did I say "Too fucking bad?" I should have. I should have barked back "Does no one in your family take taxis? Or "What are you? A man or a mouse?"

But it was I who was mouselike. I said, "I'll be down as soon as I can."

"It's a black Town Car with Jersey plates, double-parked. We might have to circle the block."

I rushed in a way I would later chastise myself for. I zipped myself into my dress, wobbled into my heels, cut minutes off the time I would have spent with hair dryer, blusher, and mascara, and grabbed my everyday pocketbook instead of transferring the essentials to a chic little evening purse I'd found on eBay. I even thought about running down eleven flights of stairs when the elevator dawdled.

The black Town Car was double-parked and my date was sitting in the back seat, frowning into his phone. What might have been dark good looks in another situation was, behind tinted glass, now suggesting villainy. I rapped on the window, waved a pathetic little wiggle of five fingers; smiled. Did he open the door? No. He said something to the driver, who scurried out of the front seat to open the very door that was at my date's elbow. I said, before stepping in, "Hi, I'm Gwen. Stephanie's friend."

How would a blind date answer in such a situation if this were, let's say, a romantic comedy and not a nightmare? "Nice to meet you"? "Sorry for the confusion"? Or "That was quick, I appreciate it"?

What he said was "Get in."

I hesitated. Did "Get in" sound gruff no matter the context or the tone? "Okay," I said. "But move over."

His next words were not to me but to the driver. "Twenty-first between Lex and Third." And then to me: "Another two minutes and I wouldn't have been here."

Did I see a little twitch from the front seat, a concerned, backward half glance as if the driver were sharing my shock?

I managed an offended "Excuse me?"

"I was here at six! It's twenty past! It's gonna take half an hour to get there in this traffic."

I said, "Our date was for seven-fifteen! You came more than an hour early."

"I called! You didn't answer."

190

"I was in the shower —"

"I left a message!"

I didn't reply. And it was a silence best described as incredulity mixed with white-hot anger of a sort I hardly recognized. We were only two or three blocks from the Batavia, inching east in traffic. The traffic light ahead obligingly turned yellow.

When we came to a full stop, I opened my door, jumped out, and slammed it behind me, but not before I heard "What the fuck?"

I had expected no pursuit, but Geoffrey was beside me, a hand on my arm. I said, loud enough for passersby to hear, "Let go or I'll scream."

"Are you okay?" a tattooed woman with a half-shaved head asked me. "Do you need help?"

"He's a blind date. The worst! Would you believe he came an hour early and it's my fault! But thank you, I live right up the street."

"If I upset you —" Geoffrey began.

"Scram," my new friend growled. "I have mace and don't think I won't use it."

The phone was ringing when I got back to the apartment. It was Geoffrey, sweet-talking my answering machine. "C'mon. Let's get a bite. I was agitated because my daughter needs the car. She and her friends are seeing —"

Anthony picked up, midsentence. "Don't call here again," he said. "And by the way, you're an asshole, and your daughter's a spoiled brat."

"You need anger management!" I yelled.

Even though Anthony was going out, he boiled some pasta for me, poured us glasses of wine, and kept me company while I ate.

That was the night I took stock of my life and recognized that it was very full. Or full enough. I had companions and champions. I had memories, a roof over my head, and a journal that was getting daily devotions in a dear-diary kind of way.

Who needs complications in an otherwise simple, happy life? Not me. Clearly, my white-hot anger had forged an ironclad new rule: no more looking and no more disappointments. Farewell, rude men, blind dates, and Match.com!

What a smart decision — and what a relief.

I avoided my e-mail, quite sure that Geoffrey would send a message of some sort, either an apology, a critique, or another overture. As I ran a bath, I did glance at my in-box. Something caught my eye, the subject line "RE: your ad," forwarded by the *New York Review of Books.* It read:

> Dear "Nervous":
>
> Hello! I am writing on behalf of my son, a single man of fifty-plus, who is also nervous about dating. He shouldn't be! He is smart and nice looking and very kind. His wife died approximately 2 yrs and 5 months ago from a quick kind of cancer, so it's time.
>
> He is an engineer who works for a good company. His two daughters are grown and not underfoot, 21 and 24 years of age, and they know I'm doing this. What else should I tell you? He is tall, with a master's degree, and owns his own apartment on the Upper East Side of Manhattan. Your ad appealed to me. I have a picture of him but don't know how to send it. Are you still available, and are you by any chance of the Jewish faith? He doesn't care.
>
> Sincerely,
> Myra Offenberg
> Queens, New York

After a five-minute meditation on how soon to answer, I pressed REPLY and wrote:

> Dear Mrs. Offenberg:
> Thank you for your inquiry. My main concern is that your son might not be okay with your playing matchmaker. Does he know and does he approve? I'm sure your granddaughters could help you upload a photo of their father. I am also widowed, a college gradu-

ate, and live in Manhattan. Not of the Jewish faith or much of any other kind.

Sincerely,

Gwen-Laura Schmidt

I sent it. I wasn't reneging on my decision to forsake men and dating. I was being polite. I'd placed an ad, and an elderly mother had answered it with hope in her heart. Good manners dictated that I acknowledge receipt of her inquiry. I wouldn't tell Anthony or Margot that my personal ad had found a reader because they would get their hopes up and misinterpret the fact that I wrote back. They'd hover around my laptop, waiting for a reply, all the while discussing my hair, its roots, and the most efficacious first-date attire. Days would go by. And in a week, when Mrs. Offenberg's nice-looking widowed engineer son failed to materialize, I'd have to push back against their pity.

31

Benefit of the Doubt

THOUGH I WAS no longer looking for a beau, the amateur sociologist in me noticed that four days had passed without a reply from Mrs. Offenberg's son. I conducted what I hoped was a casual poll at a sisters-plus-Anthony dinner on a warm April day that took us up to the roof terrace. Betsy had treated us to a smorgasbord of Chinese food and was sticking serving forks and spoons into the generous array of take-out containers.

"Suppose," I began, when we were finally seated and wine had been poured, "someone sees your ad and writes to you . . ."

"Your specific ad?" Betsy asked. "Or are we talking hypotheticals?"

"My ad. Someone answered —"

This aroused a chorus of whos and whens and a clamor for details.

I waited. I skewered a dumpling with my fork and sampled it, lollypop-style. "It was a reply, once removed," I hinted between bites.

"Meaning?" asked Anthony.

"It was a mother writing on behalf of a son."

Immediately, sides were taken. Betsy and Anthony were on the No team — forget it; what kind of wimp lets his mother ask someone out on a date?

Margot was on the Extenuating Circumstances team — perhaps . . . benefit of the doubt . . . it's very likely that he is too modest to sing his own praises in the way needed to catch someone's attention.

"Tell us what she said," Betsy ordered. "And I don't want the abridged version."

I said I could give them the gist. The engineer son was also widowed; had two more-or-less grown daughters; was fifty-plus, smart, tall, and a resident of Manhattan.

"Photo?" asked Anthony.

"No, but she said he was good-looking."

Margot coughed out a laugh.

I found myself on the cusp of being insulted. Did I not have sound judgment and good instincts? Was I not capable of reading between the lines to distinguish a decent prospect from a dreadful one?

Betsy asked, "Did you green-light it?"

"If you mean did I answer, I did. I wrote back and asked the obvious: Did she have her son's approval to speak on his behalf?" I reminded them, "I'm out of this business. I don't even *want* to meet him. I quit Match before my subscription ran out."

"So you're just making conversation?" asked Margot.

"There's nothing more to tell. I never heard back."

"Time frame?" asked Betsy.

"Four days ago."

I saw a droop of acute disappointment on Margot's face. "I don't love that," she said.

My MBA sister said, "So Gwen will write him."

"Absolutely not," I said.

"Hold on," Betsy said. "You're saying no because you're thinking in terms of your pride. But why should you care? He doesn't know you. It's not like high school where you'd have to see him in homeroom and he'd tell his friends and they'd snicker when you walked by."

Anthony liberated his legs from between table and bench, and said he was going back for sesame oil. "Don't make any decisions without me," he called from the rooftop door.

We obeyed, turning the conversation temporarily to our nephews' summer camp destinations (overnight in Vermont, day camp in New Jersey). Anthony returned quickly with the sesame oil, two bottles of beer, and my laptop.

"Good," said Betsy. "Now she can read us the original e-mail."

"Not till she eats. Everything's getting cold up here," said Margot.

Anthony said, "I'm still working on 'What does Gwen have to lose?' And I'm getting close to 'Why let this candidate drop off the face of the earth because his mother only checks her e-mail once a week?'"

"And if she doesn't answer this time," said Margot, "if she doesn't have the common decency to say, 'My son, as it turns out, is not open to my matchmaking. So sorry to have gotten your hopes up — '"

I said, fibbing, "She didn't get my hopes up. I have zero expectations."

Anthony asked us to pass the rice — the white, not the brown — and also the chicken, the tofu, and the noodles. He asked if we were planning on leftovers and if Betsy had even expected that he'd be joining us. Kudos on the selection of dishes, by the way. Especially the pork with Szechuan pickles.

"Eat up," Betsy said.

I meant to introduce other topics. I was interested in their social and work lives, yet I couldn't help returning in the next conversational break to "So? Is everyone agreeing with Betsy?"

"Everything's delicious," said Margot. "I hope the delivery guy left us a take-out menu."

"Not that," I said. "I meant — to follow up or not?"

Anthony pointed with his chopsticks toward my laptop.

"Now?" I said.

"You get Wi-Fi up here?" asked Betsy.

"Let's take a stab at it," said Anthony. "A rough draft."

Not one of them trusted my instincts or actions. I'd married late. Malformations of my husband's heart had gone undetected, and I'd slept through his death. My abstemious escort service — a terrible idea to begin with — was DOA. My personal ad had drawn only one response, and it was from an unauthorized proxy. I said, "No, thank you. I'll do it later."

"But write before the mother's bedtime," said Margot.

"BCC us?" asked Betsy.

At eight-forty-five p.m. I sent the following to Myra Offenberg: *As a conscientious correspondent, I wanted to be sure that my reply of Monday night reached you.* And hating myself even as it was uploading, I attached my best photo. I didn't include my telephone number, fearing she might befriend me on her own, and soon I'd be accepting an invitation to a matinee or a seder. Confident for a few seconds, I pressed SEND. But then the second-guessing crept in. Had I done the right thing? Was I appearing needy and undesirable? And what about the no-date, no-beau vow I'd made to myself?

There was a message waiting from Myra when I woke up, bearing the exclamation points of a high-priority dispatch. Could I call Eli myself due to his being on the shy side? Four telephone numbers including his fax line were supplied.

I wrote back. *Does he even know of my existence?*

Yes came her answer. *Do you enjoy the movies?*

Within seconds, another e-mail arrived, its subject line was "p.s.": *Forgot to mention that he likes your looks.*

Who isn't emboldened by flattery? I wrote back. *Even the shyest person can compose an e-mail.*

Again, no answer for an eternity. After thirty-six hours, I found a new sender in my in-box, an eoffenb.

Dear Ms. Schmidt,

I'm on a campaign to end maternal harassment. Would you care to meet for coffee or a drink some time?

Cordially,

Eli Offenberg

I neither forwarded it nor asked my team about strategy. Should I or shouldn't I? Would I be inviting another disappointment? Even though I didn't approve of my own actions, I pressed REPLY and surprised myself with a *Yes* and an exclamation point.

From Statenilend to MiddleSister: looking for wife ,,,I am Russian man ,,living in USA ,,NEW YORK ,, my age 66yrs ,, divorced ,looking for decent wife ,, she is beautiful with nice lips,, romance ,,serious not like play games ,,ty , . . .

32

Seriously?

T WAS A DREAM, AND from what I understand, a common one: I was on a couch I didn't recognize having energetic sex with a man I didn't know.

How eerie then to find upon waking a return e-mail from Eli Offenberg. It said, *Shall we meet for a drink or should we plunge right into dinner? The following dates are good for me* — and here was the endearing part: He reeled off an entire week of nights, all in a row, which to some people might be emblematic of unpopularity, but to me showed honesty and moxie.

I wrote back, trying to be a little wry myself. *Is a Saturday night too fraught for a first meeting? Second choice, Friday.*

His answer came instantaneously. *I can live with "fraught." What kind of food do you like?*

Did women still play hard to get? To avoid the impression that I was instant-messaging him, I left my room, made a pot of coffee, and brought my Syracuse good-luck mug back to my computer. I typed *I eat everything*, but then deleted those words in case they carried a sexual message. I next tried *I'm an omnivore*, but erased that description, too, with its connotation of huge and prehistoric. Finally, just the truth. *I like everything, especially Italian. Do you have a favorite place? I live in the Village.*

No answer immediately, but I attributed that to the hour, a few minutes after eight a.m., when an employed person would be on his way to work. To short-circuit my constant e-mail surveillance, reminiscent of my teenage vigils by the phone, I volunteered to buy stamps and return our library books.

Margot said, "No, do something more interesting than that."

Thus, for the first time, I accepted Anthony's invitation to accompany him to the gym, using the guest pass he'd been hawking since he'd moved in. He warned me that I shouldn't expect to meet anyone midmorning except retirees and young moms. The employed, the driven, and the mostly heterosexual came for their workouts between five and six a.m. or after work. I told him I didn't care. And had I mentioned that I had a date on Saturday night?

Side by side on treadmills, his moving at twice the speed of mine, he asked, "Details?"

"All I know is we're having dinner."

"Not at his place," said Anthony. "You don't go to a strange man's house on a first date."

"Not to worry. He's picking a restaurant. He asked for my preferences and I said Italian."

"Love that," said Anthony. "Italian has a high romance potential. Very *Lady and the Tramp*."

Did I feel a little proud? Was I wondering if anyone on the neighboring treadmills was listening and deeming me socially active?

Here came my answer: A young woman, running hard on my right, her big diamond engagement ring and platinum wedding band holding sway over her left hand, asked, "Did I hear that you're single?"

I said, "I'm widowed."

She didn't spend any time on that bit of biography or on condolences. She went right to "My father-in-law is single. Do you want to come to his birthday party on the fourteenth? We're trying to get him socialized."

I said, "He's not socialized?"

"I meant get him out. Dating. He's trying to get over a bad divorce."

How odd. How out of left field. The word "boundaries" came to mind. But isn't there inside every single woman's cortex the video flashing forward to her met-cute story retold as a wedding toast?

I asked where he lived and the young woman said, "Long Island."

I turned back to Anthony. "This nice woman" — I pointed and she waved — "has a divorced father-in-law and she's invited me to his birthday party."

"Which birthday?" he asked.

"Fifty-something," the woman volunteered. "I can call my husband and get his exact age."

And what was she doing now but snapping a picture of me, sweaty and perplexed — two quick flashes with her phone before I ducked.

Anthony yelled, "Seriously?"

With her blond ponytail swinging in metronomic fashion, she didn't seem to realize that Anthony's question was a rebuke. She was now manipulating the phone in her right hand, apparently e-mailing me to someone.

"Blondie!" Anthony shouted. "Did you just take a picture of my friend and e-mail it without her permission?"

"Just to my husband," she said. "It's fine. This is what we do."

I slowed my treadmill down to barely moving so I could catch every word. Anthony slowed down, too, indicating *Action ahead.*

"It's not fine," he said. "Now call your husband, and I mean this minute, and put him on speaker so we know you're not faking it, and tell him to delete that e-mail."

She didn't actually pronounce the words "Make me," but she might as well have.

I asked her name.

"Belinda," she said.

I said, "Belinda, I'd appreciate it if you did what Anthony asked."

And how did she respond? With every dope's classic comeback in all such situations. "It's a free country."

Anthony asked me what she said, and when I repeated her line, he stopped his treadmill, jumped off, and strode to hers. "Your phone," he said, his hand open. "Don't make me wrestle you for it."

I won't repeat what she said verbatim, except to characterize it as a gay slur along the lines of her being unafraid to wrestle with someone of his sexual orientation.

Can you imagine? In a gym in the West Village of Manhattan, USA?

She increased her speed until she was galloping. The show-off.

Having been in no fights outside of those in my girlhood bedroom, and then with only sisters, I didn't know how one conducts a yelling match in public. Anthony did. He got back up on his now-stationary treadmill, facing his would-be audience, and asked for everyone's attention.

"This woman, right here, in — what would I call it? — lilac? Her name is Belinda. She just directed a gay slur at me. I don't have the authority to throw her out, but I'd like all people of good will to shun her from now on. Okay?"

With everyone's hands gripping equipment, there wasn't much applause, but there were some utterances of solidarity. Belinda pretended for another few tenths of a mile that she hadn't heard a word, then dismounted. Lucky for us, she left her pink-jacketed iPhone in the concavity meant for her water bottle. Anthony got to it first. With one quick slide to unlock and some expert taps, he located and deleted my photos before its owner snatched it back.

Somehow the whole thing enlivened me. I loved Anthony more at that moment than ever before. When the awful Belinda walked away with a very precise "Fuck. You," Anthony took an extravagant bow.

I yelled after her, "It's unbelievably rude to take someone's photo while she's exercising!"

A not-so-fit man pedaling at an unattractive, recumbent angle asked, "Isn't there a rule about that, anyway?"

Belinda must have tattled on her way to the lockers because a minute later a pierced and muscled man was walking toward us. "I'm surprised at you, Anthony," he was saying. "We can't have harassment here."

"That woman violated his civil rights," I said.

"In a way you would *not* have liked," Anthony told him. "In a way our brothers take great personal offense at."

The employee looked around the room. No one seemed to be listening. "Show's over, folks," he said anyway.

A confirmation came just after six p.m. that night, which displayed excellent taste and initiative. Eli had made a reservation at a well-regarded bistro on MacDougal, which was listed — Margot knew this — in the back of our *Zagat* under "Quiet Conversation." Everyone heartily approved and considered the choice a sign of good things to come.

"Don't get your hopes up," I warned. "Not only is it a blind date, but I haven't even seen a photo."

"How will you know it's him?" Margot asked.

"I won't. I'll just ask for the Offenberg table."

"No photo? Not a good sign," said Anthony.

"It's too late to ask for one. Plus, it'll seem as if I'm saying, 'I can't meet you unless you're good-looking.'"

When Anthony snickered, Margot translated. "That was a gay sound effect for 'What else counts?'"

"This is the guy whose mother set you up?" he asked.

"More or less."

"Not loving that part," he said.

Margot asked if I had an exit strategy.

"Meaning?"

"The excuse you'll have ready if he's awful and you want to leave."

"He won't be awful."

"Now who's getting her hopes up?" Anthony asked.

Stateniland to MiddleSister: Pretty lady I wrote You I think of u for decent wife but u didn't Anser!!! Not intersted? last try,,,,,good luck to you,,,,&& me!!,,,ty,,,,

33

Bella Notte

B OTH MARGOT AND ANTHONY insisted on a little black dress, as long as it wasn't the one I'd worn to Edwin's funeral. The unanimous first choice was a V-necked jersey sheath, overnighted from Betsy's closet with an accompanying note asking if I owned a push-up bra and please no wearing hose with sling-back shoes. Approved accessories: an heirloom locket I'd received for my high school graduation, a wide acrylic bangle in Granny Smith green, and no rings, which, they claimed, would make me look nostalgic and needy. Feet: black suede heels, peekaboo toes, nails painted maroon. Purse: a black snakeskin clutch of Margot's.

My roommates' send-off was too ceremonial — hugs, compliments, and a chorus of *West Side Story*'s "Tonight," which I suspected they had rehearsed. Like a dissatisfied maestro, I signaled *No, stop.* Surely bad luck, I told them. Surely a jinx.

The weather cooperated. It was a warm night requiring no umbrella or wrap. I walked slowly to MacDougal Street, hoping to be a few casual minutes late. Nonetheless, I arrived first. The restaurant had three slate gray walls, a fourth of whitewashed brick, and undulating wooden floors, an homage to its factory roots. People half my age were at the bar drinking colorful potions in asymmetric martini glasses. "Table or seat at the bar until your party is complete?" asked the tall, ravishing, surely Ethiopian-American hostess.

"Table, please."

Once seated, I accepted the handsome oblong linen-covered menus, then pondered whether it was better to check my lipstick and risk being caught preening, or just sit there idly.

What had I done, accepting an invitation so rashly? He could still be grief-stricken. He could be resentful of maternal matchmaking. He could be dull and humorless. He could be a drunk, an embezzler, a sex offender. Why hadn't we had a screening phone call? He could have a toupee, a ponytail, a little triangle of facial hair under his bottom lip. He could have tattoos, body piercings, body odor. He could forget to show up. Trying not to look anxious should he spot me before I spotted him, I initiated what I hoped was a nonchalant perusal of the menu. So little time had passed — I'd only gotten halfway through *insalate e minestre* — when I sensed the hostess approaching and telling someone casually over her shoulder, "Your wife's already here."

I strained to hear how he'd correct her, how flustered or annoyed she had made him. But his smile was unperturbed. "Actually, a friend," he said.

"Sorry about that! Enjoy!"

I believe what he answered, very quietly, was "Thank you. I intend to."

He shook my hand before pulling out the chair opposite me. "Eli" was all he said.

"Gwen," I answered.

Here is what he did not say or appear to be suppressing: *Let's get it over with. What choice did I have? I have to be somewhere else in one hour and you're not coming with me.*

What he actually said was "Hope you haven't been waiting long."

"One minute," I said. "I only live a few blocks away."

Handsome? Some, including me, would say yes. His once-brown hair was receding, and I liked that he wasn't trying to hide that with

205

tricks. His eyes were army-fatigue khaki green, matched by the floating leaves on his winsome tie. It was a nice face, a kind face. Was he slender? No. A few pounds in the direction of well fed, and he acknowledged the fact good-naturedly when he ordered the appetizer portion of spaghetti carbonara before his veal *pizzaiola*. He was not as tall as advertised. I'd pictured six feet, and now I knew him to be five-ten. ("Six feet Jewish" was his explanation of his mother's prideful estimate.)

He asked if we should get a bottle of wine, and I of the usual one glass said, "Sure."

"Red or white?"

"I might start with a glass of prosecco."

"Brilliant. I will, too."

Where did I venture conversationally? Did I ask about his marriage, his children, his job, his extracurricular activities, his passions, his last book read, and magazines subscribed to? No.

"How's your mother?" I asked.

"My mother," he said. "My mother is, no doubt, sitting by the telephone."

I laughed. I said I had a team at home who would be waiting up, too.

"Kids? Have I asked you that?"

I said no. I lived with my sister who was divorced, and we had another boarder, Anthony, who was divorced, too — long story — and at twenty-nine was something of an honorary baby brother to Margot and me.

Next I elaborated on the subject of Anthony's baking talents, his original cupcake recipes, and their clever nomenclature.

"Is he a professional?" Eli asked.

I said no, but he could be. Gingerbread chocolate chunk! Peanut butter banana-raisin! His Scarlett O'Haras!

"Let me guess. Red velvet?"

"Exactly. With pink cream-cheese frosting. We always say that if we weren't in a recession, he could open a boutique."

"Would Anthony, by any chance, have recently baked to celebrate the passage of the Marriage Equality Act?" he asked in the kindest, most genial manner.

I said yes. Anthony was gay and single. Margot was divorced, with an ex-husband who lived in our building.

"Interesting," he said. "Though probably awkward."

"It's getting more and more amiable," I said, ending that topic there since the cataloging of Charles's crimes and moral failings would have taken us into the realm of sex and insemination. Instead, I told him, due to its never-fail interest quotient, that my sister was able to buy the apartment with her divorce settlement, then lost every cent that was left over.

"Stock market?" he asked.

Just the question I was hoping to generate, never having met anyone who *wasn't* titillated by meeting a real-life Ponzi victim or her next of kin. I said, "Believe it or not, all her money was invested with Bernie Madoff."

Eli had been swirling spaghetti around his fork, which he now put down. "Ye gods. The sister you live with? Is she doing okay? I mean emotionally?"

I said, "She's pretty great. I mean, very resilient. More than I would have been. More than I *have* been."

"Your husband."

"And your wife."

"How long?"

"More than two years now."

"What was his name?"

"Edwin. And your wife's?"

"Joanne."

We both said how sorry we were. How difficult it had been, but here we were now at this lovely restaurant on a beautiful night. Then two sentences apiece about how we'd both come out on the other side to the relief of those who worried about us.

He asked what happened.

I explained, "It was unexpected, his heart. He was alive and, we thought, healthy. And then one horrible morning, he woke up dead."

I hadn't meant that, exactly. It was a summary Margot had coined — the cynical, perked-up version that I'd never before used. Quickly I said, "That was a poor choice of words. I meant to say 'He died in his sleep.'"

After what seemed to be a withdrawal devoted to private, dirgeful thoughts, he said, "I hope you won't be offended if I say he was lucky. Joanne suffered terribly and was never the same . . . an inoperable brain tumor."

I said, "How awful. And how could I be offended? It was extremely *un*lucky in every other way, but I like to think he didn't suffer."

It was here that most people asked me for Edwin's medical history, the implication being *No stress test? No pacemaker? No statins? No signs? No angioplasty? No insight?* Instead, Eli asked, "What did Edwin do?"

"He was a New York City public school music teacher and he coached the marching band."

"So, so admirable."

Now came the dreaded choking up by the widow, who needed to be more charming and date-ready than her red eyes indicated. He reached over and touched my hand briefly. Not a clasp, but an apology. I said, "I'm fine. I was told to avoid this sort of thing on a first date."

"Me, too," he said. He lifted his glass. "To them."

We clinked glasses. I asked what Joanne did.

"Raised the girls. Did a little acting, nothing big. A commercial now and then." After a pause, he said, "It wasn't perfect. But it worked. I think overall it was a good marriage. Two great kids."

"We didn't have children," I said. "I married on the late side. Now I think we could have tried harder, seen a specialist . . . adopted. But who knew I'd be alone this early?"

He then pantomimed something I didn't translate right away. It was *Pick up your salad plate because, instead of dwelling on death, I want you to taste my carbonara.*

I lifted my own plate and said, "Try a beet. And take some walnuts."

He did, chewing and nodding thoughtfully. "Do you know how long it's been since I've eaten a beet? I did it to impress you. No one wants to have dinner with a picky eater."

Before I could assure him that a dislike of beets didn't make one a picky eater — and besides, there are worse thing to be — his phone buzzed.

"So sorry. I meant to shut it off." He checked its screen. "My older daughter, the ringleader. A text."

"Everything okay?"

He smiled. "She has a question."

I waited.

He turned the phone so I could see the green dialogue bubble, *Hvg a gd time?* it asked. Smiling still, he said, "Nosy child," then, "Not literally a child. She's twenty-four. Would you mind . . . ? I'll be quick, one word."

I didn't watch, pretending that gold, orange, and magenta beets required my full attention.

"I hope I'm being accurate" I heard him say. Then, "Gwen?"

I looked up. The screen was illuminated and there was an answer below the green bubble. Under *Hvg a gd time?* Eli's succinct answer — for the record and to my shock — was *VERY.*

34

All Ears

NOT ONLY WERE Margot and Anthony both at home, but Charles was visiting, sitting hip to thigh with Margot on the couch, and all three were feigning looks of unsolicitude when I got back from my date. "It's Saturday night," I said to Anthony. "Why aren't you out?"

"It's barely ten o'clock," he said. "To some of us, the night's still young."

Charles said, "We're watching *Harry Potter and the Half-Blood Prince—*"

"*They* are," said Anthony, phone in hand, thumbs texting.

"I'm catching up on stuff that came out when I was away," said Charles. "I did read the books, though . . . multiple copies in the prison library. This is quite a good adaptation."

I said, hoping to sound blasé, "Well, you guys enjoy. I want to get out of Betsy's dress and into my lounging clothes." I hoped Margot would follow as I made my way down the hall, unclasping earrings, conscious of being a woman in a black dress, shoes in hand as if I'd danced too many tangos at the Copacabana.

I left my door ajar, and within seconds Margot was in the room.

Planting myself in front of her, I lifted my hair off my neck — body language for *Unzip me, please.*

"Tell me everything," she said, and shut the door behind us.

I slept well. It took me a few seconds upon waking to put a caption under the sensation that something positive had occurred the night before. Eli Offenberg's face floated into view, followed immediately by the worry that I'd done too much debriefing with Margot before bed-time. I shouldn't get her hopes up. Or mine. Besides, I hadn't thanked him. Perhaps there was an overnight e-mail?

Not exactly.

Dear Ms. Schmidt,
    Just in case my son doesn't write you on his own, I wanted to let you know that he not only enjoyed your company, but the food and the atmosphere as well.
    Yours truly,
    Myra (Offenberg)

I forwarded Mrs. O's communication to Margot and Anthony, then printed out a copy in case they wouldn't have checked their e-mail before breakfast. And I'm sure it would have been the morning's hot topic if it weren't for the fact that a barefoot Charles was in the kitchen in a short seersucker bathrobe, a half carton of jumbo eggs at the ready.

My options: Pretend this was business as usual, or ask why he was opening and closing our cupboards as if he owned the place. "Can I help you?" I asked.

Without interrupting his search, he said, "A *very* good morning, and a very good night, too. At least that's what Margot told me."

So smarmy, so horrible, so uncalled for . . . until I realized he was talking about *my* date and not his time spent disrobed in our apart-ment.

He tried again. "I understand you had a successful date last night."

This is what I heard in his voice: *You, Gwen-Laura Schmidt, whose bearing and affect do not suggest good times or successful dates, have accomplished exactly that.*

I said, "Would you like to rephrase that so it doesn't sound as if a miracle occurred?"

Now he was beating the eggs, showing off with the whisk and making a racket loud enough to wake up Anthony, one undersized room away.

"I only know what your confidante told me," he said. "You'll forgive me if I take her report down a notch because she can be overly excitable."

Those two words carried a double meaning when the speaker is in his bathrobe, chest hairs on display. I had no desire to confide in him. I didn't like his being here or his helping himself to our provisions. I asked, "Are you making enough for everyone? Because that's what we do around here: communal dining. All for one and one for all."

He looked at the half-empty egg carton and back at me, which is when Anthony's door opened. After a few quick chin-ups and a dismount, he asked, "To what do we owe this honor . . . ?"

Charles smiled — unctuously, I thought — causing Anthony to say, "On second thought, I'd rather not know."

Charles asked where we kept the sauté pans, "Preferably one that's eight or nine inches."

Now at the coffee machine, Anthony turned around so we could exchange looks. Clearly his asked, *Did he just get subliminal with those inches?*

"Bottom cupboard, next to the stove," I told Charles, averting my glance so I wouldn't have to witness his bending over.

With a "Shall you and I set the table?" Anthony and I left the kitchen for the dining room where we exchanged more shrugs and head tilts in the direction of our overnight guest. Finally locating a topic we could discuss aloud, Anthony said, "I heard through the grapevine that you liked your blind date."

I said that was true. I did like him. He was very nice —

"But?"

"No *but,*" I said.

The mention of Eli, not even by name, triggered something I wouldn't have expected in Anthony. He said, "I was going to ask what this guy looked like, but suddenly I remembered that I don't know what Edwin looked like! It suddenly seems so strange to me. I've never seen a photo of him. How is that possible?"

"You've never been in my *bedroom?*" — which, of course, was the exact moment Margot joined us, coiffed and dressed in capri pants and a crisp white shirt tied bolero-style.

"What am I walking in on?" she asked.

Anthony said, "Well, miss. Your sister and I could ask you the same thing."

Margot said, "Let me get some coffee. You guys all set?"

She was gone longer than it took someone to fill a mug and add her half-and-half. Nor was there conversation coming through the swinging door.

"They must be kissing," I said.

"He's in his bathrobe. Rather unencumbered is my guess."

We left it at that till Margot returned, wearing a little less lipstick. "Everyone having scrambles?" she asked.

We understood: Inquiries not welcome.

I said, "Scrambled is fine."

"*Moi aussi,*" said Anthony.

Returning to the previous non-Charles topic, I told Anthony I would show him the program from Edwin's funeral, which was the most recent photo of him.

"No, you won't," Margot said. "Show him your wedding portrait. He looks so happy. You both do."

"I'd like that," said Anthony.

"Edwin was perfectly pleasant-looking," Margot continued. "Not a movie star, but appealing in many ways. Besides, a person's looks can grow on you. I can give a first-person account of that phenomenon."

213

"You mean the good doctor?" Anthony said. "Do we have ourselves a reconciliation?"

Margot said, "Hardly."

"He seems to have slept over," I said.

Frowning and checking the kitchen door, Margot whispered, "Nothing more than — if you must put a name on it — both of us in the right mood."

"Completely understandable," said Anthony.

Instead of launching the topic that would begin with "But you hate him," I asked, "What's taking so long in there?"

"He's trying to stretch the eggs with onions and peppers. And he found some ham in the freezer. It's going to be a western scramble, so act excited when he serves it."

After a beat, Anthony said, "I'm noticing more affection than we're used to in your voice when talking about you-know-who."

"Just being a good hostess."

Anthony said, "Okay, I'll try to act excited when the western scramble appears." He turned to me and grinned. "In the meantime, I'm way behind on your date. Description, please!"

I said, "Very nice. Intelligent. Interesting. We talked about how our spouses died, but then we moved on. He was tallish. And balding, but had a nice-shaped head. I'm pretty sure his eyes were hazel, though the lighting wasn't great. Not skinny, but not paunchy, either."

"Wearing?" Margot asked.

"A suit and tie, which I thought was a really nice gesture."

From the kitchen: "Anyone besides me like their eggs wet?"

We all said, "No."

Unsolicited, Margot murmured, "I know you're thinking I've forgiven him, but I haven't."

Our answers, simultaneously, were my "Are you sure?" and Anthony's "Coulda fooled me."

Margot put an index finger to her lips, then switched to a smile as

214

Charles came through the swinging door, eggs on a platter and an abundant stack of toast on a plate.

"This is nice, isn't it?" Margot asked, as Charles hovered at her elbow, serving her with a professional scissors grip on two serving spoons. When he was seated and eating, he picked up the printout of my e-mail.

"Myra Offenberg?" he asked.

I said, "It's nothing. A little inside joke."

Obviously unimpressed, he put it down without comment.

"Lemme see," said Margot.

Instead of complying, Charles asked if the ham he found was the Smithfield he'd brought to our party some time back.

"If it was in the freezer, in little packets . . ." said Anthony.

"Definitely your ham, no question," said Margot.

Did I not have a right to their attention on such a day? True, I'd been aiming for serene and secretive last night, but now no one seemed interested enough to pursue the topic of Eli's mother's documentation of a successful date. I reached for the printout and said, "It was very sweet of her, don't you think?"

"If it was my mother, I'd kill her," said Anthony.

"How did it end?" asked Charles.

"It didn't end."

"No, I meant — how did you two leave it?"

"We made a date for Thursday."

"Well, well, well," said Charles.

"'Well, well, well' as in 'How amazing'?" I asked.

"Would that be so off the mark?"

Margot spoke before I could manage an answer. "I don't think Charles meant 'How amazing' in terms of a successful follow-up date. Am I right, Charles? Weren't you referring to the high odds against a blind date being decent?"

"Of course," he said. "What other possible connotation could there be?"

215

"Okay then," I said. "Let's start over. On Thursday I'm meeting Eli after work."

"For a walk on the High Line, weather permitting, and then dinner," Margot supplied. "At least that was the plan as of last night."

Charles said, "I'm happy to hear that. Long overdue, if you don't mind my saying so."

I *did* mind, but he wasn't finished.

"A widower is a hot commodity at our age. My God — the ratio! Is he dating online? These guys move on if there isn't instant chemistry. We feel like kids in a candy store."

"*We?* You're still doing that?" Margot asked.

"Of course I'm not! Why would I?"

And Anthony, in not the friendliest tone, said, "I would think these dating services do background checks before they let a person sign up."

Charles said, "I think the tone of this conversation has become less than cordial."

Margot said, "Not true. But let me point out that Gwen doesn't need you to rain on her parade after a lovely date and in advance of what I'm sure will be her *second* lovely date."

Anthony said, "Once again, I haven't gotten my details! I mean Armani, Zegna, Barneys, Sears? Lips? Teeth? Eyes? Eyeglass frames? Musculature?"

Margot asked me, "How much do we love Anthony's consistency?"

"Who paid?" Charles asked.

I said, "Eli did. I made an insincere gesture in the direction of the check, but he slipped it to his side of the table and said, 'No. I don't believe in that.'"

"I like that," said Margot. "Both the impulse and the answer."

"Did you feel any chemistry?" asked Charles.

"You and your chemistry," Margot said.

"It's important," he argued. "It's the number one question. It's the hundred-thousand-dollar question. Let me put it another way: Did you want to kiss him?"

"Kissing a near stranger?" asked Margot. "Gwen's not the dreamy kind who thinks in sexual terms on a first date. She's a little guarded about those things."

I said, "I think I could be the dreamy kind."

"It's actually not a bad question," said Anthony. "I once met some-one at a bar and we were having a nice conversation, not even flirta-tious, just friendly, when I asked, 'Anyone here you'd like to kiss?' and he said very sweetly, 'Only you.'"

Of course, that led us off track once again because Margot em-barked on a new line of questioning, namely: Who was that guy, and did that start something, and were he and Anthony still in touch?

I picked up my printed e-mail. "Since I only made one copy, I'll read it aloud." I did, causing Charles to revisit, "His mother's in-volved? *That* I don't like."

I said I was getting more coffee. Charles held up his empty cup, but I ignored it. In the kitchen, I considered leaving via the service exit, slipping back around to the front door and down the hall into my room. I patted my pockets. No front door key. So I refilled my cup and returned to the Council on Social Dissection. I sensed that there had been a whispered conference, led by Margot and setting a ground rule as Miss Housebound stood on the threshold of a possible attachment. *Let's back off, guys. She thinks she has an admirer. Could we all just play along?*

DancinMan to MiddleSister: COMMUNICATION and CARING are
the foundation for forever i want to hear of your day and CARE
and know you are of the same mindset. Am a romantic, i have
plenty for both of us!!!

35

Sister Night

NEXT STOP: DISARMING BETSY. We considered a family dinner in-house with newly integrated member Charles at his most
useful and hospitable, displayed when the main course required carving or deboning. Instead, we chose an upcoming Betsy-takes-her-less-
fortunate-sisters-to-dinner night.

We were back at Elephant & Castle, midway through our entrées,
when Margot gave me the brisk nod signaling *I'm going to tell her now.*

"Bets?" she began. "Gwen and I thought you should know something that's slowly crept from the back burner to the front. It's been
bubbling for a while and when I tell you what and whom it involves,
you'll understand why I waited this long to tell you."

"Charles, obviously," said Betsy.

"Wait. Not so fast." Margot paused to push a chunk of bread through
the gravy surrounding her meatloaf. "Don't say anything until I've finished, okay?"

I knew she had a speech prepared, and Betsy's bull's-eye guess was
undercutting points one through three. Margot started over with "If
anyone had told me three years ago what I'm about to confide, I'd say,
'Never! No way! Out of the question.'"

Betsy said again, "Charles, obviously."

"It could be about a lot of things. I could have eloped or come out of the closet or adopted a kid from a Romanian orphanage."

Betsy said, "Here's what I think happened. Charles became your downstairs neighbor and before too long—What? A couple of weeks?—he came upstairs with a bottle of wine and within days had ingratiated himself back into your little family. And God knows Gwen wasn't going to say boo."

"I resent that," I said. "I'm older than you are and I say boo all the time."

"And here we have a good example of how people change," Margot said. "Gwen isn't our most assertive sister, but she's coming way out of her shell. People change. Maybe even a person can go into prison and come out a different man."

There it was: the whole story, unembroidered. Margot hadn't needed to name names to evoke the look of revulsion on Betsy's face.

Margot said, "Couples break up. Marriages dissolve. Men and women both lie and cheat and get divorced. Then time goes by—"

"Not like this! What he did was a lot worse than your garden-variety adultery! He—you'll excuse me—*fucked* his patients! You think his character and ethics and morals and bad judgment got fixed in *prison?*"

Margot sat back in her chair, crossed her arms, and stared in a way I knew meant *Counterpoint ahead.* "Betsy? Do you think Andrew is perfect?"

She and I both knew Betsy did not think that. Our ambitious sister wished her teacher-husband was applying his math skills on Wall Street instead of in a public school classroom in Crown Heights.

"Oh, no, you don't," said Betsy. "That isn't fair. If I've groused to you about things I find annoying in Andrew—and who isn't annoying after eighteen years of marriage and two children and a PhD that's taking an eternity—every one of those things is minor! You can't even compare!"

Margot turned to me. "Gwen, tell Betsy why I brought this up tonight and what I've learned in the last three years. I think she knows you'll be objective."

I motioned to the waiter, *Yes, I will have that second glass of wine after all*, then plunged ahead. "For the sake of argument," I began, "let's say that a person didn't change all that much. But can't the bad stuff be water under the bridge? If a divorced woman wanted to spend time with her ex, would he necessarily have to be a model citizen? It's not like he's dangerous. He's not a violent criminal. Couldn't it be about a warm, hard body that happens to be an elevator ride away?"

I looked to Margot. All she said was "Don't let your food get cold."

I ate a French fry and picked up my turkey burger. Margot said, "I didn't mean you shouldn't continue."

So I did. "As I was saying, the ex-husband becomes a neighbor. A friendly one. He brings her and her roommates things he can't use due to having no stove to speak of—"

"A huge tom turkey, a name-brand ham, and what was that fish?" Margot asked me. "The one I put into a bouillabaisse? Red snapper?"

"Flounder," I said. "Also expensive wines left and right."

"So he brings you things?" Betsy asked. "That's supposed to impress me—that he's good at bribery?"

Margot said, "Gwen? Tell your sister what else Charles and I have been exploring."

I asked for a hint, and Margot whispered, "Therapy."

"Right. They've been seeing a therapist, and I think what they discovered is . . . good stuff." All I knew of their therapy was Margot's initial reluctance to participate, then her liking the megaphone it gave her, and especially the discovery that Chaz's mother was newly engaged to an old high school prom date.

Betsy asked, "Where would a couples therapist even begin? I mean, who would even want to take on a husband who did what he did to his wife? Screwing around with patients! Breaking her heart and calling it artificial insemination! You two might consider that water under the bridge, but I don't! Then, hello—his arrest, the headlines, the

220

grand jury, the trial. Was this therapist amazed that you agreed to be in the same room with him?"

Margot said, "You don't think a couples therapist has clients who beat each other up and need restraining orders? He's seen it all! We're a piece of cake compared to most people. That's what he said. Piece. Of. Cake. He also said that all of that stuff, the trauma, the arrest, put me into shock. In fact, he thinks I suffered from post-traumatic stress disorder!"

Because I'd pledged to help win Betsy over and to appear supportive without too much lying or fudging, I said, "It's very possible it was PTSD. Their marriage ended with a big bang after all. With anger! Fury! Headlines! Embarrassment! Humiliation! A marriage that was never on the rocks was suddenly in a thousand little pieces. Maybe all of us are suffering from PTSD."

Excellent, Margot mouthed.

"So?" asked Betsy.

"So . . . she may be coming out of it. And if she can move on, why should we keep reliving the battles and the combat and the . . . IEDs?"

I was making it all up for no other reason than it was fun to sound more like Margot than myself. I wasn't sold on Charles, not even Charles as one-night stand. After dispensing an approving pat to my hand, Margot took over the narrative. "See?" she said. "Gwen understands. It's all about you-know-what, isn't it?"

Not certain, and not wanting to guess wrong, I waited for amplification.

"Loneliness?" Betsy asked.

"Forgiveness!" Margot yelled, startling the couple at the next table.

Betsy took a small forkful of her Cornish game hen, chewed unhappily, put her cutlery down, and said, "So you're willing to forgive the lying, the cheating, the humiliation, the sick things he did in the name of science. I heard that! I'm the one who used vacation days to sit through the trial. Science? How do you forgive all of that? Is he the last man left on earth or something?"

Margot's glance in my direction felt like a favorite-sister conspiracy. *Maybe we won't tell Betsy quite yet about the overnights and the intercourse.*

I said, "He fainted at our apartment once, and Margot thought he'd dropped dead. That puts things in perspective."

"How so?"

"It was that night, after he didn't actually die, that we noticed a thawing."

Returning to her main theme, Margot asked, "Do you think people can change, Bets?"

"In Charles's case, I'd say no. You actually *think* that a guy, a doctor, who fucked his patients is going to come out of prison, after all that time consorting with criminals, a more ethical man? Puh-leeze!"

"It was minimum security," I pointed out.

Margot said very quietly into her wineglass, "He's sorry. As sorry as someone can be without slitting his wrists."

"Charles? Ha! Do sociopaths slit their wrists?"

Margot said to me, "She's impossible — worse than I thought she'd be."

I asked her if Betsy knew about Chaz.

"Chaz?" Betsy repeated.

"Well, now she does," said Margot.

"Chaz? Is that Charles's new nickname? His new identity? He's reinventing himself?"

I checked with Margot. "You might as well finish what you started," she said.

With what I thought was great dignity, I announced, "Chaz is Charles's bastard son."

"Gwen!" Margot said.

"What? I've heard Chaz describe himself that way." And to Betsy: "He's eighteen and goes to the Fashion Institute of Technology. And even though we were all suspicious of his motives at first, we've grown quite fond of him."

"Was he one of the ones the prosecution did a DNA test on?"

Margot said, "How the hell do I know?"

I said, "You *do* know. Anthony knew from the trial transcripts. Or maybe from Facebook. And the answer is yes. His mother testified."

Betsy said, "I knew this would happen!"

Margot and I waited.

"With Charles moving into the Batavia! He'd come around with a song and dance about being sorry, repentant, a changed man. Right? Because a guy who manages to seduce dozens of patients is not a guy without charm."

Margot said, "Not *dozens* of patients . . ."

"As if anyone knows what the exact number was! Sometimes I think he wanted to get caught so people would know what a big playboy he is. And I'm not the only one who thinks that."

"Who else?" Margot asked.

"Andrew, of course."

"Andrew, of course," Margot mimicked.

"Bets? Do you think Margot likes being reminded of her husband's infidelities? You've been doing that all night — pressing the black-and-blue spot."

"Well, I'm certainly not going to roll over like you two."

I said, "Why not? It's her life. What if Charles is making her happy? Or not even happy but less lonely?"

"With a houseful of people? How lonely can she be?"

"I live in that houseful of people, too. I think I can answer that question for both of us."

Margot said, "I'm sorry I told you. You'd think you'd give me more credit and him the benefit of the doubt. Or a fraction of a benefit. You haven't spent one minute with him —"

"I went to every minute of the trial! Even that was all ego. Why didn't he plead guilty instead of putting everyone through that and himself into the headlines?"

I said, "What if Margot didn't care about his character? What if she just needed a fuck buddy?"

Margot executed the bug-eyed, overblown double take I was hoping for.

"Who taught her 'fuck buddy'?" Betsy asked.

"I learned it out in the wide world," I said.

"MiddleSister hasn't been herself lately," said Margot.

"You're not going to marry him, are you?" Betsy asked Margot. "Because I wouldn't be able to stand up for you. Andrew and I couldn't even, in good conscience, bring the boys to the wedding."

Margot said, "Fine! You don't ever have to see Charles again. Or meet the adorable Chaz, who is already making a name for himself in the hat world. And you won't have to worry about standing up for me at our nonexistent wedding because I've said no very emphatically every time he's proposed."

"I'm speechless," said Betsy.

I said, "It's hard to keep up with your single sisters, isn't it? Maybe we should do this more often." I finished the last drop of wine and asked if anyone wanted to share a dessert.

"Maybe," said Margot.

"Depends," said Betsy, reaching for the menu.

"I met someone," I said.

36

By the Time We Got to Broadway

WE WENT TO A club in the East Village that had live jazz and a two-drink minimum. Anthony had coached me in advance, knowing I preferred music that had melodies and lyrics. Just listen and appreciate every note, he advised, and don't worry about where it's been or where it's going. Also, take your signals from the keenly interested ones around you and don't clap until they do.

I wore a gauzy skirt bought ($15) special for the occasion at a second-hand clothing store on Canal and a peasanty blouse that exposed my clavicle. Eli said he'd pick me up at the Batavia, a trek from East 75th, a gesture noted and lauded by my roommates. Nonetheless, I forbade Margot to come downstairs for a formal introduction or to skulk around the lobby at the appointed hour. Only four days had passed since our first date, too early for a second opinion from someone who never held back.

My team said, "Don't wait for him downstairs. Be cool. Let the doorman call you when he arrives."

"Do you think he'll kiss me hello in front of Rafael?"

"Did he kiss you good night on Saturday?" Margot asked.

I said no. And I had appreciated that.

"Interesting," Margot said to Anthony, with a smile.

"What is?"

"That you liked *no* kiss better than a kiss."

"I'd just met him. Who wants to kiss a stranger?"

"Don't look at me," said Anthony.

"Tell her," said Margot.

"Tell me what?"

Anthony said, "I went out with your friend William."

"He called? I can't believe you didn't tell me!"

"I know that look," said Margot. "It's the wounded, left-out look. Correct? You were already asleep when he left. You know these young people. What time was the date? Something ridiculous like midnight?"

"He's in a play," said Anthony. "It was either that or wait till Monday."

"And?" I asked.

"Liked him."

"Did you kiss him or do you also not go for that sort of thing till you're engaged?" Margot asked.

Anthony said, "Ask him when you see him."

"Meaning never?"

"No, next Monday night. For dinner. I'll cook."

Margot and I both emitted happy squeals of hostess anticipation. I said, "It must say something that you invited him over this fast."

"He sort of invited himself so he could see his new friend Gwen. You made an exceedingly good impression at that workshop."

"See?" Margot said. "I want you to keep that in mind."

"What, exactly?" I asked.

"How people see you! First impressions! You made a conquest without even trying."

"She's right," said Anthony.

Margot then reminded herself that this was Thursday. Charles was scheduled for dinner. We were getting to be the most social apartment in New York City, weren't we? What should she cook, and what did we have on hand?

"Go out," said Anthony. "Isn't that the deal? One out of two nights at a decent restaurant?"

Margot said, in an uncharacteristically few words, "I don't mind staying in."

I welcomed these distractions, grateful to be off the topic of my upcoming evening. One had to manage expectations. I knew from my premarital social life that a girl could romanticize the silences between the meetings after developing an unwarranted crush on the stranger across the table.

He was dressed more casually than he had been on the previous Saturday. No tie, but a white shirt, starched and impeccably pressed. It was another beautiful evening, warm and still light. He asked how I felt about a walk to the East Village . . . we could cab it if I minded. I said, "I think a walk would be wonderful."

He tucked my hand inside his elbow, and I let it sit there. We were a throwback, I realized, arms entwined. After only a block or two of our promenade, I noticed the occasional fellow pedestrian smiling in a rather un-Village-like manner as we passed.

I volunteered that it was especially nice to be out this night because my sister-roommate was entertaining her ex-husband.

"It must have been an amicable divorce," he noted.

"No! An atrocious divorce. But it's creeping toward . . . friendly."

"Do you know what made it atrocious?"

I liked his "Do you know?" as if marital troubles were subtle and hard to discern in what must be an exceedingly discreet family. I told him that the *official* grounds had been adultery . . .

"But?"

"I guess I didn't tell you before — that Charles was a doctor who'd acted inappropriately with his patients."

Eli didn't answer. I could tell that behind his silence was delicacy, as if any follow-up question would suggest prurient interest.

"It gets worse," I said. "His specialty was infertility. He did use a sperm bank, with contributions from the educated and the handsome. But guess what?"

After a long pause, Eli said, "I'll let you tell me."

I stopped. I probably wet my lips and cleared my throat. "With some of the patients . . . it was direct deposit. Insemination without the syringe."

Finally, he asked, "Are you saying he had sex with his patients?"

"Exactly."

"Good God . . . Wait! Did I read about this? Was there a trial?"

I said yes, two years ago. A very splashy one. Then prison.

"And this is the couple who's having dinner together tonight?"

I said, "He claims to be very sorry, and she seems to have forgiven him."

"What about you? Have you forgiven him?"

"Working on it."

We passed a café on the corner of Greenwich Avenue. It had a few tables outside and a big wood-burning oven inside. He stopped to read the posted menu, then asked if I'd tried it. I said, "We mostly cook at home because we're sort of a boarding house. Dinner is part of the package." Then bravely, "You'll join us some night."

"I'd love to," he said. "And will I get to meet the famous Anthony and the notorious ex-husband?"

"There could even be another interesting guest: his son."

"*Their* son? Your nephew?"

"No, just Charles's. As in when you inseminate your patients yourself, you sometimes get a baby."

He stopped midstride. "How old and how many?"

"Eighteen going on nineteen and so far just the one who went public . . . Lucky for Charles, not all the treatments took."

"Treatments," he repeated. And with the first smile the topic had evoked, "Is that what they're called?"

Who can say when formality tilts slightly in the opposite direction?

We were adults talking about very personal things. I do know this: By the time we got to Broadway, we were holding hands.

I was surprised that an engineer in a white button-down shirt would know hipster musicians at any club, let alone one in the East Village. It was a neighborhood I rarely visited since I didn't engage in what Anthony called "clubbing." Eli knew two couples at one table and a threesome across the room. The pianist was a fellow engineer, he explained.

The early set lasted less than an hour. One of the women said they were going out for dinner, probably just pizza, and would we like to join them. Without consulting me and without a glance at his watch, Eli said, "Thanks, but I have a table waiting back in the West Village. We'd better get going."

"You can call the restaurant and cancel," said another woman with huge gold hoop earrings that looked to be a strain on her lobes.

Eli smiled. "Well, I *would* if I wanted a quorum instead of having Gwen all to myself."

Was he flirting with me? Was I supposed to hear that? I'd ask my team when I got home.

It had to have been a townhouse once, or a speakeasy. We walked down a few steps to the restaurant's entrance, up a half landing to a bar, then up another flight to a dining room with bookshelves and draperies and antique maps on the walls. There were leather banquettes and white tablecloths. It was beautiful. It was where you'd bring someone for an anniversary or on a second date if the first had had romantic potential.

Even though I'd already had two mojitos at the club, I agreed to a glass of something bubbly. Clinking his glass, I said, "I'm having a really good time."

"Go on," he said. "I'm listening."

I meant to come up with something charming, but instead I heard myself asking what Betsy had worried about aloud. "Have you dated a lot of women since your wife died?"

Eli said, eyes now on the menu, "A lot? Enough."

I said, "I'm not even sure why I asked."

He said, "Might it have been because my mother took matters into her own hands, hinting that I needed her matchmaking services . . . ironically."

"Ironically?"

"Because if I *had* told her about my social life, she wouldn't have made it her business to find her poor widowed son a date." He looked up finally, and said most solemnly, "Then one night she sent me an e-mail about you. And your photo. I was surprised she even knew how to forward something."

I waited. Such solemnity could easily take a disappointing turn. "Yes?" I prompted.

He raised his glass. A toast? It did look a little meaningful.

The room was low-lit. Our table felt private enough, and I wasn't my usual sober self. Right then, I decided to kiss Eli Offenberg. I leaned forward, raising myself an inch or two off the bench. He grasped what was about to happen and met me halfway.

37

For Love and Country

DESPITE ALL OUR efforts to forgive and forget, Betsy and I remained wary of Charles's character and intentions. An intelligent man, in therapy, occasionally self-aware and benefiting from pillow talk with our eldest sister, he knew exactly where Margot's sisters stood. Could that have contributed to the very un-Charles-like, altruistic thing he did upon the restoration of his medical license? With hair cut short, and letters of reference in hand, he went to the army recruitment office in Times Square and took the first steps toward signing up.

Weeks passed between his first visit and the army's decision, during which he jogged daily along the Hudson and rewrote his will. Often he raised the topic of how relatively safe an army doctor would be, in case we'd stopped thinking about inherent dangers. You modern ladies, he reminded us, know that there are thousands of female troops, maybe hundreds of thousands, so his specialty was essential in a way it hadn't previously been. Not that his duties would be mere pelvic exams, Pap smears, and birth-control prescriptions! Hadn't we all read about pregnant women in backward nations, with careless husbands and brutal neighbors, who'd had no prenatal care and less-than-sanitary midwives, who needed to be airlifted to clean American hospitals for emergency C-sections? Dr. Charles Pierrepont would once again be saving lives and serving his country, albeit in gynecological and obstetrical fashion.

Schooled on TV coverage of soldiers' sad departures and ecstatic homecomings, I asked Margot if she'd be one of those women waiting back home, who e-mails and Skypes and bakes, along the lines of every straight soldier's fondest wish. His personal goal, she confided, was this simple, this pragmatic: Should the unthinkable happen, he wanted Margot to be his lawfully wedded beneficiary.

She resisted at first. Many mornings at breakfast Anthony and I heard about Charles's latest effort to stage a romantic proposal — each setting and prop a little showier than the last. When a bouquet of long-stemmed yellow roses didn't do the trick, his next inducement was a path of rose petals leading up to the terrace where he was waiting, flanked by votive candles, a little velvet box in hand. Margot finally said, somewhat off the emotional mark, "Okay. I'll wear it."

The wedding would have to be soon, before the alleged deployment. There was a brief discussion about holding a ceremony in penthouse B, on the terrace, weather permitting. Strenuously objecting, Anthony cried, "Christ almighty! You never leave this place! Could we please have a wedding off-site? I'll find it. I'll plan it. There are event venues. There are churches. You're what? Protestants, Catholics, Jews? Just tell me how many guests. And where was your first one? Would you go back there?"

No, she would *not*. Margot said she had enough ambivalence about their doing this a second time and didn't want any déjà vu to spook her. Or, just as bad, the inevitable pangs caused by the missing faces of her parents and grandparents, and the memory of the unfortunate dresses we bridesmaids had been cajoled into wearing twenty-six years before. As for her own dress, she threatened to wear black or red or deepest purple, signaling nonconformity or simply because a Fashion Institute undergrad was acting as her personal shopper.

However, as soon as the unflawed, emerald-cut diamond, a bigger version of the original one, was on her finger, Margot decided to go all

232

the way. And Betsy, who'd once said she could not attend or stand up for such nuptials, nor bring her children, insisted that a new wedding dress, a symbol of a fresh start, would be her contribution and gift. I knew it was something close to patriotism that had won her over, and a grudging respect for Charles's unexpected, upcoming bravery. She and I, along with Chaz, spent three consecutive Saturdays watching Margot try on wedding dresses, which all evoked unanimous thumbs-down. At every store the salespeople asked what was so unflattering and what was it that her bridal party found so funny.

Margot said, "They can't believe I'm getting married."

"To her ex," I added.

"Don't get me started," said Betsy.

"He's joining the army," I inevitably told every consultant.

"A military wedding!" the women always repeated, revived, as if this new intelligence called for a reimagining of the day, the setting, the groom, the dress.

"This one is awful," said Betsy, now on her feet, poking her finger into the too-ample cleavage produced by the current mummy-inspired gown.

"Can you honestly say you like this one?" Margot asked the saleswoman. "You think this is *me?*"

At the last shop, the woman hurried to an adjoining room and came back with a long curtainlike veil, edged in lace, which caused Chaz to leap to his feet.

"Uh-uh. No. Sorry, that's my territory. No thanks."

"His major," said Margot. "He's won awards."

"Not quite," said Chaz.

"Commendations? Something like that?"

Chaz said, "Just A's."

"We think he'll be famous some day," said Margot.

I had noticed a thawing in Betsy, and not just in the direction of Charles. These outings were her first meetings with Chaz. She was, after all, the mother of two sons, and here was something close to their cousin and a very appealing something at that. "What if she wore a suit for the ceremony?" she asked him. "Something classic, maybe in ivory or an ice blue. Not so bridey."

"A suit can be very MOB," said the saleswoman.

"MOB?" we repeated.

"Mother of the bride," said Chaz.

"A whole other department," said the woman, "literally and figuratively."

Margot asked, "How about a plain old gorgeous dress that I'd wear to a black-tie event —"

The woman said, "In that case, I'd try Bergdorf's or Saks."

She fished a business card from the pocket of her black smock, wrote something on it, and handed the card to Margot. "This is a friend who is a personal shopper at Saks. You'll make an appointment first. I don't usually do this, but when one of my brides is marrying a soldier . . . did you tell me what branch of the service?"

Slinging the long train over her arm for an easier walk back to the dressing room, Margot called back to us, "Someone else explain."

Chaz said, "He's a doctor. So he'll be . . . like, a medic? I'm not sure."

Betsy said, "He's a board-certified physician, who will undoubtedly be assigned to that big hospital complex in Germany where the incoming seriously wounded are medivacked to."

Later, when I told Margot about Betsy's aggrandizement, her proud use of "medivac" and "board-certified," we both agreed it was progress.

Now we know: Not every doctor with an MD from Yale can be accepted into the armed forces. Charles had worried that his age would disqualify him (it didn't) and that his specialty would not be useful enough (it was). He had also feared that his medical records would reveal a recent fainting spell or elevated blood pressure or a slightly enlarged prostate. But what killed it, said the recruiter who swore that his application had gone all the way up to the Secretary of the Army, was Dr. Pierrepont's status as a felon. Outstanding traffic tickets or math errors on income tax returns might be overlooked. But when the crime was committed in his professional capacity? No, thank you, Doc. Good luck in the private sector.

Had he known all along that they wouldn't take him? Perhaps. He kept up the jogging and talked of an appeal. His next utterly uncharacteristic job outreach, or at least one that went as far as his placing a phone call, was to serve as a contract doctor with the Department of Defense. This was the juncture at which Margot said, "Enough already. Don't they send you to war zones? Aren't those the people who are mercenaries and killers?"

I was present for that discussion. I said, "And if you want to do some good and give back, how about helping poor women in a free clinic? Wasn't that your original plan?"

"My fallback. My plan B. Or maybe C."

"He wanted to wear a uniform and be a hero," Margot said. "Which makes total sense after you've been a criminal."

"It wasn't about being a hero. I wanted to serve my country. Don't I get credit for at least trying?"

I didn't say what I was thinking. *You wanted to impress Margot. You wanted a grand gesture that would undo your wrongs.*

"Betsy will be disappointed," said Margot.

"Not as disappointed as I am," said Charles. "Though let's face it — her disappointment will be that I'm less likely to be killed now in the line of duty or go MIA."

"I'll e-mail her," said Margot. "I'll tell her that you tried as hard as you could, but eventually it went all the way to the top, to the Secretary of the Army. And if she doesn't believe me, I'll show her the letter."

I said, "It's hard for any of us to get a pass from Betsy."

Margot said, "Birth order. Isn't that supposed to make us who we are? Is the baby in the family the bossiest one or is that just her?"

"In two words: *Always right*," I said.

"Always *thinks* she's right," Margot corrected.

I realized I was being disloyal in front of Charles, especially in view of Betsy's being the architect of our residential arrangement and consultant on all matters, solicited or un-. "She's always buying us presents and treats whenever we go out . . ." I began.

"And loves us," said Margot. "That's never a question."

Charles said, "I think we'd all agree, generosity aside, Betsy can be formidable."

"And I'm not?" asked Margot.

"You're plenty formidable."

"What about me?" I asked.

I interpreted Charles's smile as charitable. "Thankfully, Gwen, I count on you for being the least formidable sister." With that, he lifted his big Yale coffee mug, the one he'd recently brought from downstairs and kept in our cupboard. He continued, sounding unsteady. "By which I mean you're often kind when I haven't earned it." With that he rose and hurried away in the direction of the parlor.

Margot and I both watched until he was out of sight. When he didn't return, she said, "Go see what's wrong."

I said, "I know what's wrong. He's not used to apologizing, so he's embarrassed."

"He's a man. And a scientist. I think he's very fond of you and can't deal with the emotion."

I said, "This is new."

"It is! He ends up crying every week in front of our therapist. She thinks it's male menopause."

I said, "Which could explain his trip to the army recruitment office."

She walked to the doorway and glanced around the corner. "One of us should go in there."

"Why me? You're his fiancée."

"He was addressing you. And I sense this could be something you could build on."

Why did I say yes? Because I thought the same thing, and maybe it was the new Charles in there, the one I'd been hearing about. I took my mug of coffee with me — and his.

He was sitting opposite the TV, the volume barely audible, a bright green soccer field in high definition. He thanked me for the coffee, took a sip, swallowed, said it was cold. He looked up at me. "I ruined my life, didn't I?"

I sat down next to him on the couch, hoping to demonstrate the very qualities by which I'd distinguished myself as the least formidable sister. "You're starting over. With Margot. With work. And parole ends in what? A couple of weeks? You'll deliver babies again, like you did at Saint Vincent's. I think that's a good metaphor for a new life, don't you?"

"I don't blame you for hating me," he said.

I asked if he was forgetting I had accepted every single collect call from prison and had kept him company on those meal-plan nights when Margot and Anthony had flown the coop.

He rose and walked to the window, which overlooked West Tenth and a thin slice of Fifth Avenue. "I think you're the reason she made it through this whole mess, through my incarceration, and even why she's taking me back," he said in an uncharacteristically soft voice.

Was this humility I was hearing? I pretended to be momentarily distracted by the hullabaloo on the TV screen, men in red celebrating a goal. I finally said, "Thank you, but I'm quite sure I'm not the reason she's taking you back."

"You contributed! I mean, your circumstances did. Poor Edwin did. Margot realized that anything can happen, at any time. Life can change in an instant. You of all people know that. And you know your sister: She simply cannot be alone. Look how fast she moved you in here. Then Anthony. How do you explain a whole other boarder if it's not for additional company?"

"Rent," I said. "And adorableness."

"She cannot be alone," he repeated.

I pointed out that it might be true, but it was a moot point because soon they'd be married, which should give her a roommate for a few more decades.

"I know . . ."

"But . . . ?"

And then — because people don't change overnight; because he couldn't picture me in any other role than nursemaid and companion — he said, "If anything happens to me, can you promise me you'll move back in with Margot?"

As if on cue, Margot called from close range, "Everything okay? I'm out here flapping in the breeze. Can I come in?"

Charles whispered, "Case in point. You've never noticed this before?"

"She's very social. She likes company." And then, what finally needed to be acknowledged: "Circumstances change, you know. I may not always be the ever-available spinster sister."

I could see in his face the effort he was putting into being an unselfish conversationalist. "Your beau! Of course. How's that going? I haven't been paying much attention, given the vicissitudes of my own life lately."

I said, "I don't want to jinx anything —"

"Eli, right? The nice man with the mother? How many dates?"

I said, "I've lost count. And, yes, he's the nice man with the mother."

He was peering at me in a manner I judged to be diagnostic. "I *have* noticed you looking happy lately. It didn't register till now."

There was a quick rap on the door, and instantly Margot was in the room. "What are you two talking about?" she asked.

"Eli," I told her.

"Something's up, apparently," said Charles.

"Seriously? You just noticed a change?" asked Margot, squeezing between us on the couch.

"I commented on it before you joined us. I believe the word I used was 'happy.'"

Margot said to me, "Notice how he doesn't have to join the army to be MIA."

Charles sputtered a protest. Margot said he should open his eyes and perhaps discuss this very thing in therapy — his tendency toward self-absorption. "It's so obvious," she said. "Look at her. Anyone who was paying just a little attention would know."

Charles said, "Know what?"

"Can *I* tell him?" asked Margot. "Please."

"Okay. Sure. You deserve that honor."

I hadn't put a name, aloud, to what I'd been feeling, so how did I know that Margot would get it right? But she did.

"Gwen-Laura Schmidt is in love," Margot announced.

38

Amplifications

MARGOT HAS NOW READ everything I've written and believes I have underplayed the good while overstating the bad. She thinks I sound too modest and too mousy. "You need to say something like 'I know I gave the impression that I was unpopular and not terribly attractive, but I was never considered either of those things. In fact, I've grown into my looks, and it's a widely held belief'" — a pause while she conjured — "'that I'm the fairest sister of them all.'"

"Who said that?"

"I know for a fact that Edwin did. All the time."

"Doesn't count."

"Dad used to say something along those lines. Remember? 'A rose between two thorns'?"

"Maybe when you two were fighting."

"I don't care. Write that down," she instructed. So I did.

She'd given me carte blanche to describe these past two years: widowhood for me, singledom for both of us, and the poorhouse for Margot and Anthony. I know now that she was humoring me, letting me tell all, even the exposing of financial and marital secrets better left in the cemetery of dead headlines — because she didn't think a memoir by Gwen-Laura Schmidt would ever get published.

After I printed out the whole manuscript, I watched as she read it, both of us seated, days on end, at the dining-room table that so often represented the full geography of our social lives. She divided the pages into two piles: those she could live with (the chapters covering her own private life and romantic renaissance) and those that needed beefing up.

"For example," she said, pausing to fold one offending page into a paper airplane before launching it across the table into my chest.

I opened it and read my own words. "I love this scene," I protested.

"A kiss in a restaurant? That's it?" Had I not realized, she demanded, that a kiss was only a snapshot at the end of my second date with Eli, and how were readers supposed to know that everything didn't collapse before the third? "Remember that song from *A Chorus Line* — 'Dance 10, Looks 3'?" she asked. "Because if I was rating your pages, I'd have to say 'Roommates 10, Gwen 3.' And even that might be generous."

I said yes, she was making that quite clear.

"It might be enough of an ending in an old black-and-white movie, where the kiss is the last thing the audience sees as the music swells and the credits roll. And, yes, in a simpler world, a kiss could mean 'happily ever after.' But you're not Doris Day."

When I said, "I was trying for subtlety," she looked up. "Oh, really? Because I notice you didn't hold back when it came to Charles and me. I come across as something of a vixen." She grinned. "Which I thank you for."

I asked, "How far do I have to push it?"

"You're the writer in the family! Put in some reassurances. Put in some flesh and blood."

So here is more, dedicated to Margot, who gave me backbone but is still, apparently, the boss. My dates with Eli increased in frequency from weekly to semiweekly to what my mother would have called "an understanding." Still, everyone (Margot, Anthony, Charles, Betsy, and even Chaz) noticed that progress in certain areas was slow. Totally understandable, I reminded everyone. Eli and I often, maybe too often, referred to our dead spouses, and perhaps with that topic came a sad or dreamy look that discouraged a wandering hand. Margot and Anthony were their usual, unsubtle selves, asking after each date, "Still? Nothing?"

Thus, I did what any red-blooded woman would feel an urge to do on a beautiful moonlit summer night, back from another warm and chastely romantic date that didn't progress past first base: I sent him an e-mail. Wrote, erased, composed, deleted, revised. How to ask? To be euphemistic or direct? With a glass of Chardonnay at my fingertips, I finally wrote:

> Dear Eli,
> Thank you for another lovely evening. I just wanted to say that if you, some day, wanted to move the relationship in a horizontal direction, I would welcome that.
> xo, Gwen

He wrote back so fast that I thought I was getting an out-of-office reply.

> Dear Gwen,
> I'll be right over. (Kidding, but only due to the hour.) How's tomorrow night?
> Love, Eli

The next morning, merely walking down the hall toward the linen closet, I must have conveyed something with my expression or skin tone because Margot grabbed my wrist as she passed me.

"You look different," she said. "Flushed. What's up? You can tell me."

"Eli's cooking me dinner tonight. At his place . . ."

And with only that, she negotiated me backward into my room for a conference. Actually, it was a wordless conference; she went straight for my underwear drawer. And as soon as she completed her inventory and refreshed her lipstick, we went shopping.

• • •

So we got to the other side of this project, at his apartment, between cocktails and dinner and Egyptian cotton sheets. Who knew what I was capable of? Not this Gwen-Laura Schmidt.

Over lobsters steamed and delivered by an obliging fishmonger in his neighborhood, Eli said, "I seem to have worked up quite an appetite. And if that sounds like code for something else, it is."

I looked down at my plate, then up at him. "Lobster is just as good cold, don't you think?"

"Better, actually."

"C'mon," I said.

Later, side by side at the microwave, remelting the butter, Eli said, "I just remembered. My mother invited us for dinner this weekend. How would you feel about that?"

I said I'd like that very much. Was he sure the invitation included me?

He left the kitchen and returned with his phone. There on the screen was Myra's e-mail, enlarged and unambiguous: *When are you bringing Gwen home to meet me? Love, Mom.*

"Radar," I said.

Two days later, on a scalding Sunday, I found myself on the Number 7 train to Queens, dressed in a sundress and sandals bought for the new season Margot had dubbed the Summer of Second Chances, holding a potted orchid on my lap. Its card said only MOST GRATE-FULLY, GWEN.

Greeting us at the door with arms opened wide, Myra Offenberg looked like the vigorously retired school principal that she was, with excellent posture, a French twist, and eyeglasses on a hot-pink cord. She was taller than I, nimble, smiling, tanned. "Come in, come in. It's cool! I have cold white wine and iced tea. Sweetie? Get my wedding goblets. I didn't want to get up on a step stool. Let's have a toast to something."

I told her the apartment was lovely, adding — a line I'd had at the ready — "Eli told me you moved here from Washington Heights when he was starting first grade because the neighborhood elementary school was better."

My comment seemed to delight her. Soon enough I would realize that all questions, all topics, all answers did, too.

"We did! For the schools. Nineteen sixty-something. I'll show you his room." I followed her down a short hallway to an unlikely candidate. Its walls were a deep rose and its pale-pink lampshades looked like tutus. "Do you believe what I did? Like a cliché! I turned it into a study two minutes after he left for college. He was the worst slob — clothes everywhere. Didn't know what a hamper was for! He'd empty his pockets onto the nearest surface — pennies, quarters, Canadian coins, receipts, gum wrappers, golf tees. A pigsty! I rolled up my sleeves — I was just going to clean it up, vacuum, and then I got carried away. Voilà. The desk and adding machine were my father's. He was a CPA. The sofa converts, of course." And after only the slightest pause: "Are your parents alive?"

I said, "No, unfortunately. They died within a year of each other."

"Before your husband or after?" she asked. "No. Why did I ask that? Morbid curiosity. You seem fine. I mean, able to go full-swing into this." And with that, she tilted her head in the direction of her absent son.

He joined us, managing three monogrammed goblets. "Believe me," he said. "The walls weren't pink when I lived here." Then, in teen-lover-boy fashion, he slipped an arm around my waist and asked, "Wanna listen to some music? Ma, you leave. She's helping me with my English homework. I'll keep the door open."

Myra said, "Very funny. C'mon. I have Gouda and Triscuits."

I listened hard for hints of buyer's remorse from our matchmaker, especially for any words suggesting she'd been too hasty in promoting a match with a non-Jew. After we finished an unidentified cold green soup, she told me no, sit, Eli would clear. And while you're in there, hon, would you take the pot roast out of the oven and slice it up nice on the big oval tray that was on the counter?

"Happy to," he said. "But be nice. No third degree."

"Use the oven mitts," she said. And as soon as he'd left the dining room, she whispered, "It's written all over his face, isn't it?"

I didn't want to be presumptuous, so I said, "Something good, I hope."

"Good? Better than good. He's happy," and with that, her voice broke. She flapped one hand in front of her face, signaling *Don't mind me.*

I said, "I'm happy, too, Mrs. Offenberg."

"Myra!"

"Myra."

"You continue to be happy. He's a wonderful boy. A wonderful man. Much neater now. I'm lucky that I lived to see this," she said, waving her index finger back and forth between me and the kitchen.

I said, "I don't want to take anything for granted . . ."

She leaned closer. "I'm a widow, too."

I said, yes, I knew that —

"I had just turned seventy, maybe seventy-one, when Joe died. And even though it wasn't the biggest love story ever told, I had no desire to keep company with another man."

"But you did?"

"My high school reunion, another cliché! My fiftieth. Does that add up right? Maybe it was an odd-year reunion. Nathan Sondheim — no relation, unfortunately. We'd gone to a dance together junior or senior year, not even a prom, a semiformal. Not a word or a photo in fifty-plus years. He walked in alone. I walked in alone. Nathan recognized me immediately. And when I got home that night I dug out my high school yearbook and I saw what he'd written. Believe it or not, it said, 'Myra Lowenthal, will you marry me?' Of course, I took it as a joke because he was always something of a wisenheimer."

"How soon was this after Mr. Offenberg died?"

"Actually, it was before, but a few months later he was gone. Nathan sent a card. We had our first dinner together six, maybe seven months later. When people ask, I say it was a year."

245

"Has he since confessed that he meant it — the marriage proposal in the yearbook?"

"No! He has no recollection of it, so I haven't brought it up." She smiled. "He took me to his grandson's bar mitzvah this past April and introduced me to everyone as 'the woman to whom I'm not married.' That's how we like it."

She whispered that Eli wasn't up to speed on Nathan. Her doing. Sons can be squeamish about a mother's love life. She patted my hand as if to say *Watch this*. "Hon? How are you doing in there? Was the knife sharp enough?"

"No, but I'm almost done," he called back. "Two minutes. Do you have any parsley? Everything's the same color."

"Of course I do." She winked at me and said, "Chop it fine. And arrange the carrots and potatoes around the meat, okay?"

He called back, "Sure, I'll stall."

Myra's reply was "Don't be silly." And then to me, "Would you marry again?"

I said, "I never *thought* I would . . ."

"But?" Myra was breaking her roll into increasingly smaller pieces, to no obvious end.

"What are you hoping I'll say?" I asked her.

She took her time before answering. "Maybe something like 'But then Eli came along.'"

I took a roll and passed her the butter dish.

"Then Eli came along," I said.

Nobody was home when I got back to West Tenth Street, the first time in recent memory that penthouse B had been deserted on a weeknight. I checked the messages on my silenced phone. The first was Margot's. "We're out" was followed by a muffled side conversation with Charles. "Quiet. Sorry! We're debating sushi versus Thai, and a late movie if we can agree on which one. How was the mom? Call me." And a text from Anthony, nothing more than *Out w Wm. Won't be home. Thank U! How was dinner? How was Myra?*

I texted back the same to each: *Myra is great. So am I. Have fun. xoxo.*

A bleep told me I had a text message from Eli. It was short but perfect.

I still have it.

39

Acknowledgments

F IRST, I WANT to thank Margot for everything. In our year of co-operative living, I learned how to have fun, to give and take, and to count blessings that weren't visible to the leaky eye. I thank her for being the person who can turn vegetables from the scrap heap into full-course meals, and hot dogs and beans into a party on a roof. Is penthouse B a classroom where one learns how to charm salesmen, doormen, waiters, and strangers on the street? I might be living proof of that.

I am extremely grateful to Anthony, a perfect roommate, wise friend, and safety net. Has anyone ever treated two women, old enough to be his big sisters, as equals and social guinea pigs in the nicest, most inclusive manner? He taught us how to download music, upload photos, find decent dates and biological children online; how to squeeze frosting out of a pastry bag — all without one word of complaint about his claustrophobic, windowless back room.

Despite our urgings, he did not find his calling in cupcakes. He continues to bake, to impress, to indulge and woo with his original and delicious confections. But what I learned from our well-meaning optimism and misguided career counseling is that something done on a small, amateur scale doesn't necessarily mean employment on a larger one. We are guilty of pushing him rather than appreciating his gifts, and have apologized for ignoring his frequent reality check: A bakery needs venture capital to get off the ground, something none of our cheerleading could provide.

He is a multitalented, unflappable multitasker. Who else knows where to find a kosher caterer, a florist, a judge, Japanese lanterns, and a chuppah? If anyone reading this has a job for Anthony Sarno, our letters of reference would bedazzle your Human Resources department.

I must also thank my sister Betsy. On the whole, I recognize that bossiness is just another name for leadership, and without question, she cocaptained the team that pushed me out of the house wearing better outfits than those in my closet. And most important, it was her suggestion that put her two older sisters, who were lost at sea for different reasons, in one boat. "Win-win," she is often heard bragging about the impulse and the results.

Next I want to thank Charles. We had our issues, but here is the lesson of Dr. Pierrepont: If a person is dogged enough in his repentance, eventually forgiveness can't be denied. He refused to turn Margot's postdivorce, postincarceration hatred of him into a shoot-out; instead, he showed up, dedicated to the task and persistent, the very traits that got him through medical school, internship, residency, and prison. Hat in hand, he returned and fought, even when some of us clung to the notion of him as untrustworthy and obnoxious. If he had a family crest, its slogan would be "Love conquers all," which he would, no doubt, correct to "*Omnia vincit amor.*"

I had hoped to report that we are all gainfully employed, but that is not the case. Charles was the first to slip back into the working world, once his license was restored. A prison gynecologist is not the most prestigious or lucrative appointment for a physician, but he finds it rewarding. Never one to chase down job leads, Margot has rather smoothly transitioned back into the role of doctor's wife.

Next, I'd like to acknowledge my step-nephew, Chaz. He most generously and affectionately relies on the circumference of Margot's head to guide his constructions because so many of his projects, even the mistakes, end up in her possession. She is now officially a hat person; women often stop her on the street to ask her where these marvelous creations come from. His mother, he says, would also proudly wear his creations, but the new husband, a three-sport coach, doesn't like her being a billboard for his stepson's sissy talents. What Margot exhibits is something close to maternal pride, possibly even to motherhood, and when they're together and I'm lucky enough to be present, I see that in her eyes.

I thank Myra Offenberg deeply for subscribing to the *New York Review of Books,* and, especially, for keeping her old issues lying around, as well as for the nerve it took to e-mail me without her son's knowledge or permission. I also thank her for her huge heart and open door, welcoming a person of a different religion into her family. And I might as well thank the teenager in her building who advised her in the purchase of a computer, gave her lessons, and signed her up for Wi-Fi. So thank you, Seth Levi-Aronson. I hope we meet someday.

No less deserving of gratitude: Alison and Maddy Offenberg, Eli's daughters. Could two motherless girls have been any less possessive of their father, more interested in his love life, or any more encouraging to me? And how wise they were, pushing him out the door the night of our first date, calling after him, "It's only dinner, Dad. It's one meal. It doesn't mean you have to be buried together."

My thanks go to the Batavia's co-op board for overlooking what in less recessionary times might be considered illegal residencies, times two, and sometimes three.

I might even thank my support group. I imagine that visit, a final meeting, perhaps the one closest to Valentine's Day or New Year's Eve. I'd be something of a guest speaker, a success story, and they could call it closure. I'd tell them about my weepy widowhood and my reluctance to give it up. I'd say to the newcomers, "Do you hate coming here? I did, too."

And then I would quote Emily Dickinson. I'd say, "I should've paid better attention to that poem, the one the English teacher quoted almost the very week before she dropped out of the group. 'Hope is the thing with feathers.' Remember? She said it like punctuation, like a blessing. That line means more to me now, so if anyone's in touch with her, please send her my regards."

Eli. I saved him for last.

This is hard to write, knowing my sister will want to improve it. I have to begin with an earlier truth, unseasoned by my newfound self-esteem. I am realistic. I have my moments and some might say my charms, but still, not so many men have taken a luminous and stead-fast shine to Gwen-Laura Considine Schmidt.

I'd already had what most people ask from life: a husband, a marriage with music, an apartment with a view of the Hudson River. I ask myself, in secret, guiltily, "Was it possible that my feelings for Eli bumped Edwin down a rung? And what if the marriage I'd commemorated as a storybook romance had been more down to earth and comfortable than I previously understood?" When I confessed this to Margot, she asked, "So? Would that be so terrible? Love comes in different temperatures."

So this is what I'm getting to: Bad things happen to everyone. No one is exempt, even high above West Tenth Street, in mostly leafy, mostly beautiful Greenwich Village. I don't mean to sound pessimistic. All I am saying is, I am most appreciative. Some people think a higher power orchestrates these things, but I am satisfied with "fate" or "timing" or "luck."

Eli says, when I voice such sentiments, "But I'm the lucky one."

Imagine if my father could hear those words on the occasion of a suitor asking for my hand? I picture Daddy's face, and at that moment I believe I really could have been the rose between two thorns.

Orphan that I am now, Eli did something close to that, in a more traditional manner than I expected. He asked Margot, the family elder, to join us for lunch.

What would you guess my older sister would do and say in a public space, at the elegant restaurant chosen just for the occasion? Scream? Dance? Leap out of her chair and throw her arms around Eli, then me, and probably the closest waiter?

"I'd like your blessing —" he began.

"Is this *it?*" she whispered, clutching my hand.

"Hold on," I said.

She just stared down at her plate, long enough to worry Eli and make him regret this unnecessary chivalry.

"What's wrong?" he asked. "We thought this would be welcome news."

"Eli," she began. "Gwen . . . you two . . ."

"What?" I said. "Just say it."

Have two sisters ever been closer? Did this moment need to make perfect sense? She was crying now, and not quietly. Within seconds the maître d' glided to our table and asked if everything was all right.

"All right?" Margot echoed. "More than all right!" She asked if he could bring us something bubbly and sparkling that didn't cost a fortune. That Spanish champagne? Or Californian? Dry but not too dry? Three glasses, s'il vous plaît. Because this man across the table, this lovely man, her host, her treasured friend, had just made her the happiest sister on earth.